D0206478

Also by
Lawrence Block

Hit Man

Matthew Scudder Crime Novels

Even the Wicked
Everybody Dies
When the Sacred Ginmill Closes
A Long Line of Dead Men
The Devil Knows You're Dead
A Walk Among the Tombstones
A Ticket to the Boneyard
Out on the Cutting Edge
Eight Million Ways to Die
A Stab in the Dark
In the Midst of Death
Time to Murder and Create
The Sins of the Fathers

Short Story Collections

Some Days You Get the Bear
Like a Lamb to Slaughter
Sometimes They Bite

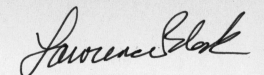

LAWRENCE BLOCK

A Dance at the Slaughterhouse

A MATTHEW SCUDDER CRIME NOVEL

AVON BOOKS
An Imprint of HarperCollins*Publishers*

This is a work of fiction. Names, characters, places, and incidents are the products of the author's imagination or are used fictitiously and are not to be construed as real. Any resemblance to actual events, locales, organizations, or persons, living or dead, is entirely coincidental.

AVON BOOKS
An Imprint of HarperCollins*Publishers*
10 East 53rd Street
New York, New York 10022-5299

Copyright © 1992 by Lawrence Block
Cover photo by Lindsay Silverman/International Stock
Interior design by Kellan Peck
Library of Congress Catalog Card Number: 91-7876
ISBN: 0-380-81373-4
www.avonbooks.com

First Avon Books Trade Paperback Printing: July 2000
First Avon Books Mass Market Printing: August 1992

Avon Trademark Reg. U.S. Pat. Off. and in Other Countries, Marca Registrada, Hecho en U.S.A.
HarperCollins® is a trademark of HarperCollins Publishers Inc.

Printed in the U.S.A.

RRD   10   9   8   7   6   5   4   3   2   1

For Philip Friedman

ACKNOWLEDGMENTS

The author is pleased to acknowledge the substantial contributions of the Virginia Center for the Creative Arts, where this book was begun, and of the Ragdale Foundation, where it was completed.

*If God should punish men according
to what they deserve, He would not leave
so much as a beast on the back of the earth.*

—THE KORAN

1

MIDWAY INTO THE FIFTH ROUND THE KID IN THE BLUE TRUNKS rocked his opponent with a solid left to the jaw. He followed it with a straight right to the head.

"He's ready to fall," Mick Ballou said.

He looked it, too, but when the kid in blue waded in the other boy slipped a punch and groped his way into a clinch. I got a look at his eyes before the referee stepped between the two fighters. They looked glazed, unfocused.

"How much time is there?"

"More than a minute."

"Plenty of time," Mick said. "Watch your man take the lad right out. For a small man he's strong as a bull."

They weren't that small. Junior middleweights, which I guess would put them somewhere around 155 pounds. I used to know the weight limits for all the classes, but it was easy then. Now they've got more than twice as many classifications, with junior this and super that, and three different governing bodies each recognizing a different champion. I think the trend must have started when someone figured out that it was easier to promote a title bout, and it's getting to the point where you rarely see anything else.

The card we were watching, however, was strictly nontitle, and a long way removed from the glamour and showmanship of championship fights staged in Vegas and Atlantic City casinos. We were, to be precise, in a concrete-block shed on a dark street in Maspeth, an industrial wasteland in the borough of Queens bordered on the south and west by the Greenpoint and Bushwick sections of Brooklyn and set off from the rest of Queens by a half-circle of cemeteries. You could live a lifetime in New York without ever getting to Maspeth, or you could drive through it dozens of times without knowing it. With its warehouses and factories and drab residential streets, Maspeth's not likely to be on anybody's short list for potential gentrification, but I suppose you never know. Sooner or later they'll run out of other places, and the crumbling warehouses will be reborn as artists' lofts while young urban homesteaders rip the rotted asphalt siding from the row houses and set about gutting the interiors. You'll have ginkgo trees lining the sidewalk on Grand Avenue, and a Korean greengrocer on every corner.

For now, though, the New Maspeth Arena was the only sign I'd seen of the neighborhood's glorious future. Some months earlier Madison Square Garden had closed the Felt Forum for renovations, and sometime in early December the New Maspeth Arena had opened with a card of boxing matches every Thursday night, with the first prelim getting under way around seven.

The building was smaller than the Felt Forum, and had a no-frills feel to it, with untrimmed concrete-block walls and a sheet-metal roof and a poured concrete slab for a floor. It was rectangular in shape, and the boxing ring stood in the center of one of the long walls, opposite the entrance doors. Rows of metal folding chairs framed the ring's three open sides. The chairs were gray, except for the first two rows in each of the three sections, which were blood red. The red seats at ringside were reserved. The rest of the arena was open seating, and a seat was only five dollars, which was two dollars less than the price of a first-run movie in Manhattan. Even so, almost half of the gray chairs remained unoccupied.

The price was low in order to fill as many of the seats as possible, so that the fans who watched the fights on cable TV wouldn't realize the event had been staged solely on their behalf. The New Maspeth Arena was a cable phenomenon, thrown up to furnish programming for FBCS, Five Borough Cable Sportscasts, the latest sports channel trying to get a toehold in the New York metro area. The FBCS trucks had been parked outside when Mick and I arrived a few minutes after seven, and at eight o'clock their coverage began.

Now the fifth round of the final prelim fight was ending with the boy in the white trunks still on his feet. Both fighters were black, both local kids from Brooklyn, one introduced as hailing from Bedford-Stuyvesant, the other from Crown Heights. Both had short haircuts and regular features, and they were the same height, although the kid in blue looked shorter in the ring because he fought in a crouch. It's good their trunks were different colors or it would have been tough to tell them apart.

"He should have had him there," Mick said. "The other lad was ready to go and he couldn't finish him."

"The boy in the white has heart," I said.

"He was glassy-eyed. What's his name, the one in blue?" He looked at the program, a single sheet of blue paper with the bouts listed. "McCann," he said. "McCann let him off the hook."

"He was all over him."

"He was, and punching away at him, but he couldn't pull the trigger. There's a lot of them like that, they get their man in trouble and then they can't put him down. I don't know why it is."

"He's got three rounds left."

Mick shook his head. "He had his chance," he said.

He was right. McCann won the remaining three rounds handily, but the fight was never closer to a knockout than it had been in the fifth. At the final bell they clung together briefly in a sweaty embrace, and then McCann bopped over to his corner with his gloves raised in triumph. The judges agreed with him. Two of them had him pitching a shutout, while the third man had the kid in white winning a round.

"I'll get a beer," Mick said. "Will you have something?"

"Not right now."

We were in the first row of gray chairs over on the right-hand side of the ring as you entered. That way I could keep an eye on the entrance, although I hadn't been looking anywhere much outside the ring. I looked over there now while Mick made his way to the refreshment stand at the far end of the hall, and for a change I saw someone I recognized, a tall black man in a well-tailored navy pinstripe suit. I stood up at his approach and we shook hands.

"I thought it was you," he said. "I ducked in before to watch a couple minutes of Burdette and McCann from the back, and I thought I saw my friend Matthew over here in the cheap seats."

"They're all cheap seats in Maspeth."

"Isn't that the truth." He put a hand on my shoulder. "First time I saw you was at the fights, wasn't it? The Felt Forum?"

"That's right."

"You were with Danny Boy Bell."

"You were with Sunny. I don't remember her last name."

"Sunny Hendryx. Sonya, her name was, but nobody ever called her that."

I said, "Join us, why don't you? My friend's getting a beer, but the whole row's empty, or almost. If you don't mind sitting in a cheap seat."

He grinned. "I got a seat," he said. "Over by the blue corner. Got to cheer my man to victory. You remember Kid Bascomb, don't you?"

"Of course I do. He was on the card the night we met, he beat some Italian kid that I don't remember at all."

"Nobody does."

"He took the heart out of him with a body punch, I remember that. The Kid's not fighting tonight, is he? He's not on the program."

"No, he's retired. He hung 'em up a couple of years ago."

"That's what I thought."

"He's sitting right over there," he said, pointing. "No, my man in the main event's Eldon Rasheed. He ought to win, but the boy he's fighting is sitting on eleven wins and two defeats, and one of those they stole the decision from him. So he's not just an opponent."

He was talking about fight strategy when Mick came back carrying two large paper cups. One held beer, the other Coke. "In case you get thirsty," he said. "I wouldn't care to stand in that long a line for a single beer."

I said, "Mickey Ballou, Chance—"

"Chance Coulter."

"A pleasure," Mick said. He was still holding on to both drinks, so they couldn't shake hands.

"Here comes Dominguez now," Chance said. The fighter came down the aisle flanked by his retinue. He wore a royal-blue robe with navy piping. He was good-looking, with a long, square-jawed face and a neat black mustache. He smiled and waved at fans, then climbed up into the ring.

"He looks good," Chance said. "Eldon may have his hands full."

"You're supporting the other one?" Mick asked.

"Yes, Eldon Rasheed. Here he comes now. Maybe we can all have a drink afterward."

I said that sounded good. Chance made his way over to his seat near the blue corner. Mick gave me both cups to hold while he settled himself in his seat. " 'Eldon Rasheed versus Peter Dominguez,' " he read. "Where do they get their names?"

"Peter Dominguez is a pretty straightforward name," I said.

He gave me a look. "Eldon Rasheed," he pronounced, as Rasheed climbed through the ropes. "Well, if it was a beauty contest, you'd have to hand it to Pedro. Rasheed looks as though God hit him in the face with a shovel."

"Why would God do a thing like that?"

"Why does God do half the things He does? Your friend Chance is a good-looking man. How do you come to know him?"

"I did some work for him a few years ago."

"Detective work?"

"That's right."

"I thought he looked like a lawyer. Dresses the part."

"Actually he's a dealer in African art."

"Carvings, like?"

"That sort of thing."

The announcer was in the ring, ballyhooing the coming bout and doing what he could to hype next week's card. He introduced a local welterweight who'd be fighting in next week's main event, then called up a few other celebrities seated at ringside, including Arthur "Kid" Bascomb. The Kid got the same lackadaisical round of applause that had greeted everyone else.

The referee got an introduction, and the three judges, and the timekeeper, and the guy whose job it was to count in the event of a knockdown. He figured to get some work tonight; the fighters were heavyweights, and both had knocked out most of their previous opponents. Eight of Dominguez's eleven wins were by knockout, and Rasheed, undefeated in ten professional bouts, had only had one fight that had gone the distance.

Dominguez got a big hand from an Hispanic contingent at the far end of the arena. Rasheed's ovation was more restrained. They huddled together in the center of the ring while the referee told them nothing that they didn't already know, then touched gloves and went back to their corners. The bell rang and the fight got under way.

The first round was largely exploratory, but both fighters landed some shots. Rasheed worked nicely off a strong left jab and went to the body effectively. He moved well for a man his size. Dominguez was awkward in comparison, an ungainly fighter, but he had a straight overhand right that was very sudden, and he caught Rasheed over the left eye with it with thirty seconds to go in the round. Rasheed shook it off, but you could see he felt it.

Between rounds Mick said, "He's strong, that Pedro. He might have stolen the round with that punch."

"I never know how they'll score it."

"A few more blows like that last and there'll be no need to keep score."

Rasheed had the edge in the second round. He stayed away from the right and landed some solid body shots. During the round I happened to notice a man sitting at ringside in the center section. I'd noticed him before, and something made me look at him again.

He was around forty-five, balding, with dark brown hair and prominent eyebrows. He was cleanshaven. He had a lumpy sort of a face, as though he might have been a fighter once himself, but if so I figured they would have introduced him. They were not exactly awash in celebrities, and anybody who'd gone three rounds in the Golden Gloves stood a good chance of being called up to take a bow for the FBCS cameras. And he was right at ringside; all he'd have had to do was climb over the ropes and bask in the applause.

There was a boy with him, and the man had one arm around him, his hand resting on the boy's shoulder while he gestured with the other hand, pointing things out in the ring. I assumed they were father and son, although I couldn't see much resemblance; the boy, in his early teens, had light brown hair with a sharply defined widow's peak. Any widow's peak the father might have had was long gone. The father wore a blue blazer and gray flannel slacks. His tie was light blue, with black or navy polka dots, big ones, close to an inch in diameter. The boy wore a red plaid flannel shirt and navy corduroy pants.

I couldn't think how I knew him.

* * *

The third round looked even to me. I didn't keep count, but I had the impression that Rasheed landed more punches. Dominguez hit him a few good shots, though, and they had more authority than the ones Rasheed got in. When the round ended I didn't look over at the man with the polka-dot tie because I was looking instead at another man.

This one was younger, thirty-two to be exact. He stood about five-eleven and he was built like a light heavyweight. He had shucked his suit jacket and tie and was wearing a white button-down shirt with a blue stripe. He approached the sort of handsomeness you see in menswear catalogs, a combination of chiseled features and attitude, spoiled by a little too much fullness in the pouty lower lip and a brutish thickness to the nose. A full head of dark hair, styled and blown dry. A tan, a souvenir of a week in Antigua.

His name was Richard Thurman, and he was producing the telecast for Five Borough Cable Sportscasts. He was standing on the ring apron now, outside of the ropes, talking to a cameraman. The girl with the placard came around, showing us that the fourth round was coming up next, and showing us a bit more than that in her abbreviated costume. The audience at home would miss that part of the show. They'd be watching a beer commercial while she showed the world what she had. She was a tall, leggy girl with a lush figure, and she was displaying a lot of skin.

She came over to the camera and said something to Thurman, and he reached out a hand and gave her a pat on the fanny. She didn't seem to notice. Maybe he was used to touching women and she was used to being touched. Maybe they were old friends. She was all pink, though, so it seemed unlikely that he'd taken her along to Antigua.

She got out of the ring and he climbed down and they rang the warning bell. The fighters got off their stools and it was time for Round Four.

In the first minute of the round Dominguez got the

straight right in and opened up a cut over Rasheed's left eye. Rasheed jabbed a lot and hammered Dominguez with body punches, and toward the end of the round snapped his head back with a good uppercut. Dominguez landed another good right at the bell. I had no idea how to score the round, and said as much to Mick.

"No matter," he said. "It'll never go ten."

"Who do you like?"

"I like the black fellow," he said, "but I don't care for his chances. Pedro's too fucking strong."

I looked over at the man and the boy. "That fellow over there," I said. "First row, sitting next to the kid. Blue jacket, polka-dot tie."

"What about him?"

"I think I know him," I said, "but I can't place him. Do you recognize him?"

"Never saw him before."

"I can't think where I know him from."

"He looks like a cop."

"No," I said. "Do you really think so?"

"I'm not saying he's a cop, I'm saying he has that look. You know who he looks like? It's an actor who plays cops, I can't think of his name. It'll come to me."

"An actor who plays cops. They all play cops."

"Gene Hackman," he said.

I looked again. "Hackman's older," I said. "And thinner. This guy's burly where Hackman's sort of wiry. And Hackman's got more hair, doesn't he?"

"Jesus help us," he said. "I didn't say he was Hackman. I said that's who he looks like."

"If it was Hackman they'd have made him come up and take a bow."

"If it was Hackman's fucking cousin they'd have made him take a bow, desperate as they are."

"But you're right," I said. "There's a definite resemblance."

"Not that he's the spitting image, mind you, but—"

"But there's a resemblance. That's not why he looks familiar. I wonder where I know him from."

"One of your meetings, maybe."

"That's possible."

"Unless that's a beer he's drinking. If he's a member of your lot he wouldn't be drinking a beer, would he now?"

"Probably not."

"Although not all of your lot make it, do they?"

"No, not all of us do."

"Well then, let's hope it's a Coke in his cup," he said. "Or if it's a beer, let's pray he gives it to the lad."

Dominguez got the better of it in the fifth round. A lot of his big punches missed, but a couple got through and hurt Rasheed. He rallied nicely at the end but the round still clearly belonged to the Latin fighter.

In the sixth, Rasheed took a straight right to the jaw and went down.

It was a solid knockdown and it brought the crowd to its feet. Rasheed was up at five and took the mandatory eight count, and when the ref motioned for them to resume fighting Dominguez rushed in swinging for the fences. Rasheed was wobbly but he showed a lot of class, ducking, slipping punches, playing for time in clinches, fighting back gamely. The knockdown came fairly early in the round, but at the end of the three minutes Rasheed was still on his feet.

"One more round," Mick Ballou said.

"No."

"Oh?"

"He had his chance," I said. "Like that fellow in the last bout, what was his name? The Irishman."

"The Irishman? What Irishman?"

"McCann."

"Ah. Black Irish, that would be. You think Dominguez is another one who doesn't know how to pull the trigger?"

"He knows how, he just didn't have what he needed. He threw too many punches. Punching tires you, especially when you don't hit anything. I think the round took more out of him than it did out of Rasheed."

"You think it'll go to the judges? They'll give it to Pedro then, unless your man Chance put the fix in."

You wouldn't fix a fight like that. There's no betting. I said, "It won't go to a decision. Rasheed'll knock him out."

"Matt, you're dreaming."

"You'll see."

"Do you want to bet? I don't want to bet money, not with you. What shall we bet?"

"I don't know."

I looked over at the father and son. Something was hovering at the edge of thought, nagging at me.

"If I win," he said, "we'll make a night of it and go to the eight o'clock mass at St. Bernard's. The butchers' mass."

"And if I win?"

"Then we won't go."

I laughed. "That's a great bet," I said. "We're already not going, so what would I be winning?"

"All right then," he said. "If you win I'll go to a meeting."

"A meeting?"

"A fucking AA meeting."

"Why would you want to do that?"

"I wouldn't want to do it," he said. "Isn't that the fucking point? I'd be doing it because I lost the bet."

"But why would I want you to go to a meeting?"

"I don't know."

"If you ever want to go," I said, "I'll be happy to take you. But I certainly don't want you to go on my account."

The father put his hand on the boy's forehead and smoothed his hair back. There was something about the gesture that hit me like a hard right hand to the heart. Mick said something but I'd gone momentarily deaf to it. I had to ask him to repeat it.

"Then I guess there's no bet," he said.

"I guess not."

The bell rang. The fighters rose from their stools.

"It's just as well," he said. "I think you're right. I think that fucking Pedro punched himself out."

That's how it turned out. It wasn't that clear-cut in the seventh round because Dominguez was still strong enough to land a few shots that got the crowd cheering. But it was easier to get the crowd on its feet than to knock Rasheed off his, and he looked as strong as ever, and confident in the bargain. Late in the round he landed a short stiff right to the solar plexus and Mick and I looked at each other and nodded. Nobody had cheered, nobody had shouted, but that was the fight, and we knew it and so did Eldon Rasheed. I think Dominguez did, too.

Between rounds Mick said, "I got to hand it to you. You saw something in the round before that I never saw. All those body punches, they're money in the bank, aren't they? They don't look like anything at all, and then all at once your man has no legs under him. Speaking of legs."

The placard girl was letting us know that Round Eight was next.

"She looks familiar, too," I said.

"You met her at a meeting," he suggested.

"Somehow I don't think so."

"No, you'd remember her, wouldn't you? A dream, then. You were with her in a dream."

"That's more like it." I looked from her to the man with the polka-dot tie, then back at her again. "They say that's one of the ways you know you're middle-aged," I said. "When everybody you meet reminds you of somebody else."

"Is that what they say?"

"Well, that's one of the things they say," I said, and they rang the bell for the eighth round. Two minutes into it Eldon Rasheed staggered Peter Dominguez with a brutal left hook to the liver. Dominguez's hands fell and Rasheed dropped him with a right cross to the jaws.

He was up at eight, but it must have been pure machismo that got him on his feet. Rasheed was all over him, and three shots to the midsection put Dominguez on the canvas again. This time the ref didn't even bother to count. He stepped between the fighters and raised Rasheed's arms overhead.

Most of the same people who'd been rooting for a Dominguez knockout were on their feet again now, cheering for Rasheed.

We were standing next to Chance and Kid Bascomb, over by the blue corner, when the ring announcer quieted the crowd and told us what we already knew, that the referee had stopped the fight after two minutes and thirty-eight seconds of the eighth round, that the winner by a technical knockout was Eldon "the Bulldog" Rasheed. There were two more four-round bouts to follow, he added, and we wouldn't want to miss a minute of the nonstop boxing action here at the New Maspeth Arena.

The boxers competing in those two four-rounders had a thankless task ahead of them, because they were going to be playing to a near-empty house. The fights were on the card as insurance for FBCS. If the prelims had finished early, one of them would have been shoehorned in before the main event; if Rasheed had kayoed Dominguez in the second round, or been knocked out himself, there would be a bout or two left to fill up the television time slot.

But it was almost eleven now, so neither of the remaining bouts would make it onto the screen. And just about everybody was heading for home, like baseball fans streaming out of Dodger Stadium in the seventh inning of a tie game.

Richard Thurman was in the ring now, helping his cameraman pack up his gear. I didn't see the placard girl anywhere. I didn't see the father and son team from ringside, either, although I looked for them, thinking I'd point them out to Chance and see if he recognized the man.

The hell with it. Nobody was paying me to figure out why some doting father looked familiar. My job was to get a line on Richard Thurman, and to find out whether or not he had murdered his wife.

2

BACK IN NOVEMBER, RICHARD AND AMANDA THURMAN HAD attended a small dinner party on Central Park West. They left the party shortly before midnight. It was a pleasant night; it had been unseasonably warm all week, so they elected to walk home.

Their apartment occupied the entire top floor of a five-story brownstone on West Fifty-second Street between Eighth and Ninth Avenues. The ground floor housed an Italian restaurant, while a travel agent and a theatrical broker shared the second floor. The third and fourth floors were both residential. There were two apartments on the third floor, one housing a retired stage actress, the other a young stockbroker and a male model. The fourth floor held a single apartment; the tenants, a retired attorney and his wife, had flown to Florida on the first of the month and wouldn't be back until the first week in May.

When the Thurmans got home, somewhere between twelve and twelve-thirty, they reached the fourth-floor landing just as a pair of burglars emerged from the attorney's empty apartment. The burglars, two large and muscular white males in their late twenties or early thirties, drew guns and herded the Thurmans into the apartment they had just ransacked. There they relieved Richard of his watch and wallet, took Amanda's jewelry, and told the two that they were a pair of worthless yuppies and they deserved to die.

They gave Richard Thurman a beating, tied him up and

taped his mouth. Then they sexually assaulted his wife in front of him. Eventually one of them struck Richard over the head with what he believed was a crowbar or pry bar and he lost consciousness. When he came to the burglars were gone and his wife was lying on the floor across the room, nude and apparently unconscious.

He rolled off the bed onto the floor and tried kicking at the floor, but it was thickly carpeted and he couldn't make enough noise to attract the attention of the tenant in the apartment below. He knocked over a lamp but no one responded to the noise it made. He made his way over to where his wife was lying, hoping to arouse her, but she did not respond and did not appear to be breathing. Her skin felt cool to him and he was afraid that she was dead.

He couldn't free his hands and his mouth was still taped. It took some doing to loosen the tape. He tried shouting but no one responded. The windows were closed, of course, and the building was an old one, with thick walls and floors. He finally managed to upend a small table and knock a telephone down onto the floor. Also on the table was a metal tool that the attorney used to tamp down the tobacco in his pipe. Thurman gripped that between his teeth and used it to ring 911. He gave the operator his name and address and said he was afraid his wife was dead or dying. Then he passed out, and that's how the police found him.

That was on the second weekend in November, Saturday night and Sunday morning. On the last Tuesday in January, I was sitting in Jimmy Armstrong's at two in the afternoon drinking a cup of coffee. Across the table from me sat a man about forty years old. He had short dark hair and a closely trimmed beard that was showing a little gray. He wore a brown tweed jacket over a beige turtleneck. He had an indoor complexion, no rare thing in the middle of a New York winter. His gaze, behind metal-framed eyeglasses, was thoughtful.

"I think that bastard killed my sister," he said. The words were angry but the voice was cool, the inflection level and neutral. "I think he murdered her and I think he's getting away with it, and I don't want that to happen."

Armstrong's is at the corner of Tenth and Fifty-seventh. It's been there a few years now, but before then it was on Ninth Avenue between Fifty-seventh and Fifty-eighth, in premises now occupied by a Chinese restaurant. In those days I just about lived in the place. My hotel was right around the corner, and I ate one or more meals a day there, met clients there, and spent most of my evenings at my usual table in the back, talking with people or brooding by myself, drinking my bourbon neat or on the rocks or, as an aid to staying awake, mixing it with coffee.

When I stopped drinking, Armstrong's was at the top of my unwritten list of people, places, and things to avoid. That became easier to do when Jimmy lost his lease and moved a block west, out of my usual daily traffic pattern. I didn't go there for a long time, and then a sober friend suggested we stop there for a late bite, and since then I've probably had half a dozen meals there. They say it's a bad idea to hang out in ginmills when you're trying to stay sober, but Armstrong's felt more like a restaurant than a ginmill anyway, especially in its current incarnation with its exposed brick walls and potted ferns overhead. The background music was classical, and on weekend afternoons they had live trios playing chamber music. Not exactly your typical Hell's Kitchen bucket of blood.

When Lyman Warriner said he was down from Boston I suggested we meet at his hotel, but he was staying at a friend's apartment. My own hotel room is tiny, and my lobby is too shabby to inspire confidence. So once again I had picked Jimmy's saloon as a place to meet a prospective client. Now a baroque woodwind quintet played on the sound system while I drank coffee and Warriner sipped Earl Grey tea and accused Richard Thurman of murder.

I asked him what the police had said.

"The case is open." He frowned. "That would seem to suggest that they're working on it, but I gather it means the reverse, that they've largely abandoned hope of solving it."

"It's not that cut-and-dried," I said. "It usually means the investigation is no longer being actively pursued."

He nodded. "I spoke to a Detective Joseph Durkin. I gather the two of you are friends."

"We're friendly."

He arched an eyebrow. "A nice distinction," he said. "Detective Durkin didn't say that he thought Richard was responsible for Amanda's death, but it was the way he didn't say it, if you know what I mean."

"I think so."

"I asked him if he could think of anything I might do to help resolve the situation. He said that everything that could be done through official channels had been done. It took me a minute before I realized he couldn't specifically suggest I hire a private detective, but that was where he was leading me. I said, 'Perhaps someone unofficial, say a private detective—' and he grinned as if to say that I'd caught on, that I was playing the game."

"He couldn't come right out and say it."

"No. Nor, I gather, could he come right out and recommend your services. 'As far as a recommendation's concerned, all I'm really supposed to do is refer you to the Yellow Pages,' he said. 'Except I should say that there's one fellow right here in the neighborhood who you won't find in the book, on account of he's unlicensed, which makes him very unofficial.' You're smiling."

"You do a good Joe Durkin imitation."

"Thank you. Pity there's not much call for it. Do you mind if I smoke?"

"Not at all."

"Are you sure? Almost everyone's quit. *I* quit, but then I started again." He seemed about to elaborate on that, then took out a Marlboro and lit it. He drew in the smoke as if it were something life-sustaining.

He said, "Detective Durkin said you were unorthodox, even eccentric."

"Were those his words?"

"They'll do. He said your rates are arbitrary and capricious, and no, those weren't his words either. He said you don't furnish detailed reports or keep track of expenses." He leaned forward. "I can live with that. He also said when you get your teeth in something you don't let go, and that's what I want. If that son of a bitch killed Amanda I want to know it."

"What makes you think he did?"

"A feeling. I don't suppose that's terribly scientific."

"That doesn't mean it's wrong."

"No." He looked at his cigarette. "I never liked him," he said. "I tried to, because Amanda loved him, or was in love with him, or whatever you want to call it. But it's difficult to like someone who clearly dislikes you, or at least I found it difficult."

"Thurman disliked you?"

"Immediately and automatically. I'm gay."

"And that's why he disliked you?"

"He may have had other reasons, but my sexual orientation was enough to place me beyond the pale of his circle of potential friends. Have you ever seen Thurman?"

"Just his photo in the newspapers."

"You didn't seem surprised when I told you I was gay. You knew right away, didn't you?"

"I wouldn't say I knew. It seemed likely."

"On the basis of my appearance. I'm not setting traps for you, Matthew. Is it all right if I call you Matthew?"

"Certainly."

"Or do you prefer Matt?"

"Either one."

"And call me Lyman. My point is that I look gay, whatever that means, although to people who haven't been around many homosexuals my own gayness, if you will, is probably a good deal less evident. Well. My take on Richard Thurman, based on *his* appearance, is that he's so deep in the closet he can't see over the coats."

"Meaning?"

"Meaning I don't know that he's ever acted out, and he may very well not be consciously aware of it, but *I* think he prefers men. Sexually. And dislikes openly gay men because he fears we're sisters under the skin."

The waitress came over and poured me more coffee. She asked Warriner if he wanted more hot water for his tea. He told her he would indeed like more hot water, and a fresh tea bag to go with it.

"A pet peeve," he told me. "Coffee drinkers get free refills. Tea drinkers get free hot water, but if you want another tea bag they charge you for a second cup. Tea costs them less than coffee anyway." He sighed. "If I were a lawyer," he said, "I might mount a class-action suit. I'm joking, of course, but somewhere in our litigious society, someone is probably doing just that."

"I wouldn't be surprised."

"She was pregnant, you know. Almost two months. She'd been to the doctor."

"It was in the papers."

"She's my only sibling. So the bloodline dies out when I go. I keep thinking that should trouble me, but I don't know that it does. What does trouble me is the idea of Amanda dying at the hands of her husband, and of him getting away with it. And of not knowing for sure. If I knew for sure—"

"What?"

"It would trouble me less."

The waitress brought his tea. He dunked the fresh tea bag. I asked him what might have motivated Thurman to kill Amanda.

"Money," he said. "She had some."

"How much?"

"Our father made a lot of money. In real estate. Mother found ways to piss away a good deal of it, but there was still some left when she died."

"When was that?"

"Eight years ago. When the will cleared probate Amanda and I each inherited slightly in excess of six hundred thousand dollars. I rather doubt that she spent it all."

By the time we were through it was getting close to five o'clock and the bar business was beginning to pick up as the first of the Happy Hour set arrived. I had filled several pages in my pocket notebook and had begun turning down coffee refills. Lyman Warriner had switched from tea to beer and was halfway through a tall glass of Prior dark.

It was time to set a fee, and as always I didn't know how much to ask for. I gathered that he could afford whatever I charged him but that didn't really enter into my calculations. The number I settled on was $2500, and he didn't ask me how I'd arrived there, just took out a checkbook and uncapped a fountain pen. I couldn't remember the last time I'd seen one.

He said, "Matthew Scudder? Two *t*'s, two *d*'s?" I nodded and he wrote out the check and waved it to dry the ink. I told him that he might have a refund coming if things went faster than I expected, or that I might ask for more money if it seemed appropriate. He nodded. He didn't seem terribly concerned about this.

I took the check, and he said, "I just want to know, that's all."

"That might be the most you can hope for. Finding out that he did it and turning up something that'll stand up in court are two different things. You could wind up with your suspicions confirmed and your brother-in-law still getting away with it."

"You don't have to prove anything to a jury, Matthew. Just prove it to me."

I didn't feel that I could let that go. I said, "It sounds as though you're thinking of taking matters into your own hands."

"I've already done that, haven't I? Hiring a private detective. Not letting matters take their own course, not allowing the mills of God to grind in their traditionally slow fashion."

"I wouldn't want to be part of something that winds up with you on trial for Richard Thurman's murder."

He was silent for a moment. Then he said, "I won't pretend it hasn't occurred to me. But I honestly don't think I would do it. I don't think it's my style."

"That's just as well."

"Is it? I wonder." He motioned for the waitress, gave her twenty dollars and waved away change. Our check couldn't have come to more than a quarter of that, but we'd taken up a table for three hours. He said, "If he killed her, he was exceedingly stupid."

"Murder is always stupid."

"Do you really think so? I'm not sure I agree, but you're more the expert than I. No, my point is that he acted prematurely. He should have waited."

"Why?"

"More money. Don't forget, I inherited the same amount Amanda did, and I can assure you I haven't pissed it away. Amanda would have been my heir, and the beneficiary of my insurance." He took out a cigarette, put it back in the pack. "I wouldn't have had anyone else to leave it to," he said. "My lover died a year and a half ago, of a four-letter disease." He smiled thinly. "Not gout. The other one."

I didn't say anything.

"I'm HIV-positive," he said. "I've known for several years. I lied to Amanda. I told her I'd been tested and I was negative, so I had nothing to worry about." His eyes sought mine. "That seemed like an ethical lie, don't you think? Since I wasn't about to have sex with her, why burden her with the truth?" He took out the cigarette but didn't light it. "Besides," he said, "there was a chance I might not get sick. Having the antibody may not necessarily mean having the virus. Well, scratch that. The first telltale purple blotch appeared this past August. KS. That's Kaposi's sarcoma."

"I know."

"It's not the short-term death sentence it was a year or two ago. I could live a long time. I could live ten years, even more." He lit the cigarette. "But," he said, "somehow I have a feeling that's not going to happen."

He stood up, got his topcoat from the rack. I reached for mine and followed him out to the street. A cab came along right away and he hailed it. He opened the rear door, then turned to me once more.

"I hadn't got around to telling Amanda," he said. "I thought I'd tell her at Thanksgiving, but of course by then it was too late. So she didn't know, and of course he wouldn't have known, so he couldn't have realized the financial advantage in delaying her murder." He threw his cigarette away. "It's ironic," he said, "isn't it? If I'd told her I was dying, she might be alive today."

3

I GOT UP THE NEXT MORNING AND PUT WARRINER'S CHECK IN the bank and drew some walking-around money while I was at it. We'd had a little snow over the weekend but most of it was gone now, with just a little gray residue left at the curbs. It was cold out, but there wasn't much wind and it wasn't a bad day for the middle of winter.

I walked over to Midtown North on West Fifty-fourth, hoping to catch Joe Durkin, but he wasn't there. I left word for him to call me and walked on down to the main library at Forty-second and Fifth. I spent a couple of hours reading everything I could find about the murder of Amanda Warriner Thurman. While I was at it I looked for her and her husband in the *New York Times Index* over the past ten years. I read their wedding announcement, which had appeared four years ago September. She would already have come into her inheritance by then.

I had already learned when they were married from Warriner, but it never hurts to confirm things a client tells you. The announcement furnished me with other information Warriner hadn't given me—the names of Thurman's parents and others in the wedding party, the schools he'd attended, the jobs he'd held before he went with Five Borough Cable.

Nothing I turned up told me that he had or hadn't murdered his wife, but I hadn't figured to solve the case with two hours of library research.

I called Midtown North from a pay phone on the corner.

Joe hadn't come back. I had a Sabrett hot dog and a knish for lunch and walked over to the Swedish church on Forty-eighth, where there's a twelve-thirty meeting on weekdays. The speaker was a commuter who lived with his family on Long Island and worked for one of the Big Six accounting firms. He'd been sober ten months and couldn't get over how wonderful it was.

"I got your message," Durkin said. "I tried you at your hotel but they said you were out."

"I was on my way there now," I said. "I thought I'd take a chance, see if I'd catch you in."

"Well, today's your lucky day, Matt. Have a seat."

"A fellow came to see me yesterday," I said. "Lyman Warriner."

"The brother. I figured he'd call you. You gonna do something for him?"

"If I can," I said. I had palmed a hundred-dollar bill and I tucked it between his fingers. "I appreciate the referral."

We were alone in the office, so he felt free to unfold the bill and look at it. "It's a good one," I assured him. "I was there when they printed it."

"Now I feel better," he said. "No, what I was just thinking is I shouldn't even take this from you. You want to know why? Because it's not just a case of throwing a couple of bucks your way and keeping the citizen happy. I'm glad you took the guy on. I'd love to see you do him some good."

"You think Thurman did his wife?"

"Do I think? I fucking know it."

"How?"

He considered the question. "I don't know," he said. "Cop instinct. How's that?"

"It sounds good to me. Between your cop instinct and Lyman's feminine intuition, I figure Thurman's lucky to be walking around free."

"Have you met the guy, Matt?"

"No."

"See if you don't read him the same way I did. He's one phony son of a bitch, I swear to God. I caught that case, I was the first person in there after the blues who responded to the 911 call. I saw him then, when he was still in shock and bleeding from a head wound and with his face red and raw from where he'd worked the tape off of his mouth. I saw him I don't know how many times over the next couple of weeks. Matt, he never rang true. I just did not buy that he was sorry she was dead."

"That wouldn't necessarily mean he killed her."

"That's a point. I've known killers who were sorry their victim was dead and I suppose it works the other way around. And I'm not setting myself up as Joseph Durkin the Human Polygraph. I can't always tell when somebody's lying. But with him it's easy. If his lips are moving, he's feeding you a line of shit."

"All by himself?"

He shook his head. "I don't see how. The woman was raped fore and aft with signs of forced entry. Semen deposited vaginally was definitely not from the husband. Different blood type."

"And in back?"

"No semen deposited anally. Maybe the guy in back was practicing safe sex."

"Rape in the modern age," I said.

"Well, it's all those leaflets the Surgeon General mailed out, raising the level of public consciousness and all. Anyway, from the looks of it you got your two burglars just the way the husband told it."

"Any other physical evidence besides semen?"

"Short and curlies. Seem to be two types, one that's definitely not the husband's, the other that's a possible. The thing is, you can't tell too much from pubic hair. You can tell both samples are from male Caucasians but that's about all you can get. Plus it doesn't prove anything if some of the hairs *are* Thurman's, because they were married, for Christ's sake, and it's not unheard of to carry your husband's pubic hair around in your bush for a day or two."

I thought for a moment. I said, "In order for Thurman to have done it solo—"

"Couldn't happen."

"Sure it could. All he needed was some foreign semen and pubic hair."

"How would he come by that? Blow a sailor and spit in a Glad bag?"

I thought fleetingly of Lyman Warriner's perception of Thurman as a closet case. "I suppose that's as good a way as any," I said. "I'm just running through what's remotely possible and what isn't. One way or another he obtained specimens of foreign semen and hair. He went to the party with his wife, came home—"

"Climbed three flights of stairs and told her to wait a minute while he forced entry to the Gottschalk apartment. 'Look, honey, I learned this neat way to open doors without the key.' "

"The door was forced?"

"Jimmied."

"That could have been done after."

"After what?"

"After he'd killed her and before he called 911. Say he had a key to the Gottschalk place."

"That's not what the Gottschalks say."

"He could have had one without them knowing about it."

"They had a couple of locks on the door."

"He could have had a couple of keys. 'Hang on, honey, I promised Roy and Irma I'd water the plants.' "

"That's not their names. Alfred Gottschalk, that's the lawyer. I forget the wife's name."

" 'I promised Alfred and Whatsername I'd water the plants.' "

"At one in the morning?"

"What's the difference? Maybe he says he wants to borrow a book from the Gottschalks, something he's been wanting to read. Maybe they're both a little giddy from the party and he tells her they'll sneak into the Gottschalk apartment and screw in their bed."

" 'It'll be exciting, honey, like before we were married.' "

"That's the idea. He gets her in there, he kills her, he makes it look like rape, he plants the physical evidence, the sperm and the pubic hairs. Did they find anything under her nails, anything to suggest she scratched anybody?"

"No, but he didn't say anything about her fighting them off. And you had two of them, so one could hold her hands while the other made whoopee."

"Let's get back to the idea of him doing it all by himself. He kills her and fakes the rape. He sets the stage in the Gottschalk apartment, makes it look like the place was burglarized. Did you get the Gottschalks to come up and see what was missing?"

He nodded. "He came up, Alfred. He said his wife's been ill, she's supposed to avoid unnecessary travel. They keep a couple hundred dollars cash in the refrigerator for emergencies, and that was gone. There was some jewelry missing, heirloom stuff, cuff links and rings he'd inherited but doesn't wear. Jewelry of hers, but he couldn't describe it because he didn't know what she'd taken to Florida and what was in the safe-deposit box. The good stuff was all in the bank or in Florida, so he didn't expect the loss would amount to much, but he'd have to have Ruth make up a detailed list of what was missing. That's the wife's name, Ruth. I knew it would come to me."

"What about furs?"

"She doesn't own any. She's an animal-rights activist. Not that she'd need a fur coat in the first place, spending six months and a day in Florida every year."

"Six months and a day?"

"Minimum, so they qualify as Florida residents for tax purposes. There's no state income tax in Florida."

"I thought he was retired."

"Well, he still has an income. From investments and so on."

"Anyway, no furs," I said. "Anything bulky? A stereo, a television set?"

"Nothing. There were two TVs, a big rear-projection set in the living room and a smaller model in the back bedroom. They unplugged the bedroom set and moved it into the living room but left it there. The way it reads, they were planning on taking the set and they either forgot it in the excitement or decided not to risk looking suspicious, not with a dead woman in the apartment."

"Assuming they knew she was dead."

"They beat her face in and wrapped her panty hose around her neck. They damn well knew she was in worse shape than before she ran into them."

"So they took some cash and some jewelry."

"That's what it looks like. That's all Gottschalk could come up with. Thing is, Matt, they turned the apartment upside down."

"The lab crew?"

"No, the burglars. They gave it a very thorough toss and made a mess doing it. Every drawer dumped, books off the shelves, that kind of thing. Not like they were searching for a secret stash, no mattresses slashed or cushions cut open, but a very thorough job all the same. I would guess they were looking for cash, and not a couple hundred dollars in the butter-keeper compartment in the refrigerator."

"What did Gottschalk say?"

"What could he say? 'I had a hundred grand in unreported cash and the bastards found it.' He said there wasn't anything really valuable in the apartment, except for some artwork, and they never touched that. He had some framed prints, signed and numbered stuff, Matisse and Chagall and

I forget what else, and he had a floater policy covering them. I think the value of all the art came to something like eighty grand. The thieves took some of the stuff off the wall, probably looking for a wall safe, but they didn't steal any of it."

"Say he did it himself," I said.

"We're back to that, huh? Go ahead."

"The place is really ransacked, so it looks like a bona fide burglary, but all he has to stash is a wad of cash and a handful of jewelry. Did you search him?"

"Thurman?" He shook his head. "Man's all beat up, hands tied behind his back, his wife's lying there dead, how are you gonna strip search him, look up his asshole for somebody's platinum cuff links? Anyway, your scenario, he could have stowed everything in his own apartment."

"I was just going to say that."

"Still with your scenario, he gets into the Gottschalk place with a key, two keys, whatever it takes, he does his wife, he fakes the rape scene, he steals the cash and the jewelry and takes them upstairs, rolls them up in a pair of socks and stashes them in his sock drawer. Then he comes back downstairs and uses a pry bar on the door, makes it look like forced entry. Then I suppose he goes back upstairs and stashes the pry bar, because we didn't find it in the Gottschalk place."

"Did you search Thurman's apartment?"

"That we did," he said. "With his permission. I told him there was a good possibility the burglars had started in his place and worked their way down, which I knew they hadn't because there was no sign of forced entry at the Thurman apartment. Of course they could have got in from the fire escape, but the hell with what they could have done, because nobody had been in there. But I searched it just the same, looking for anything that might have been lifted from downstairs."

"And you didn't find anything."

"Not a thing, but I don't know what that proves. I didn't

have a chance to fine-comb the place. And he could have added the Gottschalks' jewelry to his and his wife's jewelry boxes and I wouldn't have known the difference, because I didn't know what I was looking for. And the cash, a couple hundred dollars in cash, he could have stuck that in his fucking wallet."

"I thought the burglars took his wallet."

"Yeah, right. His watch and his wallet. They left it on the first floor on their way out of the building, just dropped it at the foot of the stairs. Stripped the cash but left the credit cards."

"He could have run down himself and left it there."

"Or stood at the stairs and dropped it over the railing. Saved himself running up and down."

"And the jewelry they supposedly took from his wife—"

"He could have put right back in her jewelry box. And his Rolex, well, who knows? Maybe he wasn't wearing it in the first place. Maybe he rolled it up in a sock."

I said, "Then what? He beats himself up, ties his hands behind his back, tapes his mouth—"

"I think if I was doing it I might tape my mouth before I tied my hands behind my back."

"You're a better planner than I am, Joe. How was he tied? Did you see him when he was still tied up?"

"No, dammit," he said, "and that's the one thing that never stops bothering me. I wanted to chew the hell out of the two uniforms who cut him loose, but what could you expect them to do? Here's a guy, respectable-looking man, nicely dressed, he's all tied up and hysterical on the floor and his wife's lying there dead, and how are you gonna tell him he has to stay that way until a detective gets to the scene? Of course they cut him loose. I'd have done the same thing in their position, and so would you."

"Sure."

"But I fucking well wish they hadn't. I wish I'd had a

look at him first. Still sticking with your scenario, that he pulled it all off on his own, your question is could he have tied himself up. Right?"

"Right."

"His legs were tied. It's not hard to do that yourself. His hands were tied behind his back, and you would think that would be impossible, but it's not, not necessarily." He opened a drawer, rooted around, and came up with a set of cuffs. "Put your hands out, Matt." He fastened the cuffs around my wrists. "Now," he said, "bend forward and get one leg at a time through there. Sit on the edge of the desk. Go ahead, you can do it."

"Jesus."

"You see this on television all the time, a guy's cuffed, hands behind his back, and he sort of jumps through the circle of his own arms and he's still cuffed but his hands are in front of him. Okay, now stand up and work your hands up behind your back."

"I don't think this is going to work."

"Well, it would help if you were a little skinnier. Thurman's got maybe a thirty-inch waist and no ass at all."

"Has he got long arms? It'd be easier if my arms were a few inches longer."

"I didn't check his sleeve length. That'd be a good place for you to start your investigation, now that I think of it. Go to all the Chinese laundries in the neighborhood, see if you can find out his shirt size."

"Open the cuffs, will you?"

"Gee, I don't know," he said. "I kind of like the effect, the way you're sort of grabbing your own ass, can't stand up straight and can't sit down. I hate to interfere."

"Come on."

"I was sure I had a key somewhere. Hey, no problem, we can just ankle on down to the front desk, somebody must have a key. Oh, all right." He produced a key, unlocked the handcuffs. I straightened up. My shoulder was sore, and I had pulled a muscle slightly in one thigh. "I don't know," he said. "They make it look a lot easier on television."

"No kidding."

"The thing is," he said, "without seeing how he was tied, I don't know what kind of a job they did of immobilizing him, or if it was something he could have done himself. I'm gonna drop your scenario and assume that there were burglars and they tied him up. You know what bothers me?"

"What?"

"He was still tied when the cops got there. He rolled off the bed, he knocked a table over, he made a telephone call—"

"With a pipe tool clamped firmly between his teeth."

"Yeah, right. He did all that, and he even worked the tape most of the way off his mouth, which I guess you could do."

"I would think so."

"You want me to get a roll of tape and we'll see if you can do it? Just a little joke, Matt. You know what your problem is? You got no sense of humor."

"I was wondering what my problem was."

"Well, now you know. Seriously, he does all the other stuff but he doesn't work his hands loose. Now sometimes you can't unless you're Houdini. If you've got no mobility and there's no give in the bonds, there's not much you can do. But he was able to move around, and how good a job could these guys have done on him, given that they were pretty amateurish when it came to burglary? I wish I'd seen how he was tied, because my hunch is that he probably could have worked his way free, but that he chose not to try. And why would he make that choice?"

"Because he wanted to be tied up when the cops got there."

"Exactly, because that alibied him for the murder. If he gets loose we can say he could have killed her, he wasn't really tied up in the first place. But now, the way things stand, what we can say is he stayed tied up because he wanted to be found that way. It doesn't prove anything because if you look at it that way he's damned if he does and damned if he doesn't, but as far as his motivation—"

"I know what you mean."

"So I wish I'd seen him before they cut him loose."

"So do I. How was he tied?"

"I just said—"

"I mean what did they use? Cord, clothesline, what?"

"Oh, right. They used a kind of household twine, pretty strong stuff, like you'd use to wrap a package. Or to tie up your girlfriend, if you happened to be into that kind of thing. Did they bring it with them? I don't know. The Gottschalks had a drawer in the kitchen with pliers and screwdrivers and the usual odds and ends of household hardware. The old man couldn't say whether they might have had a ball of twine in there or not. Who remembers that sort of thing, especially when you're seventy-eight years old and you live half the year in one place and the rest of the time somewhere else? The burglars dumped that drawer, so if there was twine in it they would have seen it."

"What about the tape?"

"Ordinary adhesive tape, white, kind you'd find in your medicine chest."

"Not in mine," I said. "In mine you'd find a bottle of Rexall aspirin and a thing of dental floss."

"Well, the kind you'd find in your medicine chest if you happened to live like a human being. Gottschalk said he thought they had adhesive tape, and there wasn't any in the bathroom. They didn't leave the roll behind, or the twine either."

"I wonder why not."

"I don't know. String savers, I guess. They took the pry bar, too. If I just left a woman dead in an apartment, I don't think I'd want to walk down the street carrying burglar's tools, but if they were geniuses—"

"They'd be in some other line of work."

"Right. Why take the stuff? If Thurman was in on it, and

if he was the one who bought the stuff, maybe they were afraid it could be traced. If they used what they found in the apartment . . . I don't know, Matt, the whole thing's so fucking speculative, you know?"

"I know. You bat around the whys and what ifs, though, and sometimes something shakes loose."

"Which is why we're batting them around."

"Did he describe the burglars?"

"Oh, sure. A little hazy on the details, but consistent from one interrogation to another. He didn't contradict himself enough to amount to anything. The descriptions are in the files, you'll see them for yourself. What they were, they were two big white guys about the same age as Thurman and his wife. They both had mustaches, and the bigger one had his hair long in the back, the way some of them wear it, with like a little tail growing down there?"

"I know how you mean."

"A really classy style, marks you right away as a member of the upper crust. Like the spades with those high flattops, looks like they got a fez stuck on their heads, like they trim it with hedge clippers. Class all the way. What was I saying?"

"The two burglars."

"Yeah, right. He went through the books of mug shots, very cooperative, very eager, but he didn't spot them. I sat him down with a police artist. I think you know him. Ray Galindez?"

"Sure."

"He's good, but his sketches always come out looking Hispanic to me. There's copies in the file. I think one of the papers ran them."

"I must have missed it."

"I think it was *Newsday*. We got a couple calls and wasted a little time checking them out. Nothing. You know what I think?"

"What?"

"I don't think he did it all by himself."

"No, neither do I."

"I mean you can't positively rule it out, because he could have found a way to tie himself up, and he could have managed to lose the pry bar and the tape and the twine. But I don't think that's what happened. I think he had help."

"I think you're right."

"He makes arrangements with a couple of skells, says here's a key to the front door, make it easy on yourselves, walk on in and go up three flights and bust into the fourth-floor apartment. Not to worry, there's nobody home, there won't be anybody home upstairs either. Make yourselves at home, dump the drawers, throw the books on the floor, and help yourselves to all the cash and jewelry you can find. Just so you're ready to go at twelve-thirty or one, whatever time we get home from the party."

"And they walk home because he doesn't want to get there too early."

"Maybe, or maybe they just walk home because it's a nice night. Who knows? They get to the Gottschalks' floor and she says, 'Oh, look, Ruth and Alfred's door is open,' and he shoves her through it and they grab her and knock her out and fuck her and kill her. Then he says, 'Hey, asshole, you don't want to walk down the street middle of the night carrying a television set, you can buy ten TVs with what I'm paying you for this.' So they leave the set, but they take the twine and tape and pry bar because maybe they can be traced. No, that's bullshit, how do you trace drugstore and hardware store shit like that?"

"They take the stuff because that way we'll know he couldn't have done it himself, because how could the twine and tape walk out of there under their own power?"

"Right, okay. But first before they take anything out of there they knock him around a little, and they do some fairly impressive superficial damage, you'll see photos we took of him in the file. Then they tie him up and tape him up, his mouth, and maybe they rip it halfway off for him so he'll be able to make the call when it's time."

"Or maybe they've got him tied loosely enough that he can get a hand free and do what he has to do and then slip it back under the twine."

"I was coming to that. Jesus, don't I wish those blues had been a little slower to cut him loose."

I said, "Anyway, they clear out and he waits as long as he can and then calls 911."

"Right. I don't see any holes in that."

"No."

"I mean, show me some other way it makes sense that he's alive. They just killed her, she's lying there dead, so why would they tie him up when it's so much easier to kill him?"

"They already tied him up and taped his mouth before they did her."

"Oh, right, that's his story. Even so, why leave him alive? He can ID the both of them all day long, and they're already going to hang for doing her—"

"Not in this state."

"Don't remind me, will you? Point is they're already down for Murder Two for doing her, they don't make it any worse for themselves by doing him while they're at it. They got the pry bar, all they gotta do is hit him a lick upside the head, as our little brown brothers would say."

"Maybe they did."

"Did what?"

"Hit him hard enough so that they thought he was dead. Remember, they just killed her, and maybe they didn't plan on it, so—"

"You mean if he's telling the truth."

"Right, playing devil's advocate for a minute. They killed her unintentionally—"

"Just happened to get her panty hose accidentally wrapped around her throat—"

"—and they don't exactly panic, but they're in a hurry,

they hit him a shot and he's unconscious and they think he's probably dead, that hard a shot with a steel bar ought to kill a man, and all they want to do is get the fuck out, they don't want to take his pulse, see if he's got enough breath left to fog a mirror."

"Shit."

"You see what I mean."

He sighed. "Yeah, I see what you mean. That's why it's an open file. The evidence is inconclusive and the facts we've got'll support any theory you want." He stood up. "I want some coffee," he said. "Can I get you some?"

"Sure," I said. "Why not?"

"I don't know why the coffee's so bad," he said. "I really don't. We used to have this machine, you know, coin-operated, and you can never get a halfway decent cup of coffee out of one of them. But we chipped in and bought one of these electric drip pots, and we use premium coffee, and it comes out tasting like this. I think there must be some law of nature, you're in a station house, the coffee has to taste like shit."

It didn't taste that bad to me. He said, "If we ever clear this one, you know how it'll happen."

"A snitch."

"A snitch hears something and passes it on, or one of the geniuses steps on his cock and we pick him up for something heavy, and he tries to do himself some good by ratting out his partner. And Thurman, assuming we're right and it was his game."

"Or even if it wasn't."

"What do you mean?"

I said, " 'She was alive and kicking when we left there, man. We put the pork to her but I swear she liked that part of it, an' we sure didn't wrap no stockings around her neck. Musta been her husband, decided to get hisself an instant divorce.' "

"Jesus, that's just how they'd say it."

"I know. That's what they'd say if Thurman was a hundred percent innocent. 'Wasn't me killed her, she was alive when I left.' And it could even be true."

"Huh?"

"Say it was a crime of opportunity. The Thurmans come home, walk in on a robbery in progress. The skells rob them and beat him up and rape her because they're animals, so why not act like it? Then they leave, and Thurman gets a hand free, and his wife's unconscious and he thinks she's dead—"

"But she's not dead, but it gives him an idea—"

"—and her panty hose is right there on the bed next to her, and next thing you know it's around her neck and this time she really is dead."

He thought about it. "Sure," he said. "Could be. The medical examiner set the time of death at around one o'clock, which squares with Thurman's story, but if he did her right after they left and then stalled a while, the time he was supposed to be unconscious and then struggling to free himself, well, that would all fit."

"Right."

"And nobody could implicate him. They could say she was alive when they left, but that's something they'd say anyway." He finished his coffee and threw the Styrofoam cup at the wastebasket. "Fuck this," he said. "You can go around and around. I think he did it. Whether he planned it or it fell in his lap, I think he did it. All that money."

"She inherited better than half a million, according to the brother."

He nodded. "Plus the insurance."

"He didn't say anything about insurance."

"It's possible nobody told him. They took out policies payable to each other shortly after they were married. Hundred-thousand-dollar straight life, double indemnity for accidental death."

"Well, that sweetens it a little," I said. "Raises the ante by two hundred kay."

He shook his head.

"Am I figuring wrong?"

"Uh-huh. She got pregnant in September. Soon as they found out, he got in touch with his insurance agent and raised the amount of their coverage. A baby coming, increased responsibilities. Makes sense, right?"

"What did he raise it to?"

"A million on his own life. After all, he's the breadwinner, his income's gonna be tough to replace. Still, her role's important, so he boosted her coverage to a half mil."

"So her death—"

"Meant an even million in insurance, because they still had the double-indemnity clause, plus all of her property that he'll inherit. Round it off, call it a total of a million and a half."

"Jesus."

"Yeah."

"Jesus Christ."

"Yeah, right. He's got means and motive and opportunity, and he's a heartless little fuck if I ever saw one, and I couldn't find a shred of evidence to show that he's guilty of a single fucking thing." He closed his eyes for a moment, then looked up at me. "Can I ask you something?"

"Sure."

"Do you use the dental floss?"

"Huh?"

"Aspirin and dental floss, you said that's all you've got in your medicine chest. Do you ever use it?"

"Oh," I said. "When I remember. My dentist nagged me into buying it."

"Same here, but I never use it."

"Neither do I, really. The good news is we'll never run out."

"That's it," he said. "We got a fucking lifetime supply."

4

THAT EVENING I MET ELAINE MARDELL IN FRONT OF A THEATER on Forty-second Street west of Ninth Avenue. She was wearing tight jeans and square-toed boots and a black leather motorcycle jacket with zippered pockets. I told her she looked great.

"I don't know," she said. "I was trying for off-Broadway, but I think I may have achieved off-off-Broadway."

We had good seats down front, but the theater was too small to have any bad seats. I don't remember the title of the play, but it was about homelessness, and the playwright was against it. One of the actors, Harley Ziegler, was a regular at Keep It Simple, an AA group that meets evenings at St. Paul the Apostle, just a couple of blocks from my hotel. In the play Harley was a wino who lived in a cardboard packing case. He gave a convincing performance, and why not? A few years ago he'd been playing the role in real life.

We went backstage afterward to congratulate Harley and ran into half a dozen other people I knew from meetings. They invited us to join them for coffee. Instead we walked ten blocks up Ninth to Paris Green, a restaurant we both liked. I had the swordfish steak and Elaine ordered linguini al pesto.

"I don't know about you," I said. "It seems to me you wear a lot of leather for a heterosexual vegetarian."

"It's one of those wacky little inconsistencies wherein lies the secret of my charm."

"I was wondering about that."

"Now you know."

"Now I know. There was a woman killed half a block from here a few months ago. She and her husband interrupted burglars in their downstairs neighbors' apartment and she wound up raped and murdered."

"I remember the case."

"Well, it's my case now. Her brother hired me yesterday, he thinks the husband did it. The couple whose apartment it was, the downstairs neighbors, he's this Jewish lawyer, retired, lots of dough, and she didn't have any furs stolen. You know why?"

"She was wearing them all at once."

"Uh-uh. She's an animal-rights activist."

"Oh yeah? Good for her."

"I suppose. I wonder if she wears leather shoes."

"Probably. Who cares?" She leaned forward. "Look," she said, "you could refuse to eat bread because yeast give their lives to make it. You could pass up antibiotics because what right do we have to murder germs? So she wears leather but she doesn't wear fur. So what?"

"Well—"

"Besides," she said, "leather's neat and fur's tacky."

"Well, that settles it."

"Good. Did the husband do it?"

"I don't know. I walked past the building earlier today. I can point it out to you later, it's on our way if I walk you home. Maybe you'll pick up some vibrations, solve the case just by walking past the murder site."

"But you didn't."

"No. He had a million and a half reasons to kill her."

"A million and a half—"

"Dollars," I supplied. "Between insurance and her own holdings." I told her about the Thurmans and what I'd learned from Joe Durkin and Lyman Warriner. "I'm not sure what I can do that the police haven't already done," I said.

"Just poke around, I guess. Knock on doors, talk to people. Be nice if I could find out he's been having an affair, but of course that was the first thing Durkin looked for and he couldn't turn up a thing."

"Maybe he's got a boyfriend."

"That would fit with my client's theory, but gay people have a tendency to think the whole world is gay."

"While you and I know the whole world is morose."

"Uh-huh. You want to go to Maspeth tomorrow night?"

"Speaking of what? Moroseness?"

"No, I just—"

"Or should it be morosity? Because Maspeth does sound pretty morose, although I shouldn't say that because I don't actually think I've ever been there. What's in Maspeth?" I told her and she said, "I don't like boxing much. It's not a moral issue, I don't care if two grown men want to stand around and hit each other, but I'd just as soon change the channel. Anyway, I've got a class tomorrow night."

"What is it this semester?"

"Contemporary Latin American Fiction. All the books I've been telling myself I really ought to read, and now I have to."

In the fall she'd studied urban architecture, and I'd gone with her a couple of times to look at buildings.

"You'll be missing the architecture of Maspeth," I said. "Although I haven't really got a good reason to go myself, to tell you the truth. I don't have to travel that far to get a look at him. He lives right here in the neighborhood and his office is at Forty-eighth and Sixth. I think I'm just looking for an excuse to go to the fights. If the New Maspeth Arena had squash matches instead of boxing I'd probably stay home."

"You don't like squash?"

"I like Orange Squash okay. I've never actually seen squash played, so what do I know? Maybe I'd like it."

"Maybe you would. I met a fellow once who's a nationally ranked squash player. A clinical psychologist from Schenectady, he was in town for a tournament at the New York Athletic Club. I never saw him play, though."

"I'll let you know if I run into him in Maspeth."

"Well, you never know. It's a small world. Did you say the Thurmans lived just a block from here?"

"Half a block."

"Maybe they used to come here. Maybe Gary knows them." She frowned. "Knew them. Knows him, knew her."

"Maybe. Let's ask him."

"You ask," she said. "I can't seem to get the verbs right."

After we'd settled the tab we went over to the bar. Gary was behind it, a tall lanky man with a droll manner and a beard that hung from his lower jaw like an oriole's nest. He said it was good to see us and asked when I would have some work for him. I told him it was hard to say.

"Once this gentleman entrusted me with a matter of grave importance," he told Elaine. "It was an undercover assignment and I acquitted myself well."

"I'm not surprised," she said.

I asked about Richard and Amanda Thurman. They came in occasionally, he said, sometimes with another couple, sometimes just the two of them. "He'd have a vodka mart before dinner," he said. "She'd have a glass of wine. Sometimes he'd come in by himself and have a quick beer at the bar. I don't remember the brand. Bud Light, Coors Light. Something light."

"Has he been in since the murder?"

"Only once that I saw him. A week, two weeks ago, he and another fellow came in and had dinner one night. That's the only time I've seen him since it happened. He lives very near here, you know."

"I know."

"Just halfway down the block." He leaned over the bar, dropped his voice. "What's the story? Is there a suspicion of foul play?"

"There'd have to be, don't you think? The woman was raped and strangled."

"You know what I mean. Did he do it?"

"What do you think? Does he look like a killer to you?"

"I've been in New York too long," he said. "Everybody looks like a killer to me."

On our way out Elaine said, "You know who might like to go to the fights tomorrow? Mick Ballou."

"He might at that. You want to stop at Grogan's for a minute?"

"Sure," she said. "I like Mick."

He was there, and glad to see us, and enthusiastic at the idea of driving out to Maspeth to watch grown men stand around hitting each other. We didn't stay long at Grogan's, and when we left I flagged a cab, so we didn't walk past the building where Amanda Thurman had died, to her husband's horror or with his complicity.

I stayed the night at Elaine's apartment, and I spent the next day starting to poke into the corners of Richard Thurman's life. I was back at my hotel in time to watch the five o'clock news on CNN. Then I took a shower and got dressed, and when I went downstairs Mick's silver Cadillac was parked out front next to a fire hydrant.

"Maspeth," he said. I asked him if he knew how to get there. "I do," he said. "There was a man who had a factory out there, a Romanian Jew he was. He had a dozen women working for him, putting together bits of metal and plastic, making staple removers."

"What's that?"

"Say you've stapled some papers together and you want to take them apart. You take one of his things and it nips the staple and draws it right out. He had some women assembling the creatures and others packing them a dozen to a box and shipping them all over the country." He sighed. "He was a gambler, though, and he borrowed money and couldn't pay it back."

"What happened?"

"Ah, that's a long story," he said. "I'll have to tell it to you one of these days."

Now, five hours later, we were heading back to Manhattan on the Queensboro Bridge. He hadn't said anything more about the factory owner in Maspeth. Instead, I was telling him about the Cable TV executive.

He said, "The things people do to each other."

He had done his share. One of the things he'd done, according to neighborhood legend, was kill a man named Farrelly and carry his head around in a bowling bag, lugging it in and out of a dozen Hell's Kitchen saloons. Some people said he never opened the bag, just told everybody what it contained, but there were others who swore they'd been there to see him haul out the head by the hair, saying, "Will you look at poor Paddy Farrelly? And isn't he the ugliest bastard you ever saw?"

In the newspapers they say he's known as the Butcher Boy, but it's only the newspapers that call him that, just as no one but a ring announcer ever called Eldon Rasheed the Bulldog. The Farrelly story probably has something to do with the sobriquet, but so does the bloodstained butcher's apron Mick likes to wear.

The apron belonged to his father. The senior Ballou had come over from France and worked cutting up carcasses in the wholesale meat markets on West Fourteenth Street. Mick's mother was Irish, and he got his speech from her and his looks from the old man.

He is a big man, tall and heavily built, with a massive monolithic quality to him that suggests a prehistoric monument, a stone head from Easter Island. His own head is like a boulder, the skin scarred by acne and violence, the cheeks starting to show the broken capillaries that years of drinking will earn you. His eyes are a startling green.

He is a hard drinker, a career criminal, and a man with blood on his hands as well as his apron, and there are people, he and I among them, who wonder at our friendship. I would be hard put to explain it, but neither could I easily explain my relationship with Elaine. It may be that all friendships are ultimately inexplicable, although some of them are harder to figure than others.

Mick invited me back to Grogan's for coffee or a Coke but I begged off. He admitted he was tired himself. "But one night next week we'll make a night of it," he said. "And at closing time we'll lock the doors and sit in the dark telling old stories."

"That sounds good to me."

"And go to mass in the morning."

"I don't know about that part of it," I said. "But the rest sounds good."

He dropped me in front of the Northwestern and I stopped at the desk on my way upstairs. There weren't any messages. I went on up and went to bed.

Waiting for sleep to come I found myself remembering the man I'd seen in Maspeth, the father who'd sat with his son in the front row of the center section. I knew I'd seen him somewhere and I still couldn't think where. The boy wasn't familiar to me, just the father.

Lying there in the dark it struck me that what was remarkable was not that the man looked familiar. I see people every day whom I sense I've seen before, and no wonder; New York teems with people, and thousands upon thousands of them pass through my field of vision every day, on the street, down in the subway, at a ballpark or in a theater or, say, a sports arena in Queens. No, what was unusual was not the sense of recognition but the urgency of the whole thing. For some reason I evidently felt it was very important that I place this man, that I figure out who he was and how I knew him.

Sitting there, his arm around the boy, his hand gripping the kid's shoulder, his other hand pointing at this and at that as he explained the ring action. And then another image, the hand moving to the boy's forehead, moving to smooth the light brown hair.

I focused on the image, wondering what could invest it with such urgency, and my mind fastened on it and then wandered down some other corridor, and I slept.

I awoke a few hours later when a garbage-collection crew made a noisy job of picking up at the restaurant next door. I used the bathroom and came back to bed. Images flickered in my mind's eye. The placard girl, tossing her head, straightening her shoulders. The father, his face animated. The hand on the boy's forehead. The girl. The father. The girl. The hand moving, smoothing the hair—

Christ!

I sat up. My heart was pounding, my mouth dry. I had trouble catching my breath.

I reached over, switched on the bedside lamp. I looked at the clock. It was a quarter to four, but I was done sleeping for the night.

5

SIX MONTHS EARLIER, ON AN OPPRESSIVELY HOT TUESDAY NIGHT around the middle of July, I was at my regular evening meeting in the basement of St. Paul's. I know it was a Tuesday because I had undertaken a six-month commitment to help stack the chairs after the Tuesday meetings. The theory holds that service of that sort helps you keep sober. I don't know about that. My own feeling is that not drinking keeps you sober, but stacking chairs probably doesn't do any harm. It's hard to pick up a drink while you've got a chair in each hand.

I don't remember anything specific about the meeting itself, but during the break a fellow named Will came up to me and said he'd like to talk with me after the meeting. I said that would be fine, but I wouldn't be able to leave right away, that I had to hang around for a few minutes to put the chairs away.

The meeting resumed, ending at ten o'clock with the Lord's Prayer, and the cleanup went quicker than usual because Will gave me a hand with the chairs. When we were done I asked him if he wanted to go someplace for coffee.

"No, I have to get home," he said. "This won't take that long, anyway. You're a detective, right?"

"More or less."

"And you used to be a cop. I heard you qualify when I was a month or so sober. Look, would you do me a favor? Would you take a look at this?"

He handed me a brown paper bag folded to make a compact parcel. I opened it and took out a videocassette in one of those semi-rigid translucent plastic cases the rental shops use. The label identified the picture as *The Dirty Dozen*.

I looked at it and then at Will. He was around forty, and he did some sort of work that involved computers. He was sober six months at the time, he'd come in right after the Christmas holidays, and I'd heard him qualify once. I knew his drinking story but not much about his personal life.

"I know the movie," I said. "I must have seen it four or five times."

"You've never seen this version."

"How is it different?"

"Just take my word for it. Or rather don't take my word, take the film home and look at it. You have a VCR, don't you?"

"No."

"Oh," he said, and he looked lost.

"If you could tell me what's so special about the movie—"

"No, I don't want to say anything, I want you to see it without any preconceptions. Shit." I gave him time to sort it out. "I'd say to come over to my apartment but I really can't do that tonight. Do you know anybody who has a VCR you could use?"

"I can think of someone."

"Great. Will you look at it, Matt? And I'll be here tomorrow night, and we can talk about it then."

"You want me to look at it tonight?"

"Could you do that?"

"Well," I said, "I'll try."

I had planned on joining the crowd at the Flame for coffee, but instead I went back to my hotel and called Elaine. "If this doesn't work just say so," I said, "but a fellow just gave me a movie and said I had to watch it tonight."

"Somebody gave you a movie?"

"You know, a cassette."

"Oh, I get it. And you want to watch it on my whatcha-macallit."

"Right."

"My VCR."

"If you're sure you don't mind."

"I can stand it if you can. The only thing is I'm a mess, I don't have makeup on."

"I didn't know you wore makeup," I said.

"Is that right."

"I thought that was natural beauty."

"Oh, boy," she said. "Some detective."

"I'll be right over."

"The hell you will," she said. "You'll give me fifteen minutes to gild the lily or I'll tell the doorman to throw you out on your ass."

It was more like half an hour by the time I walked over there. Elaine lives on East Fifty-first Street between First and Second Avenues. Her apartment is on the sixteenth floor, and from her living-room window you can look out across the East River at a fairly panoramic view of the borough of Queens. I suppose you could see Maspeth if you knew where to look for it.

She owns her apartment. The building went co-op a few years ago and she bought it. She also owns a fair amount of rental property, two-family houses and apartment buildings, some but not all of them in Queens. She has other invest-ments as well, and she could probably live decently off her investment income if she were to retire from her profession. But she hasn't chosen to do so, not yet.

She's a call girl. We met years ago, when I was a cop with a gold shield in my wallet and a house and a wife and kids in Syosset, which is far out on Long Island on the other side of Queens, much too remote to be seen from Elaine's window. She and I developed a relationship based, I suppose, on mutual need, which may be the basis of most if not all relationships, if you look deeply enough.

We did things for each other. I did for her the things a cop could do for someone in her position—warned off a predatory pimp, put the fear of God into a drunk client who was giving her a hard time, and, when another client was ungracious enough to drop dead in her bed, I dumped the body where it would do no harm to his reputation, or to hers. I did cop things for her and she did call-girl things for me, and it lasted for a surprisingly long time because we genuinely liked each other.

Then I stopped being a cop, gave up the detective's gold shield about the same time I let go of the house and the wife and the kids. Elaine and I rarely saw anything of each other. We might have lost track of each other altogether if either of us had moved, but we both stayed put. My drinking got worse, and finally after a few trips to detox I began to get the hang of not drinking.

I had been doing that for a couple of years, a day at a time, and then one day some trouble came at Elaine out of the past. It came specifically from a part of the past we had shared, and it wasn't just her trouble, it belonged to both of us. Dealing with it brought us together again, though it was hard to say just what that meant. She was, certainly, a very close friend. She was also the only person I saw with any frequency with whom I had a history, and for that reason alone she was important to me.

She was also the person I was sleeping with two or three nights a week, and just what that meant and just where it was going was beyond me. When I talked about it with Jim Faber, my AA sponsor, he told me to take it a day at a time. If you make it a habit to give advice like that in AA, before you know it you have a reputation as a sage.

The doorman called upstairs on the intercom, pointed me to the elevator. Elaine was waiting in the doorway, her hair in a ponytail, wearing hot-pink pedal pushers and a lime-green sleeveless blouse with the top buttons unbuttoned. She sported oversized gold hoop earrings and enough makeup to look marginally sluttish, which was an effect she never achieved unintentionally.

I said, "See? Natural beauty."

"So glad you appreciate it, meestair."

"It's that simple unspoiled look that gets me every time."

I followed her inside and she took the cassette from me. "*The Dirty Dozen*," she read. "This is the movie you absolutely positively have to see tonight?"

"So I'm told."

"Lee Marvin against the Nazis? That *Dirty Dozen*? You could have told me and I could have run down the whole plot for you over the phone. I saw it when it first came out and I couldn't tell you how many times I've seen it on television. Everybody's in it, Lee Marvin, Telly Savalas, Charles Bronson, Ernest Borgnine, and what's his name, he was in *M*A*S*H*—"

"Alan Alda?"

"No, the movie *M*A*S*H*, and not Elliott Gould, the other one. Donald Sutherland."

"Right, and Trini Lopez."

"I forgot about Trini Lopez. He gets killed right away when they parachute in."

"Don't spoil it for me."

"Very funny. Robert Ryan's in it, isn't he? And Robert Webber, he died just recently, he was such a good actor."

"I know Robert Ryan's dead."

"Robert Ryan died years ago. They're both gone, both Roberts. You've seen this movie, haven't you? Of course you have, everybody has."

"Time and time again."

"So why do you have to see it now? Business?"

I wondered myself. Will had made sure I was a detective before handing it to me. "Possibly," I said.

"Some business. I wish I got paid to watch old movies."

"Do you? I wish I got paid to screw."

"Nice, very nice. Be careful what you pray for. You're really gonna watch this or is that a gun in your pocket?"

"Huh?"

"Mae West. Forget it. Can I watch with you, or will that impede your concentration?"

"You're welcome to watch," I said, "but I'm not sure what we're going to be watching."

"*The Dirty Dozen, n'est-ce pas?* Isn't that what it says on the label?" She slapped herself on the forehead, Peter Falk's Columbo pretending to be struck by the obvious. "Counterfeit labels," she said. "You're doing more trademark-infringement work, right?"

I had been working per diem for a large investigations agency, hassling street vendors for selling *Batman* knock-offs, T-shirts and visors and such. Decent pay, but it was mean work, rousting new arrivals from Dakar and Karachi who didn't have a clue what they were doing wrong, and I hadn't had the heart for it. "I don't think that's exactly it," I said.

"Copyright, I mean. Somebody knocked off the packaging and stuck it on a bootleg tape. Am I right?"

"I don't think so," I said, "but you can keep right on guessing. The only thing is I'll have to watch the tape to know if you're right or wrong."

"Oh," she said. "Well, what the hell. Let's watch it."

It started off looking like just what the label promised. The opening credits rolled and Lee Marvin went from cell to cell. We were introduced to the twelve American soldiers who would make up the dirty dozen, killers and rapists and all-around fuck-ups under death sentences for their crimes.

"To my untrained eye," Elaine said, "this looks remarkably like the movie I remember."

It went on looking like it for ten minutes or so, and I was beginning to wonder if Will might have problems beyond

mere alcoholism and chemical dependency. Then the screen
went abruptly blank right in the middle of a scene and the
soundtrack cut out. The screen stayed blank for perhaps ten
seconds, and then it showed a slender young man with a
boyishly open, midwestern sort of face. He was cleanshaven,
and his light brown hair was parted at the side and neatly
combed. He was naked except for a canary-yellow towel
around his middle.

His wrists and ankles were shackled to an X-shaped
metal frame that stood at a 60-degree angle to the floor. In
addition to the metal shackles at his wrists and ankles, leather
cuffs had been fitted around each leg just above the knee and
each arm just above the elbow, and there was a matching
leather belt around his waist, part of it obscured by the yellow towel. All of these devices looked to be holding him
quite securely in place.

He did not appear to be particularly uncomfortable, and
he had a tentative smile on his face. He said, "Is that thing
running? Hey, am I supposed to say anything or what?"

A male voice off-camera told him to shut up. The young
man's mouth was open and he closed it. I could see now that
he was no more than a boy, not so much cleanshaven as
beardless. He was tall, but he didn't look to be more than
sixteen or so. There was no hair on his chest, although he did
have a pale tuft in each armpit.

The camera stayed on the boy, and a woman moved into
the frame. She was about as tall as the boy but looked taller
because she was standing erect, not spreadeagled and tied to
a crossframe. She wore a mask, the sort of device the Lone
Ranger wore, but hers looked to be of black leather. That
made it a match for the rest of her outfit, skintight black
leather pants open at the crotch and black gloves that covered
her clear to the elbows. She wore black shoes with three-inch
spike heels and silver trim at the toes, and that was all she
wore. She was naked above the waist, and the nipples of her
small breasts were erect. They were also scarlet, the same

shade as her full mouth, and I suspected she'd daubed them with lipstick.

"There's that simple unspoiled look you go for," Elaine said. "This is shaping up to be dirtier than *The Dirty Dozen*."

"You don't have to watch."

"What did I tell you before? I can stand it if you can. I used to have a client who liked to watch bondage films. They always struck me as pretty silly. Would you ever want me to tie you up?"

"No."

"Or to tie me up?"

"No."

"Maybe we're missing something. Fifty million perverts can't be wrong. Ah, here we go."

The woman unfastened the boy's towel and tossed it aside. Her gloved hand caressed him, and he became aroused at once.

"Ah, youth," Elaine said.

The camera moved in for a close-up of her hand gripping him, manipulating him. Then it pulled back and she released him and tugged at each finger of the glove in turn, finally removing it.

"Gypsy Rose Lee," Elaine said.

The nails of the ungloved hand were painted with a polish that matched the lipstick on her mouth and nipples. She held the long glove in her bare hand and struck the boy across the chest with it.

"Hey," he said.

"Shut up," she said. She sounded angry. She swung the glove again and hit him across the mouth. His eyes widened. She hit him on the chest, then struck his face again.

He said, "Hey, watch it, huh? I mean, that really hurt."

"I bet it did," Elaine said. "Look, she marked his face. I think she's getting carried away with the role."

The man off-camera told the boy to be quiet. "He told you to shut up," the woman said. She leaned across the boy's body, rubbing herself against him. She kissed his mouth, touched the fingertips of her bare hand to the mark her glove had left on his cheek. She moved lower and trailed kisses across his chest, her lipstick marking him where she kissed him.

"Hot stuff," Elaine said. She had been sitting on a chair, but now she came over and sat beside me on the couch and put her hand on my thigh. "Guy told you you had to watch this tonight, huh?"

"That's right."

"He tell you to have your girlfriend around while you watched it? Hmmm?"

Her hand moved on my leg. I covered it with my hand, stopped its movement.

"What's the matter?" she said. "I'm not allowed to touch?"

Before I could answer, the woman on the screen took the boy's penis in her gloved hand. Then, with her other hand, she swung the glove and struck him hard across the scrotum.

He said, "*Owww!* Jesus, cut that out, will you? That hurt! Let me down, let me off this thing, I don't want to do this anymore—"

He was going on in that vein when the woman, her face a mask of cold fury, stepped forward and drove her knee into his unprotected groin.

He screamed. The same off-camera male voice said, "Tape his mouth, for Christ's sake. I don't want to listen to that shit. Here, get out of the way, I'll take care of it myself."

I had assumed the male voice belonged to the cameraman, but there was no break in the filming while the voice's owner stepped into the picture. He looked to be wearing a skin diver's wet suit, but when I said as much to Elaine she corrected me.

"It's rubber wear," she said. "Black rubber. They have it custom-made."

"Who does?"

"Rubber freaks. She's into leather, he's into rubber. 'Can This Marriage Be Saved?' "

He was wearing a black rubber mask as well, actually more of a hood that covered his entire head. There was a hole for each eye, and another for his nose and mouth. When he turned I saw that there was an opening as well at the crotch of the rubber suit. His penis protruded, long and limp.

"The man in the rubber mask," Elaine intoned. "What has he got to hide?"

"I don't know."

"You couldn't skin-dive in that thing, not unless you wanted the fish to give you a blow job. I can tell you one thing about this guy. He's not Jewish."

He had by this time covered the boy's mouth with several lengths of tape. Now the Leather Girl handed him her glove, and he left more red marks on the boy's skin. His hands were large, with dark hair on their backs. The rubber suit stopped at the wrists, and because his hands were nearly the only exposed part of him, I noticed them more than I might have otherwise. He was wearing a massive gold ring on the fourth finger of his right hand. It was set with a large polished stone I couldn't identify. It was either black or dark blue.

He dropped to his knees now and took the boy in his mouth. When he had restored him to an erect state he drew back and wrapped a rawhide thong tightly around the base of the boy's penis. "Now it'll stay hard," he told the woman. "You stop the vein, the blood flows in but it can't flow out."

"Like a roach motel," Elaine murmured.

The woman straddled the boy, taking him into the opening in her leather pants and the corresponding opening in her flesh. She rode him while the man caressed them in turn, now cupping her bare breasts, then tweaking the boy's nipples.

The boy's face kept changing expression. He was frightened but he was also excited. He winced in pain when they hurt him, but the rest of the time he looked wary, as if he wanted to enjoy what was happening but he was afraid of what might happen next.

Watching, Elaine and I had ceased to comment on what we were seeing, and her hand had long since withdrawn from my thigh. There was something about the performance that stifled commentary as surely as the square of white tape quieted the boy.

I was beginning to have a very bad feeling about what we were watching.

My apprehension was confirmed when the pace of Leather Woman's ride picked up. "Come on," she urged, breathless. "Do his tits."

Rubber Man moved out of the frame. He came back holding something, and at first I couldn't see what it was. Then I recognized it as a gardener's implement, something you'd use to prune a rosebush.

Still riding the boy, she worked one of his nipples between her thumb and forefinger, rolling it, pulling at it. The man laid one hand on the boy's forehead. The boy's eyes were rolling wildly. Gently, tenderly, the man's hand moved to smooth back the light brown hair.

With his other hand he positioned the pruning shears. "Now!" the woman demanded, but he waited, and she had to say it again.

Then, still stroking the boy's forehead, still smoothing his hair, he tightened his grip on the pruning shears and cut off the boy's nipple.

I triggered the remote and the screen went blank. Elaine had her arms folded so that each hand was cupping the opposite elbow. Her upper arms were pressed against her sides and she was trembling slightly.

I said, "I don't think you want to watch the rest of this."

She didn't respond right away, just sat there on the couch, breathing in and out, in and out. Then she said, "That was real, wasn't it?"

"I'm afraid so."

"They cut him, they, what do you call it, pruned, that's it, they pruned his nipple. If they got him to a hospital right away they could reattach it. Didn't one of the Mets—"

"Bobby Ojeda. Last year, it was the tip of one finger."

"On his throwing hand, wasn't it?"

"His pitching hand, yes."

"And he was rushed to the hospital. I don't know if it would work with a nipple." Deep breaths, in and out. "I don't suppose anybody rushed this kid to the hospital."

"No, I don't suppose so."

"I feel like I could pass out or throw up or something."

"Bend over and put your head between your knees."

"And then what, kiss my ass goodbye?"

"If you're feeling faint—"

"I know, to get the blood back in my head. I was just making a joke. 'She must be all right, Nurse, she's making jokes.' I'm okay, though. You know me, I was brought up right, I'm a good date, I never faint and I never puke and I never order the lobster. Matt, did you know that was going to happen?"

"No idea."

"Clip, and his nipple's gone, and the blood just oozing out, trailing down across his chest. Flowing in a sort of zig-zaggy line, like an old river. What's the word when a river does that?"

"I don't know."

"Meandering, that's it. Blood meandering down his chest. Are you going to watch the rest of it?"

"I think I'd better."

"It's going to get worse, isn't it?"

"I think so, yes."

"Will he bleed to death?"

"Not from a cut like that."

"What happens? The blood just clots?"

"Sooner or later."

"Unless you've got hemophilia. I don't think I can watch any more of this."

"I don't think you should try. Why don't you wait for me in the bedroom."

"And you'll tell me when it's safe to come out?"

I nodded. She stood up, looking unsteady on her feet at first, then getting hold of herself and walking from the room. I heard the bedroom door click shut and still waited, in no great hurry myself to see what happened next. After a minute or two, though, I worked the remote and turned the whole thing back on again.

I watched it all the way through to the end. About ten minutes in I heard Elaine's bedroom door open but I kept my eyes on the set. I was aware of it when she passed behind me to reclaim her seat on the couch. I didn't look over at her, though, or say anything. I just sat there, bearing witness.

When it ended the screen went blank again, and then we were abruptly plunged back into the action of *The Dirty Dozen*, with the major's gang of cutthroats and sociopaths unleashed on a castle full of Nazi officers enjoying R-and-R in occupied France. We sat and watched the damn thing all the way through to the end, watched Telly Savalas have his wild-eyed psychotic break, watched our heroes fire guns and hurl grenades and raise all-around hell.

After the final frame, after the credit roll, Elaine walked over to the set and pressed Rewind. With her back to me she said, "How many times did I say I must have seen this movie? Five or six? Every single time I find myself hoping this time it'll be different and John Cassavetes won't get killed at the end. He's a rotten person but it breaks your heart when he gets killed, doesn't it?"

"Yes."

"Because they've pulled it off and they're in the clear and then a last bullet comes from out of nowhere and just like that the man's dead. John Cassavetes is dead, too, isn't he? Didn't he die last year?"

"I think so."

"And Lee Marvin's dead, of course. Lee Marvin and John Cassavetes and Robert Ryan and Robert Webber. Who else?"

"I don't know."

She was standing in front of me now, glaring down at me. "Everybody's dead," she said angrily. "Have you noticed that? People keep dying left and right. Even the fucking ayatollah died, and I thought that raghead sonofabitch was going to live forever. They killed that boy, didn't they?"

"That's what it looked like."

"That's what it was. They tortured him and fucked him and tortured him some more and fucked him some more, and then they killed him. That's what we just saw."

"Yes."

"I'm all mixed up," she said. She went over and threw herself down on the chair. "*The Dirty Dozen*, people get killed left and right, all those Germans and some of our guys, and so what? You see it and it's nothing. But this other thing, those two creeps and that kid—"

"It was real."

"How could anybody *do* anything like that? I wasn't born yesterday, I'm not particularly naive. At least I don't think I am. Am I?"

"I never thought so."

"I'm a woman of the world, for Christ's sake. I mean, let's come right out and say it, I'm a whore."

"Elaine—"

"No, let me finish, baby. I'm not debasing myself, I'm only stating a fact. I happen to be in a profession where you don't necessarily see people at their best. I know the world is full of weirdos and nut jobs. I'm aware of that. I know people are kinky, I know they like to play dress-up and wear leather and rubber and fur and tie each other up and play mind-fuck games and all the rest of it. And I know there are people who lose it and go off the chart and do terrible things. I almost got killed by one of them, do you remember?"

"Vividly."

"Me too. Well, okay. Fine. Welcome to the world. There are days when I think somebody ought to pull the plug on the whole human race, but okay, in the meantime I can live with it. But I just can't get my mind around this shit, I really can't."

"I know."

"I feel dirty," she said. "I need a shower."

6

I WOULD HAVE CALLED WILL FIRST THING THE NEXT MORNING but I didn't know how to get hold of him. I knew deeply personal things about him, I knew he started drinking cough syrup at twelve, I knew his fiancé had broken up with him because he'd gotten into a drunken argument with her father, I knew his current marriage had hit a rocky stretch when he sobered up. But I didn't know the guy's last name or where he worked, so I had to wait until the eight-thirty meeting.

He got to St. Paul's just after the meeting started, and on the break he made a beeline for me and wanted to know if I'd had a chance to see the film. "Sure," I said, "it's always been one of my favorites. I especially liked the part where Donald Sutherland impersonates a general and reviews the troops."

"Jesus," he said, "I specifically wanted you to watch that particular film, the cassette I gave you last night. Didn't I tell you?"

"Just a little joke," I said.

"Oh."

"I saw the thing. It wasn't my idea of a good time, but I saw it all the way through."

"And?"

"And what?"

I decided we could get along without the second half of the meeting. I took his arm and led him outside and up a flight of stairs to street level. Across Ninth Avenue a man and woman were arguing about money, their voices carrying far and wide on the warm air. I asked Will where the cassette had come from.

"You saw the label," he said. "The video-rental place around the corner from me. Sixty-first and Broadway."

"You rented it?"

"That's right. I've seen it before, Mimi and I have both seen it several times, but we caught one of the sequels on cable last week and we wanted to look at the real thing again. And you know what we saw."

"Right."

"A fucking snuff film. That's what they're called, isn't it?"

"I think so."

"I never saw one before."

"Neither did I."

"Really? I thought being a cop and a detective and all—"

"Never."

He sighed. "Well, what do we do now?"

"What do you mean, Will?"

"Do we go to the cops? I don't want to get in trouble but I wouldn't feel right just looking the other way, either. I guess what I'm saying is I want your advice on how to proceed."

They were still yelling at each other on the far side of the avenue. Leave me alone, the man kept saying. Leave me the fuck alone.

I said, "Let me get a clear picture of how you wound up with the film. You walked into the store, you picked it off the shelf—"

"You don't pick the actual cassette off the shelf."

"You don't?"

He explained the procedure, how they had a cardboard sleeve that they displayed, and you took that to the counter and exchanged it for the cassette that went with it. He had a membership there, so they checked the film out to him and collected the charge for an overnight rental, whatever it was. A couple of dollars.

"And this was at Broadway and Sixty-first?"

He nodded. "Two, three doors from the corner. Right next to Martin's Bar." I knew the bar, a big open room like a Blarney Stone, with low-priced drinks and hot food on a steam table. Years ago they'd had a sign in the window touting their Happy Hour, with drinks at half price from 8 to 10 A.M. That's got to be some Happy Hour at eight in the morning.

"How late are they open?"

"Eleven, I think. Midnight on weekends."

"I'll go talk to them," I said.

"Now?"

"Why not?"

"Well, I don't know. Do you want me to come with you?"

"There's no need."

"You're sure? Because in that case I think I'll go back for the rest of the meeting."

"You might as well."

He turned away, then back again. "Oh, Matt? I was supposed to bring the film back yesterday, so they may want to charge for an extra day. Whatever it comes to, just let me know and I'll reimburse you."

I told him that wasn't something he had to worry about.

The video-rental store was where Will had told me it would be. I stopped at my room first and had the cassette with me when I walked in. There were four or five customers browsing, a man and a woman behind the counter. They were both in their thirties, and he had a two- or three-day growth of beard. I figured he was the manager. If she was in charge, she probably would have told him to go home and shave.

I walked over to him and said I wanted to speak to the manager. "I'm the owner," he said. "Will that do?"

I showed him the cassette. "I believe you rented this," I said.

"That's our label, so it must be one of ours. *The Dirty Dozen*, always a popular favorite. Something wrong with it? And are you sure it's the tape or has it been a while since you cleaned your heads?"

"A customer of yours checked this out two days ago."

"And you're returning it for him? If it was two days there'll be a late charge. Let me look it up." He went over to a computer terminal and keyed in a code number from the label. "William Haberman," he said. "According to this it was three days ago, not two, so that means he owes us four dollars and ninety cents."

I didn't reach for my wallet. I said, "Are you familiar with this particular tape? Not the film itself but the individual cassette?"

"Should I be?"

"There's another film recorded over half of it."

"Let me see that," he said. He took the cassette from me and pointed at one edge. "See right there? Your blank cassette has a tab there. You record something you want to save, you break the tab off and you can't record over it by mistake. A commercial cassette like this comes with a gap where the tab would be so you can't ruin it by accidentally hitting the Record button, which people would do all the time otherwise, geniuses that they are. But if you bridge the gap with a piece of Scotch tape, then you're back in business. You sure that's not what your friend did?"

"I'm very sure."

He looked suspicious for a moment, then shrugged. "So he wants another copy of *Dozen*, right? No problem, it's a popular title, we've got multiple copies. Not an even dozen, dirty or otherwise, but enough." He was on his way to get one when I stopped him with a hand on his arm.

"That's not the problem," I said.

"Oh?"

"Someone recorded a pornographic movie over the middle section of *The Dirty Dozen*," I said. "Not just the usual X-rated romp but an extremely violent and sadistic specimen of kiddie porn."

"You're kidding."

I shook my head. "I'd like to know how it got there," I said.

"Jesus, I'll bet you would," he said. He reached to touch the cassette, drew his hand away as if it were hot. "I swear I had nothing to do with it. We don't carry any X-rated stuff, no *Deep Throat*, no *Devil in Miss Jones*, none of that garbage. Most rental shops have a section or at least a few titles, you get married couples who want some visual foreplay, they're not the type to patronize the cesspools on Times Square. But when I opened up I decided I didn't want to have anything to do with that kind of material. I don't want it in my store." He looked down at the cassette but made no move to touch it. "So how did it get here? That's the big question, isn't it?"

"Someone probably wanted to make a copy of another tape."

"And he didn't have a blank cassette handy so he used this one instead. But why use a rental tape and then turn it in the next day? It doesn't make sense."

"Maybe someone made a mistake," I suggested. "Who was the last person to rent it?"

"Before Haberman, you mean. Let's see." He consulted the computer, frowned. "He was the first," he said.

"It was a brand-new tape?"

"No, of course not. Does it look like a new tape? I don't know, you get everything on computer and you can keep records like never before, and then it does something like this. Oh, *wait* a minute. I know where this tape came from."

A woman, he explained, had brought in a whole shopping bag full of videocassettes, most of them good solid classics. "There were all three versions of *The Maltese Falcon*, if you can believe that. One from 1936 called *Satan Met a Lady*, with Bette Davis and Warren William. Arthur Treacher plays

Joel Cairo, and the Sydney Greenstreet role is played by a fat lady named Alison Skipworth, believe it or not. And then there's the original 1931 version, with Ricardo Cortez playing Spade as a real slimeball, nothing like the hero Bogart made him into in 1940. That was called *The Maltese Falcon,* but after they released the Huston version the first one was retitled. *Dangerous Female,* they called it."

The woman had said she was a landlady. A tenant of hers had died and she was selling off some of his things to recoup the back rent he owed.

"So I bought the lot," he said. "I don't know if he really owed back rent or she just saw a chance to pick up a couple of dollars, but I knew she wasn't a burglar, she hadn't gone and stolen the tapes. And they were in good condition, the ones I looked at." A rueful smile. "I didn't look at all of them. I certainly didn't look at this one."

"That would explain it," I said. "If he owned the tape, whoever he was—"

"And he had a tape to copy, and maybe it was the middle of the night so he couldn't go out and buy a blank cassette. Sure, that makes sense. He wouldn't record on a rental cassette, but this one didn't become a rental cassette until I bought it from her, and by then he had already dubbed something else onto it." He looked at me. "Really kiddie porn? You weren't exaggerating?"

I said I wasn't. He said something about the kind of world it was, and I asked the woman's name.

"No way I'd remember it," he said, "assuming I ever knew it in the first place, which I don't think I did."

"Didn't you write her a check?"

"Probably not. I think she wanted cash. People generally do. There's a chance I wrote out a check. Do you want me to see?"

"I'd appreciate it."

He took time out to wait on a customer, then went into

a back room and emerged a few minutes later. "No check," he said. "I didn't think there would be. I found my memo of the transaction, which is amazing enough. She had thirty-one cassettes and I gave her seventy-five dollars. That sounds low, but these were used items, and it's the overhead that's everything in this business."

"Did you have her name on the transaction memo?"

"No. The date's June fourth, if that's any help. And I've never seen the woman before or since. I gather she lives in the neighborhood, but I don't know anything more about her than that."

He couldn't come up with anything else, and I couldn't think of any more questions to ask him. He said that Will had a one-night rental of *The Dirty Dozen* coming, an unimpaired copy, and at no charge.

When I got back to my hotel I looked up Will's number— it was easy now that I knew his last name. I called him and told him he could pick up his free movie whenever he wanted.

"As far as the other movie goes," I said, "there's nothing for either of us to do. Some guy copied a tape onto his own cassette of *The Dirty Dozen* and it wound up finding its way into circulation. The man whose tape it was is dead and there's no way of finding out who he was, let alone tracing the tape back from him. Anyway, items like that get passed around and around like that, with people interested in that sort of thing copying each other's tapes because that's the only way to get the stuff, it's not available on the open market."

"Thank God for that," he said. "But is it all right to just forget about it? A boy was killed."

"The original tape could be ten years old," I said. "It could have been shot in Brazil." Not likely, not with everybody speaking American English, but he let it pass. "It's a pretty horrible piece of tape, and my life would be every bit as rich and fulfilling if I'd never seen it, but I don't see that there's anything to be done about it. There are probably hundreds of similar tapes around the city. Dozens, anyway. The only thing special about this one is that you and I happened to see it."

"There's no point in taking it to the police?"

"None that I can see. They'd confiscate it, but then what? It would just go in a storeroom somewhere, and meanwhile you'd have to answer a lot of questions about how it happened to wind up in your hands."

"I don't want that."

"Of course not."

"Well," he said. "Then I guess we just forget about it."

Except that I couldn't.

What I had seen and the manner in which I had seen it made a fairly deep impression on me. I had been speaking the truth when I told Will I had never seen a snuff film. I heard rumors from time to time—that they'd confiscated one in Chinatown, for instance, and they'd set up a projector at the Fifth Precinct and screened it. The cop I heard it from said the cop who'd told him had left the room when the girl in the film had her hand cut off, and maybe it happened just that way, but cops' stories get improved with the telling the same as saloon stories about Paddy Farrelly's head. I knew there were films like that, and I knew there were people who would make them and others who would watch them, but the world they lived in had never before impinged upon my own.

And so there were things that stayed with me, and they were not what I might have expected. The boy's laconic air when the filming began—"Is that thing running? Am I supposed to say anything?" His surprise when the party got nasty, and his inability to believe what was happening.

The man's hand on the boy's forehead in the midst of it all, gentle, solicitous, smoothing the hair back. It was a gesture repeated intermittently through the proceedings, until the final cruelty was inflicted and the camera panned to a drain set in the floor a few yards from the boy's feet. We had seen the drain before but now the camera made a special point of seeking it out, a black metal grid set in a black-and-white checkerboard floor. Blood, red as the female performer's lipstick, red as her long fingernails and the tips of her little breasts, flowed across the squares of black and white, flowed into the drain.

That was the final shot, no people in it, just the floor tiles and the drain and the blood flowing. Then a white screen, and then Lee Marvin again, making the world safe for democracy.

For a few days, maybe as much as a week, I found myself thinking about what I had seen. I didn't do anything about it, though, because I couldn't think what to do. I had stashed the cassette in my safe-deposit box without looking at it a second time—once was enough—and, while it seemed like something I ought to hang on to, what was there to do with it? What it was, really, was a videotape in which two unidentifiable persons had sexual relations with one another and with a third person, also unidentified, whom they mistreated, presumably against his will, and almost certainly killed. There was no way to tell who they were or where and when they did what they did.

One day after a noon meeting I walked down Broadway to Forty-second Street, where I spent a couple of hours on the nasty stretch between Broadway and Eighth. I walked in and out of a lot of porno shops. I was self-conscious at first, but I got over it, and I took my time and browsed in the S-and-M sections. Each shop had some—bondage, discipline, torture, pain, each with a few sentences of description and a still photo on the outside to whet your appetite.

I didn't expect to see our version of *The Dirty Dozen* offered commercially. Censorship in the Times Square shops is minimal, but kiddie porn and murder are still prohibited, and what I'd seen was both of those. The boy might have been old enough to pass, and a good editor could conceivably have trimmed the worst of the violence, but it still seemed unlikely that I'd run across a soft version offered for sale.

There was a possibility, though, that Rubber Man and Leather Woman had made other films, separately or together. I didn't know if I would recognize them but I thought I might, especially if they appeared again in the same costumes. So that's what I was looking for, if indeed I was looking for anything.

On the uptown side of Forty-second Street, perhaps five doors east of Eighth Avenue, there was a hole-in-the-wall shop much like the others, except that it seemed to specialize in sadomasochistic material. It had all the other specialties as well, of course, but its S-and-M section was proportionately larger. There were videos ranging from $19.98 all the way up to $100, and there were photo magazines with names like *Tit Torture*.

I looked at all of the videocassettes, including the ones made in Japan and Germany and the aggressively amateurish ones with crude computer-printed labels. Before I was halfway through I had ceased really looking for Rubber Man and his heartless partner. I wasn't looking for anything. I was just letting myself soak up this world to which I'd been so abruptly introduced. It had always been here, less than a mile from where I lived, and I had always known of it, but I'd never let myself sink into it before. I'd never had reason to.

I got out of there, finally. I must have been in the shop for close to an hour, looking at everything, buying nothing. If this bothered the clerk he kept his annoyance to himself. He was a dark-skinned young man from the Indian subcontinent, and he kept his face expressionless and never said a word. In fact no one in the shop ever spoke, not he, not I, not any of the other customers. Everyone was careful to avoid eye contact, browsing, buying or not buying, and moving into and through and out of the store as if genuinely unaware of anyone else's presence. Now and then the door would open and close, now and then there'd be a jingly sound as the clerk counted out change into somebody's palm, quarters for the video booths at the back. Otherwise all was silence.

I took a shower as soon as I got back to my hotel. That helped, but I still carried the aura of Times Square around with me. I went to a meeting that night and took another shower and went to bed. In the morning I had a light breakfast and read the paper, and then I walked down Eighth Avenue and turned left on the Deuce.

The same clerk was on duty, but if he recognized me he kept it to himself. I bought ten dollars' worth of quarters and went into one of the little booths in back and locked the door. It doesn't matter which booth you select because each contains a video terminal hooked into a single sixteen-channel closed-circuit system. You can switch from channel to channel at will. It's like watching television at home, except the programming is different and a quarter buys you a scant thirty seconds of viewing time.

I stayed in there until my quarters were gone. I watched men and women do various things to one another, each some variation on an overall theme of punishment and pain. Some of the victims seemed to be enjoying the proceedings, and none looked to be in any real distress. They were performers, willing volunteers, troupers putting on a show.

Nothing that I saw was much like what I'd seen at Elaine's.

When I got out of there I was ten dollars poorer and felt about that many years older. It was hot and humid out, it had been like that all week, and I wiped sweat off my forehead and wondered what I was doing on Forty-second Street and why I'd come there. They didn't have anything I wanted.

But I couldn't seem to get off the block. I wasn't drawn to any other porno stores, nor did I want any of the services the street had to offer. I didn't want to buy drugs or hire a sexual partner. I didn't want to watch a kung fu movie or buy basketball sneakers or electronic equipment or a straw hat with a two-inch brim. I could have bought a switchblade knife ("Sold only in kit form; assembly may be illegal in some states") or some fake photo ID, printed while-U-wait, $5 black-and-white, $10 color. I could have played Pac-Man or Donkey Kong, or listened to a white-haired black man with a bullhorn who had absolute conclusive proof that Jesus Christ was a full-blooded Negro born in present-day Gabon.

I walked back and forth, back and forth. At one point I crossed Eighth and had a sandwich and a glass of milk at a stand-up lunch counter in the Port Authority bus terminal. I hung out there for a while—the air-conditioning was a blessing—and then something drove me back onto the street.

One of the theaters had a pair of John Wayne movies, *The War Wagon* and *She Wore a Yellow Ribbon*. I paid a dollar or two, whatever it cost, and went inside. I sat through the second half of one film and the first half of the other and went outside again.

And walked some more.

I was lost in thought and not paying attention when a black kid stepped up next to me and asked me what I was doing. I turned to look at him and he stared up at me with a challenging look in his eyes. He was fifteen or sixteen or seventeen, around the same age as the boy murdered in the film, but he looked far more streetwise.

"I'm just looking in a store window," I said.

"You been lookin' in every window," he said. "You been up and down the block time and time again."

"So?"

"So what you lookin' *for?*"

"Nothing."

"Walk on down to the corner," he said. "Down to Eighth, and then around the corner and wait."

"Why?"

"Why? So all these people don't be lookin' at us, that's why."

I waited for him on Eighth Avenue, and he must have run around the block or taken a shortcut through the Carter Hotel. Years ago it was the Hotel Dixie, and it was famous for one thing—the switchboard operator answered every call, "Hotel Dixie, so what?" I think they changed the name about the same time that Jimmy Carter took the presidency away from Gerald Ford, but I could be wrong about that, and if it's true it's probably coincidence.

I was standing in a doorway when he approached, walking south from Forty-third Street, his hands in his pockets and his head cocked to one side. He was wearing a denim jacket over a T-shirt and jeans. You would have thought he'd be roasting in that jacket, but the heat didn't seem to bother him.

He said, "I seen you yesterday and I seen you all day today. Back an' forth, back an' forth. What you lookin' for, man?"

"Nothing."

"Shit. Everybody on the Deuce be lookin' for somethin'. First I thought you was a cop, but you ain't a cop."

"How do you know?"

"You ain't." He took a long look at me. "Are you? Maybe you are."

I laughed.

"What you laughin' at? You actin' strange, man. Man asks do you want to buy reefer, do you want to buy rock, you just give your head a quick little shake, you don't even look at the man. You want any kind of drugs?"

"No."

"No. You want a date with a girl?" I shook my head. "A boy? Boy *and* a girl? You want to see a show, you want to *be* a show? Tell me what you want."

"I just came here to walk around," I said. "I had some things to think about."

"Sheeeee," he said. "Come on down to the Deuce to think. Put on my thinkin' cap, come on down to the Street. You don't say what you really want, how you gonna get it?"

"I don't want anything."

"Tell me what you want, I help you get it."

"I told you, there's nothing I want."

"Well, shit, plenty of shit *I* want. Say you gimme a dollar."

There was no menace to him, no intimidation. I said, "Why should I give you a dollar?"

"Just 'cause you an' me be friends. Then maybe on account of we friends, I be givin' you a jay. How's that sound?"

"I don't smoke dope."

"You don't smoke dope? What *do* you smoke?"

"I don't smoke anything."

"Then gimme a dollar an' I won't give you nothin'."

I laughed in spite of myself. I glanced around and no one was paying attention to us. I got out my wallet and handed him a five.

"What's this for?"

"'Cause we're friends."

"Yeah, but what do you want? You want me to go somewhere with you?"

"No."

"You just givin' me this here."

"No strings. If you don't want it—"

I reached for the bill and he snatched it away, laughing. "Hey now," he said. "You don't be givin' an' takin' back. Didn't your mama teach you better'n that?" He pocketed the bill, cocked his head and gave me a look. "I still ain't got you figured out," he said.

"There's nothing to figure," I said. "What's your name?"

"My name? Why you want to know my name?"

"No reason."

"You can call me TJ."

"All right."

" 'All right.' What's *your* name?"

"You can call me Booker."

"What you say, Booker?" He shook his head. "Shit, you some-thin', man. Booker. One thing you ain't, you ain't no Booker."

"My name's Matt."

"Matt," he said, trying it out. "Yeah, that's cool. Matt. Matt. An' that's where it's at, Matt."

" 'And that's the truth, Ruth.' "

His eyes lit up. "Hey," he said. "You hip to Spike Lee? You seen that movie?"

"Sure."

"I swear you hard to figure."

"There's nothing to figure."

"You got some kind of a jones. I just can't make out what it is."

"Maybe I haven't got one."

"On this street?" He whistled tonelessly. He had a round face, a button nose, bright eyes. I wondered if my five dollars would go for a vial of crack. He was a little chubby for a crack head and he didn't have the look they get, but then they don't get it right away.

"On the Deuce," he said, "everybody got a jones. They got a crack jones or a smack jones, a sex jones or a money jones, a speed-it-up or a slow-it-down jones. Man ain't got some kind of a jones, what he be doin' here?"

"And what about you, TJ?"

He laughed. "Oh, I got me a jones jones," he said. "I all the time got to be knowin' what kind of a jones the other dude's got, and that be *my* jones, an' that's where it's at, Matt."

I spent a few minutes more with TJ, and he was the best five-dollar cure I could have found for the Forty-second Street blues. By the time I headed back uptown I had shaken off the pall that had cloaked me all day. I had a shower and ate a decent dinner and went to a meeting.

The next day the phone rang while I was shaving, and I rode the subway to Brooklyn and got some work from a Court Street lawyer named Drew Kaplan. He had a client who was charged with vehicular homicide in a hit-and-run death.

"He swears he's innocent," Kaplan said, "and I personally happen to think he's full of shit, but on the chance that he's actually telling his attorney the truth, we ought to see if there's a witness somewhere who saw somebody else run over the old lady. You want to give it a go?"

I put in a week on it, and then Kaplan told me to let it go, that they'd offered to let his client plead to reckless endangerment and leaving the scene.

"And they'll drop the homicide charge," he said, "and I very strongly advised him to go for it, which he finally agreed to do once he got it into his head that this way he won't be serving any time. They're gonna ask for six months but I know the judge'll agree to probation, so I'll say yes to the deal tomorrow unless you just happened to find the perfect witness since I talked to you last."

"I found somebody just this afternoon."

"A priest," he said. "A priest with twenty-twenty vision who holds the Congressional Medal of Honor."

"Not quite, but a strong solid witness. The thing is, she's positive your guy did it."

"Jesus Christ," he said. "This is somebody the other side doesn't know about?"

"They didn't as of two hours ago."

"Well, let's for God's sake not tell them now," he said. "I'll close it out tomorrow. Your check, as they say, is in the mail. You're still a guy who doesn't have a license and doesn't submit reports, right?"

"Unless you need something for the record."

"As a matter of fact," he said, "what I need in this case

is to not have something for the record, so you won't submit a report and I'll forget this conversation that we never had."

"Fine with me."

"Great. And Matt? Somewhere along the line you ought to think about getting yourself a ticket. I'd give you more work, but there's stuff I can't use you on unless you've got a license."

"I've been thinking about it."

"Well," he said, "if your status changes, let me know."

Kaplan's check was generous, and when it came I rented a car and drove up to the Berkshires with Elaine to spend some of it. When we got back Wally at Reliable called and I got two days' work in connection with an insurance claim.

The film I'd seen became part of the past, and my emotional connection to it faded. It had affected me because I had seen it, but in truth it had nothing to do with me or I with it, and as time passed and my life got back on its usual course, it became in my mind what it in fact was—i.e., one more outrage in a world that overflowed with them. I read the paper every morning, and every day there were fresh outrages to take the sting out of the old ones.

There were images from the film that still came to my mind now and then, but they no longer held the same charge for me. And I didn't get back to Forty-second Street, and I didn't run into TJ again, and scarcely thought of him. He was an interesting character, but New York is full of characters, they're all over the place.

The year went on. The Mets faded and finished out of the race, and the Yankees were never in it. Two California teams met in the Series, and the most interesting thing that happened during it was the San Francisco earthquake. In November the city got its first black mayor, and the following week Amanda Warriner Thurman was raped and murdered three flights above an Italian restaurant on West Fifty-second Street.

Then I saw a man's hand smooth a boy's light brown hair, and it all came back.

7

I HAD EATEN BREAKFAST AND READ TWO NEWSPAPERS BY THE time the bank opened. I got the cassette from my safe-deposit box and called Elaine from a pay phone on the street.

She said, "Hi. How were the fights?"

"Better than I expected. How was your class?"

"Great, but there's a ton of stuff I've got to read. And there's one little airhead in the class who gets her hand up every time the instructor comes to the end of a sentence. If he doesn't find a way to shut her up I may have to kill her."

I asked if I could come over. "I'd like to use your VCR for about an hour," I said.

"That's fine," she said, "if you come over right away, and if it's really not much more than an hour. And if it's more fun than the last cassette you brought me."

"I'll be right over," I said.

I hung up and stepped to the curb and caught a cab right away. When I got there she took my coat and said, "Well, how did it go last night? Did you see the killer?" I must have stared, and she said, "Richard Thurman. Wasn't he supposed to be there? Isn't that why you went to Maspeth?"

"I wasn't thinking about him. He was there, yes, but I'm no closer to knowing if he killed her. I think I saw another killer."

"Oh?"

"The man in the rubber suit. I saw a man and I think it was him."

"Was he wearing the same outfit?"

"He was wearing a blue blazer." I told her about the man, and the boy he'd had with him. "So it's the same tape as last time," I said. "I don't think you'll want to watch it again."

"Not for anything. What I think I'll do, I was figuring I might do this anyway, I'll run out and buy books for my class. It shouldn't take me more than an hour. You know how to work the VCR, don't you?" I said I did. "And I'll be back in time to get ready for my appointment. I've got somebody coming at eleven-thirty."

"I'll be out of here by then."

I waited until she was out the door, then got the VCR going and fast-forwarded past the *Dirty Dozen* footage. She let herself back in a few minutes before eleven, almost exactly an hour after she'd left. By then I'd watched the show twice. It ran a half hour, but the second time around I'd worked the Fast Forward button, getting through it in half the time. I'd rewound the thing and was standing at the window when she came back.

She said, "I just spent a hundred dollars on books. And I couldn't find half of what's on the list."

"Couldn't you get paperbacks?"

"These *are* paperbacks. I don't know when I'm going to find time to read all of these." She upended the shopping bag on the couch, picked up a book and tossed it back onto the pile. "At least they're in English," she said, "which is a good thing, since I don't happen to read Spanish or Portuguese. But are you really reading something if you read it in translation?"

"If it's a good translation."

"I suppose so, but isn't it like seeing a movie with subtitles? What you're reading just isn't the same as what they're saying. Did you watch that thing?"

"Uh-huh."

"And? Was it him?"

"I think so," I said. "It would be a lot easier to say if he

hadn't had that goddam hood on. He must have been swel-
tering in a skintight rubber suit and a rubber hood."

"Maybe the open crotch had a cooling effect."

"He looked right to me," I said. "The one gesture, his
hand on the boy's hair, that's what finally rang a bell for me,
but there were other points of correspondence. The way he
held himself, the way he moved, these are things you can't
cover up with a costume. The hands looked right. The gesture, stroking the boy's hair, that was just as I remembered
it." I frowned. "I think it was the same girl, too."

"What girl? You didn't mention a girl. You mean his partner in crime, the one with the little tits?"

"I think she was the placard girl. Strutting around the
ring between rounds with a sign telling what round was
coming up."

"I don't suppose she was wearing her leather drag."

I shook my head. "She was dressed for the beach, showing a lot of leg. I didn't pay much attention to her."

"I'll bet."

"I mean it. There was something faintly familiar about
her but I didn't study her face."

"Of course not. You were too busy looking at her ass."
She put a hand on my arm. "I'd love to hear more," she said.

"But you're expecting company. I'll clear out. Do you
mind if I leave the tape? I don't want to carry it around all
day or make a special trip to get rid of it."

"No problem. And I hate to rush you, but—"

I gave her a kiss and left.

When I got out to the street I had the urge to plant myself
in a doorway and see who showed up. She hadn't come right
out and said that her appointment was with a john, but neither had she said otherwise, and I had been careful not to
ask. Nor did I really want to lurk in the shadows trying to
spot her lunch date, and speculating just what he would have

her do to earn the price of all those translations from the Spanish and Portuguese.

Sometimes it bothered me. Sometimes it didn't, and sometimes I thought that it ought to bother me more or less than it did. Someday, I thought, not for the first time, I would have to get it all sorted out.

In the meantime I walked over to Madison and took a bus thirty blocks uptown. Chance's gallery was one flight up over a shop that sold expensive clothing for children. The window featured a charming scene from *Wind in the Willows*, with the animals wearing the shop's fashions. Rat wore a moss-green jumper that probably cost as much as a whole shelf full of contemporary Latin American fiction.

The brass plate downstairs read, L. CHANCE COULTER/AFRICANA. I climbed a flight of carpeted stairs. The gilt-edged black lettering on the door bore the same legend, along with BY APPOINTMENT ONLY. I didn't have an appointment, but maybe I wouldn't need one. I rang, and after a moment the door was opened by Kid Bascomb. He was wearing a three-piece suit, and he smiled broadly when he saw who it was.

"Mr. Scudder!" he said. "It's good to see you. Is Mr. Coulter expecting you?"

"Not unless he has a crystal ball. I took a chance he'd be in."

"He'll be glad to see you. He's on the telephone but come right in, Mr. Scudder, and make yourself comfortable. I'll just tell him you're here."

I made my way around the room, looking at the masks and statues. I didn't know the field, but you didn't need much expertise to sense the quality of the pieces on display. I was standing in front of what the label identified as a Senufo mask from the Ivory Coast when the Kid returned to tell me that Chance would be with me in a minute. "He's on the phone with a gentleman in Antwerp," he said. "I believe that's in Belgium."

"I believe you're right. I didn't know you were working here, Kid."

"Oh, for some time now, Mr. Scudder." Last night in Maspeth I'd told him to call me Matt, but it was a lost cause. "You know I retired from the ring. I wasn't good enough."

"You were damned good."

He grinned. "Well, I met three in a row who was better. Were better. I retired, and then I looked for something to do, and Mr. Chance said to see if I liked working for him. Mr. Coulter, I mean."

It was an easy mistake for him to make. When I first met Chance that one syllable was the only name he had, and it wasn't until he went into the art business that he added an initial in front and a surname after.

"And do you like it?"

"It beats getting hit in the face. And yes, I like it very much. I'm learning things. There's never a day I don't learn something."

"I wish I could say the same," Chance said. "Matthew, it's about time you came to see me. I thought you were going to join us last night, you and your friend. We all trooped downstairs to Eldon's dressing room and when I turned around to introduce you you weren't there."

"We decided not to make a long night of it."

"And it did turn out to be a long night. Do you still have a taste for good coffee?"

"Do you still get that special blend?"

"Jamaican Blue Mountain. The price is outrageous, of course, but look around you." He indicated the masks and statues. "The price of everything is ridiculous. Black, right? Arthur, could you bring us some coffee? And then you'll want to get at those invoices."

He had first served me Jamaican coffee at his home, a converted firehouse on a quiet street in Greenpoint. His Polish neighbors thought the house belonged to a housebound retired physician named Levandowski, and that Chance was the good doctor's houseman and chauffeur. Instead Chance lived there alone in a house with a full weight gym and an eight-foot pool table and walls lined with museum-quality African art.

I asked if he still had the firehouse.

"Oh, I couldn't bear to move," he said. "I thought I'd have to sell in order to open this place, but I found a way. After all, I didn't have to purchase stock. I had a house jammed full of it."

"Do you still have a collection?"

"Better than ever. In a sense it's all my collection, and in another sense everything I have is for sale, so it's all store stock. Do you remember that Benin bronze? The queen's head?"

"With all the necklaces."

"I overpaid for her at auction, and every three months when she didn't sell I raised the price. It finally got so high somebody couldn't resist her. I hated to see her go, but then I took the money and bought something else." He took my arm. "Let me show you some things. I was in Africa for a month this spring, I spent two full weeks in Mali, in the Dogon country. A sweetly primitive people, their huts reminded me of the Anasazi dwellings at Mesa Verde. See, that piece is Dogon. Square holes for eyes, everything very straightforward and unapologetic."

"You've come a long way," I said.

"Oh, my," he said. "Haven't I just?"

When I first met Chance he was successful, but in another line of work. He had been a pimp, though hardly the traditional figure with the pink Cadillac and the floppy purple hat. He'd hired me to find out who killed one of his girls.

"I owe it all to you," he said. "You put me out of business."

That was true in a sense. By the time I'd done what he hired me to do, another of his girls was dead and the rest were off his string. "You were ready for a career change anyway," I told him. "You were having a mid-life crisis."

"Oh, I was too young for that. I'm *still* too young for that. Matthew? You didn't just drop in to be sociable."

"No."

"Or for the coffee."

"Or that either. There was somebody I saw at the fights last night. I thought maybe you might be able to tell me who he is."

"Somebody with me? Somebody in Rasheed's corner?"

I shook my head. "Somebody sitting first row ringside in the center section." I sketched a diagram in midair. "Here's the ring, here's where you were sitting right by the blue corner. Here's where Ballou and I were. The guy I'm interested in was sitting right about here."

"What did he look like?"

"White man, balding, say five-eleven, say a hundred and ninety pounds."

"Cruiserweight. How was he dressed?"

"Blue blazer, gray trousers. Blue polka-dot tie with large dots on it."

"The tie's the first thing that doesn't sound like everybody else. I might have noticed a tie like that, but I don't believe I ever saw it."

"He had a boy with him. Early teens, light brown hair. Might have been his son."

"Oh, I did see them," Chance said. "At least I saw a father and son in the front row, but I couldn't tell you what either one of them looked like. The only reason I noticed them at all is he might have been the only child in the place."

"But you know who I mean."

"Yes, but I can't tell you who he is." He closed his eyes. "I can almost picture him, you know what I mean? I can just about see him sitting there, but if you asked me to describe him I don't think I could do it, beyond parroting back the description you just gave. What did he do?"

"Do?"

"It's some kind of case, isn't it? I thought you were in Maspeth just to watch the fights, but I guess you were working, weren't you?"

On another case, but there was no reason to go into all that. "I had business there," I said.

"And this fellow's a part of it but you don't know who he is."

"He might be a part of it. I have to identify him in order to know."

"I get you." He considered it. "He was right up in front," he said. "Must be a real fan. Maybe he goes all the time. I was about to say I haven't seen him at the Garden or anywhere else, but the truth is I've only been getting to the fights regularly since I bought an interest in Rasheed."

"You have a big piece of him, Chance?"

"Very small, what you'd call minimum participation. You still like him? You said you did last night."

"He's impressive. He got hit too much with the right hand, though."

"I know he did. The Kid was saying the same thing. That Dominguez, though, his right came over the top very quickly."

"He was sudden, all right."

"He was indeed. And then, suddenly, he was gone." He smiled. "I love boxing."

"So do I."

"It's brutal, it's barbaric. I can't justify it. But I don't care. I love it."

"I know. Have you been to Maspeth before, Chance?"

He shook his head. "Way at the ass end of nowhere, isn't it? It's actually not that far from where I am in Greenpoint, except I didn't leave from Greenpoint when I went out there, and I didn't go to Greenpoint when I left there, so it didn't make me a whole lot of difference. I only went there because we had the fight there."

"Will you be going back?"

"If we get another booking there, and if I don't have something else requiring my presence. Next bout scheduled is three weeks from this coming Tuesday in Atlantic City." He smiled. "Donald Trump's place, it should be a little more luxurious than the New Maspeth Arena."

He told me who Rasheed was matched up with and said I ought to come down. I said I'd try. They wanted Rasheed to fight every three weeks, he said, but it was working out more like once a month.

"I'm sorry I can't help you," he said. "I could ask around if you'd like. The people in Rasheed's corner, they're at the fights all the time. You still at the hotel?"

"Same place."

"If I hear anything—"

"I appreciate it, Chance. And, you know, it's nice to see how everything's turned out."

"Thank you."

At the door I said, "Oh, I almost forgot. Do you know anything about the placard girl?"

"The what?"

"You know. Prances around the ring holding up the number of the next round."

"They call that a placard girl?"

"I don't know. I suppose you could call her Miss Maspeth. I just wondered—"

"If I knew anything about her. I can tell you she had long legs."

"I noticed that myself."

"And skin, I seem to remember she had a lot of skin. I'm afraid that's the extent of my knowledge, Matthew. I'm out of that business, thanks to you."

" 'Out of that business.' You think she looked like a working girl?"

"No," he said, "I think she looked like a nun."

"One of the Poor Clares."

"I was thinking a Sister of Charity. But you could be right."

8

THERE'S A SALOON CALLED HURLEY'S ON SIXTH AVENUE, diagonally across the street from the glass and steel tower where Five Borough Cable Sportscasts had a suite of offices. People from NBC have gone there for years, and Johnny Carson made the place famous back when he did his show live from New York; it was the site of all of his Ed McMahon drinking jokes. Hurley's is still in its original location, housed in one of the only older buildings still standing on that stretch of Sixth. Television people still patronize the place, to kill an hour or an afternoon, and one fairly frequent visitor was Richard Thurman. He often came in at the end of the workday and stayed long enough to have one drink, sometimes two, before heading on home.

I didn't have to be the world's greatest detective to learn this, because it was in the file Joe Durkin had let me read. I got to Hurley's around four-thirty and stood at the bar with a glass of club soda. I'd had the thought of trying to pump the bartender but the place was crowded and he was far too busy for that sort of exploratory conversation. Besides, we'd have had to shout at each other in order to be heard.

The fellow next to me wanted to talk about the Super Bowl, which had taken place the preceding Sunday. It was too one-sided to sustain a conversation for long, and it turned out we'd both turned it off at halftime. That common bond moved him to buy me a drink, but his enthusiasm dimmed when he found out I was drinking soda water and winked out altogether when I tried to turn the conversation to box-ing. "That's no sport," he said. "A couple of ghetto kids try-ing to beat each other to death. Why not pull the stops out, give 'em both guns and let 'em shoot each other."

A little after five I saw Thurman come in. He was with another man about his age and they found standing room down at the far end of the bar from me. They ordered drinks, and after ten or fifteen minutes Thurman left by himself.

A few minutes later so did I.

The restaurant on the ground floor of Thurman's building on West Fifty-second was called Radicchio's. I stood across the street and established that there were no lights on in the top-floor apartment. The one a flight below, the Gottschalk place, was also dark, with Ruth and Alfred in West Palm Beach for the season.

I had skipped lunch, so I had an early dinner at Radic-chio's. There were only two other tables occupied, both by young couples deep in earnest conversation. I felt like calling Elaine and telling her to hop in a cab and join me, but I wasn't sure that would be a good idea.

I had some veal and a half-portion of farfalle, I think it's called, a bowtie-shaped pasta which they served with a spicy red sauce. The small salad that came with the meal held plenty of the bitter leaf that had given the restaurant its name. A line on the menu advised me that a dinner without wine was like a day without sunshine. I drank water with my meal, and espresso afterward. The waiter brought an un-requested bottle of anisette to my table. I motioned for him to take it away.

"Is no charge," he assured me. "You put a drop in your 'spresso, makes it taste good."

"I wouldn't want it to taste that good."

"*Scusi?*"

I motioned again for him to take the bottle and he shrugged and carried it back to the bar. I drank my espresso and tried not to imagine it tasting of anisette. Because it wasn't the taste that something in me yearned for, any more than it was the taste that prompted them to bring the bottle to the table. If anise improved the flavor of coffee people would add a spoonful of seeds to the coffee grounds, and nobody does.

It was the alcohol, that's what called to me, and I suppose it had been crooning to me all day long, but its siren song had grown stronger in the past hour or two. I wasn't going to drink, I didn't want to drink, but some stimulus had triggered a cellular response and awakened something deep within me, something that would always be there.

If I do go out, if I go and pick up a drink one of these days, it'll be a quart of bourbon in my room, or maybe a bottle of Mick's twelve-year-old Irish. It won't be a demitasse of espresso with a spoonful of fucking anisette floating on the top.

I looked at my watch. It was barely past seven, and the meeting at St. Paul's doesn't get under way until eight-thirty. But they open the doors an hour before the meeting starts, and it wouldn't hurt me to get there early. I could help set up chairs, put out the literature and the cookies. On Friday nights we have a step meeting, with the discussion centering on one of the Twelve Steps that comprise AA's spiritual program. This week we'd be back on the First Step. "We admitted we were powerless over alcohol—that our lives had become unmanageable."

I caught the waiter's eye and signaled for the check.

At the end of the meeting Jim Faber came up to me and confirmed our dinner date for Sunday. He's my sponsor and we have a standing date for Sunday dinner, unless one of us has to cancel.

"I think I'll stop at the Flame," he said. "I'm in no rush to get home."

"Something the matter?"

"It'll keep until Sunday. How about you, you want to get some coffee?"

I begged off and walked up to Sixty-first and over to Broadway. The video store was open, and looked unchanged since six months ago. It had more of a crowd this time; though, with people looking to insure themselves against an empty weekend. There was a short line at the counter and I joined it. The woman in front of me took home three movies and three packages of microwave popcorn.

The owner still needed a shave. I said, "You must sell a lot of popcorn."

"It's a good item for us," he agreed. "Most of the shops carry it. I know you, don't I?"

I gave him a card. It had my name and phone number and nothing else. Jim Faber had printed up a whole box of them for me. He looked at it and at me, and I said, "Back in July. A friend of mine rented a copy of *The Dirty Dozen*, and I—"

"I remember. What's the matter now? Don't tell me it happened again."

"Nothing like that. But something's come up that makes it important for me to trace the source of that cassette."

"I think I told you. An old woman brought it in along with a whole batch of others."

"You told me."

"And did I tell you I never saw her before or since? Well, it's been six months and I still haven't seen her. I'd love to help you, but—"

"You're busy now."

"That's for sure. It's always like this on Friday nights."

"I'd like to come back when it's quieter."

"That'd be better," he said, "but I don't know what I'd be able to tell you. I didn't have any more complaints, so I think that one tape must have been the only one with a dirty movie dubbed on top of it. As far as locating the woman, the source of it, you know everything I know."

"You may know more than you realize. What's a good time tomorrow?"

"Tomorrow? Tomorrow's Saturday. We open at ten in the morning and it's pretty quiet before noon."

"I'll come at ten."

"You know what? Make it nine-thirty. I generally get here early to catch up on the paperwork. I'll let you in and we can have a half hour before I open up."

The next morning I read the *Daily News* with my eggs and coffee. An elderly Washington Heights woman had been killed watching television, struck in the head by a stray bullet from a drive-by shooting on the street outside her apartment. The intended victim had undergone emergency surgery at Columbia Presbyterian and was in critical condition. He was sixteen years old, and police believed the shooting was drug-related.

The woman was the fourth bystander killed so far this year. Last year the city had set a record, with thirty-four bystanders gunned down. If present trends continued, the *News* announced, that record could fall in mid-September.

On Park Avenue, a handful of blocks from Chance's gallery, a man had leaned out the window of an unmarked white van to snatch the handbag of a middle-aged woman who was waiting for the light to change. She'd had the bag's strap looped around her neck, presumably to make it harder to steal, and when the van sped off she was dragged and strangled. A sidebar to the main article advised women to carry their bags in a manner that would minimize physical risk if the bag were stolen. "Or don't carry a purse at all," one expert suggested.

In Queens, a group of teenagers walking across the Forest Park golf course had come upon the body of a young woman who had been abducted several days earlier in Woodhaven. She'd been doing her grocery shopping on Jamaica Avenue when another van, a light blue one, pulled up at the curb.

Two men jumped out of the back, grabbed her, hustled her into the van, and climbed in after her. The van was gone before anyone could think to get the number. A preliminary medical examination disclosed evidence of sexual assault and multiple stab wounds to the chest and abdomen.

Don't watch television, don't carry a purse, don't walk down the street. Jesus.

I got to the video store at nine-thirty. The owner, freshly shaved and wearing a clean shirt, led me to his office in the back. He remembered my name and introduced himself as Phil Fielding. We shook hands, and he said, "Your business card didn't say, but are you some kind of investigator? Something like that?"

"Something like that."

"Just like in the movies," he said. "I'd like to help if there was anything I could do, but I didn't know anything the last time I saw you and that was six months ago. I stayed around last night after we closed and checked the books on the chance that I might have the woman's name somewhere, but it was no go. Unless you've got an idea, something I haven't thought of—"

"The tenant," I said.

"You mean her tenant? The one who owned the tapes?"

"That's right."

"She said he died. Or did he skip out on the rent? My memory's a little vague, it wasn't a high-priority thing for me to remember. I'm pretty sure she said she was selling his things to recoup back rent that he owed."

"That's what you said in July."

"So if he died or just left town—"

"I'd still like to know who he was," I said. "Do many people own that many films on videocassette? I had the impression that most people rented them."

"You'd be surprised," he said. "We sell a lot. Children's classics, especially, even in this neighborhood where not that many people have kids. *Snow White, The Wizard of Oz.* We sold a ton of *E.T.* and we're selling *Batman* now, but it's not as strong as I would have predicted. A lot of people will buy the occasional favorite film. And of course there's a big market for exercise videos and instructional stuff, but that's a whole other area, that's not movies."

"Do you think many people would own as many as thirty films?"

"No," he said. "I'm guessing, but I'd say it'd be rare to own more than half a dozen. That's not counting exercise videos and football-highlight films. Or pornography, which I don't carry."

"What I'm getting at is that the tenant, the owner of these thirty cassettes, was probably a film buff."

"Oh, no question," he said. "This guy had all three versions of *The Maltese Falcon.* The original 1931 version with Ricardo Cortez—"

"You told me."

"Did I? I'm not surprised, it was fairly remarkable. I don't know where he got that stuff on video, I've never been able to find it in the catalogs. Yeah, he was a buff."

"So he probably rented films besides the ones he owned."

"Oh, I see what you're getting at. Yeah, I think that'd be a sure bet. A lot of people buy an occasional film, but everybody rents them."

"And he lived in the neighborhood."

"How do you know that?"

"If his landlady lived around here—"

"Oh, right."

"So he could have been a customer of yours."

He thought about it. "Sure," he said, "it's possible. It's even possible we had conversations about *film noir,* but I can't remember anything."

"You've got all your members programmed into your computer system, haven't you?"

"Yeah, it makes life a whole lot simpler."

"You said she brought in the bag of cassettes the first week in June. So if he was a customer, his account would have been inactive for the past seven or eight months."

"I could have a lot of accounts like that," he said. "People move, they die, some kid on crack breaks in and steals their VCR. Or they start doing business with somebody down the block and stop coming here. I've had people, I don't see them for months, and then they start coming in again."

"How many accounts do you figure you have that have been inactive since June?"

"I have no idea whatsoever," he said. "But I can certainly find out. Why don't you have a seat? Or browse around, maybe you'll find a movie you want to see."

It was past ten by the time he was finished, but no one had come knocking on the door. "I told you the mornings were slow," he said. "I came up with twenty-six names. These are people whose accounts have been inactive since the fourth of June, but who did rent at least one tape from us during the first five months of the year. Of course if he was sick a long time, stuck in the hospital—"

"Let me start with what you've got."

"All right. I copied the names and addresses for you, and phone numbers when they gave them. A lot of people won't give out phone numbers, especially women, and I can't say I blame them. I also have credit-card numbers, but I didn't copy those down because I'm supposed to keep that information confidential, although I suppose I could stretch a point if there's someone you can't trace any other way."

"I don't think I'll need it." He had copied the names on two sheets of lined notebook paper. I scanned them and asked if any of the names had struck a chord.

"Not really," he said. "I see so many people all day every day that I only remember the regulars, and I don't always recognize them or remember their names. With these twenty-six people I looked up what they'd checked out during the last year, that's what took me so long. I thought maybe one person would shape up very definitely as a film buff, with rental choices that made sense in terms of what he owned, but I couldn't find anything that looked like a buff profile."

"It was worth a try."

"That's what I thought. I'm pretty sure it was a man, that the landlady referred to her tenant as him, and some of the twenty-six are women, but I put everybody down."

"Good." I folded the sheets of paper, tucked them into my breast pocket. "I'm sorry to have put you to so much trouble," I said. "I appreciate it."

"Hey," he said, "when I think of all the pleasure you guys have brought me on the screen, how could I turn you down?" He grinned, then turned serious. "Are you trying to bust a porn ring? Is that what this is all about?" When I hesitated he assured me that he understood if I couldn't talk about it. But would I at least drop by when it was all over and tell him how it had turned out?

I said I would.

I had twenty-six names, only eleven with phone numbers. I tried the phone numbers first, because it's so much easier when you can do this sort of thing without walking all over the city. It was frustrating, though, because I couldn't seem to complete a call, and when I did I succeeded only in getting a recording. I got three answering machines, one with a cute message, the others simply repeating the last four digits of the number and inviting me to leave a message. Four times I got the NYNEX computer-generated voice telling me that the number I had reached was no longer in service. On one occasion it supplied a new number; I wrote it down and called it, and nobody answered.

When I finally got a human voice I barely knew how to respond. I looked quickly at my list and said, "Uh, Mr. Ac-cardo? Joseph Accardo?"

"Speaking."

"You're a member of the video-rental club"—what was its name?—"at Broadway and Sixty-first."

"Broadway and Sixty-first," he said. "Which one's that?"

"Next to Martin's."

"Oh, right, sure. What did I do, not bring something back?"

"Oh, no," I said. "I just noticed there's been no activity in your account in months, Mr. Accardo, and I wanted to invite you to come in and check out our selection."

"Oh," he said, surprised. "Well, that's very nice of you. I'll be sure and do that. I got in the habit, going to this place near where I work, but I'll stop by one of these nights."

I hung up the phone and crossed Accardo off the list. I had twenty-five names left and it looked as though I was going to have to do them on foot.

I called it a day around four-thirty, by which time I'd managed to cross off ten more names. It was a slow process, slower than I might have expected. The addresses were all pretty much within walking distance, so I could get around without too much trouble, but that didn't mean I could establish whether or not a particular person still lived at a particular address.

I was back in my hotel room by five. I showered and shaved and sat in front of the TV. At seven I met Elaine at a Moroccan place on Cornelia Street in the Village. We both ordered the couscous. She said, "If the food tastes as good as the room smells, we're in for a treat. What's the best place in the world to get couscous?"

"I don't know. Casablanca?"

"Walla Walla."

"Oh."

"Get it? Couscous, Walla Walla. Or, if you wanted couscous in Germany, you'd go to Baden-Baden."

"I think I get the premise."

"I knew you would, you've got that kind of mind. Where would you get couscous in Samoa?"

"Pago Pago. Excuse me, will you? I'll be back in a minute, I have to make peepee."

The couscous was terrific and the portions were large. While we ate, I told her how I'd spent the day. "It was frustrating," I said, "because I couldn't just check the doorbells to determine whether or not the person I was looking for lived there."

"Not in New York."

"Of course not. A lot of people leave the slot next to their bell blank on general principles. I suppose I should understand that, I'm in a program that places a premium on anonymity, but some people might find it a little strange. Other people have names on the doorbell but the names aren't theirs, because they're living in an illegal sublet and they don't want anybody to find out. So if I'm looking for Bill Williams, say—"

"That's William Williams," she said. "The couscous king of Walla Walla."

"That's the guy. If his name's not on the bell, that doesn't mean he's not there. And if his name *is* on the bell, that doesn't mean anything either."

"Poor baby. So what do you do, call the super?"

"If there's a resident super, but in most of the smaller buildings there isn't. And the super's no more likely to be home than anybody else. And a superintendent doesn't necessarily know the names of the tenants, as far as that goes. You wind up ringing bells and knocking on doors and talking to people, most of whom don't know much about their neighbors and are very cautious about disclosing what they do know."

"Hard way to make a living."

"Some days it certainly seems that way."

"It's a good thing you love it."

"Do I? I suppose so."

"Of course you do."

"I guess. It's satisfying when you can keep hammering away at something until it starts to make sense. But not everything does." We were on dessert now, some kind of gooey honey cake, too sweet for me to finish. The waitress had brought us Moroccan coffee, which was the same idea as Turkish coffee, very thick and bitter, with powdery grounds filling the bottom third of the cup.

I said, "I put in a good day's work. That's satisfying. But I'm working on the wrong case."

"Can't you work on two things at once?"

"Probably, but nobody's paying me to investigate a snuff film. I'm supposed to be determining whether or not Richard Thurman killed his wife."

"You're working on it."

"Am I? Thursday night I went to the fights, with the excuse that he was producing the telecast. I established several things. I established that he's the kind of guy who will take off his tie and jacket when he's working. And he's spry, he can climb up onto the ring apron and then drop down again without breaking a sweat. I got to watch him give the placard girl a pat on the ass, and—"

"Well, that's something."

"It was something for him. I don't know that it was anything much for me."

"Are you kidding? It says something if he can play grab-ass with a tootsie two months after his wife's death."

"Two and a half months," I said.

"Same difference."

"A tootsie, huh?"

"A tootsie, a floozie, a bimbo. What's wrong with tootsie?"

"Nothing. He wasn't exactly playing grab-ass. He just gave her a pat."

"In front of millions of people."

"They should be so lucky. A couple hundred people."

"Plus the audience at home."

"They were watching a commercial. Anyway, what would it prove? That he's a coldhearted son of a bitch who puts his hands on other women while his wife's body has barely had time to settle in the grave? Or that he doesn't have to put on an act because he's genuinely innocent? You could see it either way."

"Well," she said.

"That was Thursday. Yesterday, relentless fellow that I am, I drank a glass of club soda in the same gin joint with him. It was a little like being at opposite ends of a crowded subway car, but we were both actually in the same room at the same time."

"That's something."

"And last night I had dinner at Radicchio's, on the ground floor of his apartment building."

"How was it?"

"Nothing special. The pasta was pretty good. We'll try it sometime."

"Was he in the restaurant?"

"I don't even think he was in the building. If he was home he was sitting in the dark. You know, I called his apartment this morning. I was making all those other calls so I called him."

"What did he have to say?"

"I got his machine. I didn't leave a message."

"I hope he'll find that as frustrating as I always do."

"One can only hope. You know what I ought to do? I ought to give Lyman Warriner his money back."

"No, don't do that."

"Why not? I can't keep it if I don't do anything to earn it, and I can't seem to think of a way to do that. I read the file the cops built on the case, and they already tried everything I could think of and more."

"Don't return the money," she said. "Honey, he doesn't give a damn about the money. His sister got killed and if he thinks he's doing something about it he'll have a chance to die in peace."

"What am I supposed to do, string him along?"

"If he asks, tell him these things take time. You won't be asking him for more money—"

"God, no."

"—so he'll have no reason to think that you're hustling him. You don't have to keep the money, if you don't feel you've done anything to earn it. Give it away. Give it to AIDS research, give it to God's Love We Deliver, there are plenty of places to give it to."

"I suppose."

"Knowing you," she said, "you'll find a way to earn it."

There was a movie she wanted to see at the Waverly but it was Saturday night and there was a long line that neither of us felt like standing in. We walked around for a while, had some cappuccino on Macdougal Street, and listened to a girl folksinger in a no-cover club on Bleecker.

"Long hair and granny glasses," Elaine said. "And a long gingham gown. Who said the sixties were over?"

"All her songs sound the same."

"Well, she only knows three chords."

Outside I asked her if she felt like listening to some jazz. She said, "Sure, where? Sweet Basil? The Vanguard? Pick a place."

"I was thinking maybe Mother Goose."

"Uh-huh."

"What's that supposed to mean?"

"Nothing. I like Mother Goose."

"So do you want to go?"

"Sure. Do we get to stay even if Danny Boy's not there?"

Danny Boy wasn't there, but we hadn't been there long before he showed up. Mother Goose is at Amsterdam and Eighty-first, a jazz club that draws a salt-and-pepper crowd.

They keep the lights low, and the drummer uses brushes and never takes a solo. It and Poogan's Pub are the two places where you can find Danny Boy Bell.

Wherever you find him, he tends to stand out. He's an albino Negro, his skin and eyes both extremely sensitive to sunlight, and he has arranged his life so he and the sun are never up at the same time. He is a small man who dresses with flair, favoring dark suits and flamboyant vests. He drinks a lot of Russian vodka, straight up and ice-cold, and he often has a woman with him, usually every bit as flashy as his vest. The one tonight had a mane of strawberry blond hair and absolutely enormous breasts.

The maître d' led them to the ringside table where he always sits. I didn't think he'd noticed us, but at the end of the set a waiter appeared at our table and said that Mr. Bell hoped we would join him. When we got there Danny Boy said, "Matthew, Elaine, it's so nice to see you both. This is Sascha, isn't she darling?"

Sascha giggled. We made conversation, and after a few minutes Sascha sashayed off to the ladies' room.

"To powder her nose," Danny Boy said. "As it were. The best argument for legalizing drugs is people wouldn't keep running to the lavatory all the time. When they figure out the man-hours cocaine is costing American industry, they really ought to factor in those rest-room trips."

I waited until Sascha's next trip to the ladies' room to bring up Richard Thurman. "I sort of assumed he killed her," Danny Boy said. "She was rich and he wasn't. If only the fellow was a doctor I'd say there was no doubt at all. Why do you suppose doctors are always killing their wives? Do they tend to marry bitches? How would you explain it?"

We kicked it around some. I said maybe they were used to playing God, making life-and-death decisions. Elaine had a more elaborate theory. She said people who went into the healing professions were frequently individuals who were trying to overcome a perception of themselves as hurting people. "They become doctors to prove they're not killers," she said, "and then when they experience stress they revert to what they think of as their basic nature, and they kill."

"That's interesting," Danny Boy said. "Why would they have that perception in the first place?"

"A birth thought," she said. "The mother almost dies when they're born, or experiences a great deal of pain. So the child's thought is *I hurt women* or *I kill women*. He tries to compensate for this by becoming a doctor, and later on when push comes to shove—"

"He kills his wife," Danny Boy said. "I like it."

I asked what data she had to support the theory, and she said she didn't have any, but there were lots of studies on the effects of birth thoughts. Danny Boy said he didn't care about data, you could find data to prove anything, but the theory was the first one he'd ever heard that made sense to him, so screw the data. Sascha had returned to the table during the discussion but it went on without interruption, and she didn't seem to be paying any attention.

"About Thurman," Danny Boy said. "I haven't heard anything specific. I haven't listened all that hard. Should I?"

"Be good to keep an ear open."

He poured himself a few ounces of Stoly. At both of his places, Poogan's and Mother Goose, they bring him his vodka in a champagne bucket packed with ice. He looked down into the glass, then drank it down like water.

He said, "He's with a cable channel. A new sports channel."

"Five Borough."

"That's right. There's some talk going around about them."

"What?"

He shook his head. "Nothing very specific. Something shaky or shady about it, some dubious money backing it. I'll see what else I hear."

A few minutes later Sascha left the table again. When she

was out of earshot Elaine leaned forward and said, "I can't stand it. That child has the biggest tits I've ever seen in my life."

"I know."

"Danny Boy, they're bigger than your head."

"I know. She's special, isn't she? But I think I'm going to have to give her up." He poured himself another drink. "I can't afford her," he said. "You wouldn't believe what it costs to keep that little nose happy."

"Enjoy her while you can."

"Oh, I shall," he said. "Like life itself."

Back in her apartment, Elaine made a pot of coffee and we sat on the couch. She stacked some solo piano recordings on the turntable—Monk, Randy Weston, Cedar Walton. She said, "She was something, wasn't she? Sascha. I don't know where Danny Boy finds them."

"K Mart," I suggested.

"When you see something like that you have to figure silicone, but maybe they're like Topsy, maybe they just growed. What do you think?"

"I didn't really notice."

"Then you better start going to more meetings, because it must have been the vodka that was making you drool." She drew closer to me. "What do you think? Would you like me better if I had huge tits?"

"Sure."

"You would?"

I nodded. "Longer legs would be nice, too."

"Is that a fact. What about trimmer ankles?"

"Wouldn't hurt."

"Really. Tell me more."

"Cut it out," I said. "That tickles."

"Does it really. Tell me what else you've got on your wish list. How about a tight pussy?"

"That would be too much to hope for."

"Oh, boy," she said. "You're really asking for it, aren't you?"

"Am I?"

"Oh, I hope so," she said. "I certainly hope so."

Afterward I lay in her bed while she turned the stack of records and brought back two cups of coffee. We sat up in bed and didn't say much.

After a while she said, "You were pissed yesterday."

"I was? When?"

"When you had to get out of here because I had somebody coming over."

"Oh."

"Weren't you? Pissed?"

"A little bit. I got over it."

"It bothers you, doesn't it? That I see clients."

"Sometimes it does. Most of the time it doesn't."

"I'll probably stop sooner or later," she said. "You can only keep on pitching for so long. Even Tommy John had to pack it in, and he had a bionic arm." She rolled onto her side to face me, put a hand on my leg. "If you asked me to stop, I probably would."

"And then resent me for it."

"You think so? Am I that neurotic?" She thought it over. "Yeah," she said, "I probably am."

"Anyway, I wouldn't ask you."

"No, *you'd* rather have the resentment." She rolled over and lay on her back, gazing up at the ceiling. After a moment she said, "I'd give it up if we got married."

There was silence, and then a cascade of descending notes and a surprising atonal chord from the stereo.

"If you pretend you didn't hear that," Elaine said, "I'll pretend I didn't say it. We never even say the L word and I went and said the M word."

"It's a dangerous place," I said, "out there in the middle of the alphabet."

"I know. I should learn to stay in the F's where I belong. I don't want to get married. I like things just the way they are. Can't they just stay that way?"

"Sure."

"I feel sad. That's crazy, what the hell have I got to feel sad about? All of a sudden I'm all weepy."

"That's okay."

"I'm not going to cry. But hold me for a minute, okay? You big old bear. Just hold me."

9

SUNDAY AFTERNOON I FOUND MY FILM BUFF.

His name, according to Phil Fielding's records, was Arnold Leveque, and he lived on Columbus Avenue half a dozen blocks north of the video store. His building was a tenement that had thus far escaped gentrification. Two men sat on the stoop drinking beer out of cans in brown paper bags. One of them had a little girl on his lap. She was drinking orange juice out of a baby bottle.

None of the doorbells had Leveque's name on it. I went out and asked the two men on the stoop if Arnold Leveque lived there. They shrugged and shook their heads. I went inside and couldn't find a bell for the super, so I rang bells on the first floor until someone buzzed me in.

The hallway smelled of mice and urine. At the far end a door opened and a man stuck his head out. I walked toward him, and he said, "What do you want? Don't come too close now."

"Easy," I said.

"You take it easy," he said. "I got a knife."

I held my hands at my sides, showing the palms. I told him I was looking for a man named Arnold Leveque.

He said, "Oh, yeah? I hope he don't owe you money."

"Why's that?"

"'Cause he's dead," he said, and he laughed hard at his joke. He was an old man with wispy white hair and deep eye sockets, and he looked as though he'd be joining Leveque before too many months passed. His pants were loose and he held them up with suspenders. His flannel shirt hung on him, too. Either he got his clothes at a thrift shop or he'd lost a lot of weight recently.

Reading my mind, he said, "I been sick, but don't worry. It ain't catching."

"I'm more afraid of the knife."

"Ah, Jesus," he said. He showed me a French chef's knife with a wooden handle and a ten-inch carbon-steel blade. "Come on in," he said. "I ain't about to cut you, for Christ's sake." He led the way, setting the knife down on a little table near the door.

His apartment was tiny, two narrow little rooms. The only illumination came from a three-bulb ceiling fixture in the larger room. Two of the bulbs had burned out and the remaining one couldn't have been more than forty watts. He kept the place tidy but it had a smell to it, an odor of age and illness.

"Arnie Leveque," he said. "How'd you know him?"

"I didn't."

"No?" He yanked a handkerchief out of his back pocket and coughed into it. "Dammit," he said. "The bastards cut me from asshole to appetite but it didn't do no good. I waited too long. See, I was afraid of what they'd find." He laughed harshly. "Well, I was right, wasn't I?"

I didn't say anything.

"He was okay, Leveque. French Canadian, but he musta been born here because he talked like anybody else."

"Did he live here a long time?"

"What's a long time? I been here forty-two years. Can you believe that? Forty-two years in this shithole. Be forty-three years in September, but I expect to be out of here by then. Moved to smaller quarters." He laughed again and it turned into a coughing fit and he reached for the handkerchief. He got the cough under control and said, "Smaller quarters, like a box about six feet long, you know what I mean?"

"I guess it helps to joke about it."

"Naw, it don't help," he said. "Nothing helps. I guess Arnie lived here about ten years. Give or take, you know? He kept to his room a lot. Of course the way he was you wouldn't expect him to go tap-dancing down the street." I must have looked puzzled, because he said, "Oh, I forgot, you didn't know him. He was fat as a pig, Arnie was." He put his hands out in front of him and drew them apart as he lowered them. "Pear-shaped. Waddled like a duck. He was up on three, too, so he had two flights of stairs to climb if he went anywhere."

"How old was he?"

"I don't know. Forty? It's hard to tell when somebody's fat like that."

"What did he do?"

"For a living? I don't know. Had a job he went to. Then he wasn't going out so much."

"I understand he liked movies."

"Oh, he sure did. He had one of those things, what the hell do they call it, you watch movies on your TV set."

"A VCR."

"It woulda come to me in a minute."

"What happened to him?"

"Leveque? Ain't you paying attention? He died."

"How?"

"They killed him," he said. "What do you think?"

It was a generic *they*, as it turned out. Arnold Leveque had died on the street, presumably the victim of a mugging. It was getting worse every year, the old man told me, what with people smoking crack and living on the street. They would kill you for subway fare, he said, and think nothing of it.

I asked when all this had happened, and he said it must

have been a year ago. I said that Leveque had still been alive in April—Fielding's records indicated his most recent transaction had been on the nineteenth of that month—and he said he didn't have that good a head for dates anymore.

He told me how to find the super. "She don't do much," he said. "She collects the rents, that's about all." When I asked his name he said it was Gus, and when I asked his last name a sly look came over his face. "Just Gus is good enough. Why tell you my name when you ain't told me yours?"

I gave him one of my cards. He held it at arm's length and squinted at it, reading my name aloud. He asked if he could keep the card and I said he could.

"When I meet up with Arnie," he said, "I'll tell him you was looking for him." And he laughed and laughed.

Gus's last name was Giesekind. I found that out by checking his mailbox, which shows I'm no slouch as a detective. The super's name was Herta Eigen, and I found her two doors up the street where she had a basement apartment. She was a small woman, barely five feet tall, with a Central European accent and a wary, suspicious little face. She flexed her fingers as she talked. They were misshapen by arthritis but moved nimbly enough.

"The cops came," she said. "Took me downtown somewhere, made me look at him."

"To identify him?"

She nodded. " 'That's him,' I said. 'That's Leveque.' They bring me back here and I got to let them into his room. They walked in and I walked in after them. 'You can go now, Mrs. Eigen.' 'That's all right,' I said. 'I'll stay.' Because some of them are all right but some of them would steal the money off a dead man's eyes. Is that the expression?"

"Yes."

"The *pennies* off a dead man's eyes. Pennies, not money." She sighed. "So they finish poking around and I let them out and lock up after them, and I ask what do I do now, will somebody come for his things, and they say they'll be in touch. Which they never were."

"You never heard from them?"

"Nothing. Nobody tells me if his people are coming for his belongings, or what I'm supposed to do. When I didn't hear from them I called the precinct. They don't know what I'm talking about. I guess so many people get murdered nobody can bother to keep track." She shrugged. "Me, I got an apartment, I got to rent it, you know? I left the furniture, I brought everything else down here. When nobody came I got rid of it."

"You sold the videocassettes."

"The movies? I took them over on Broadway, he gave me a few dollars. Was that wrong?"

"I don't think so."

"I wasn't stealing. If he had family I would give it all to them, but he had nobody. He lived here for many years, Mr. Leveque. He was here already when I got this job."

"When was that?"

"Six years ago. Wait a minute, I'm wrong, seven years."

"You're just the superintendent?"

"What else should I be, the queen of England?"

"I knew a woman who was a landlady but she let on to the tenants that she was only the super."

"Oh, sure," she said. "I own the building, that's why I live in the basement. I'm a rich woman, I just have this love for living in the ground like a mole."

"Who does own the building?"

"I don't know." I looked at her and she said, "Sue me, I don't know. Who knows? There's a management company that hired me. I collect the rent, I give it to them, they do whatever they want with it. The landlord I never met. Does it matter who it is?"

I couldn't see how. I asked when Arnold Leveque had died.

"Last spring," she said. "Closer than that I couldn't tell you."

I went back to my hotel room and turned on the TV. Three different channels had college basketball games. It was too frenzied and I couldn't bear to watch. I found a tennis match on one of the cable channels and it was restful by comparison. I don't know that it would be accurate to say that I watched it, but I did sit in front of the set with my eyes open while they hit the ball back and forth over the net.

I met Jim for dinner at a Chinese restaurant on Ninth Avenue. We often had Sunday dinner there. The place never filled up and they didn't care how long we sat there or how many times they had to refill our teapot. The food's not bad, and I don't know why they don't do more business.

He said, "Did you happen to read the *Times* today? There was an article, an interview with this Catholic priest who writes hot novels. I can't think of his name."

"I know who you mean."

"He had this telephone poll to back him up, and he said how only ten percent of the married population of this country have ever committed adultery. Nobody cheats, that's his contention, and he can prove it because somebody called a bunch of people on the phone and that's what they told him."

"I guess we're in the grip of a moral renaissance."

"That's his point." He picked up his chopsticks, mimed a drumroll. "I wonder if he called my house."

"Oh?"

Avoiding my eyes, he said, "I think Beverly's seeing somebody."

"Somebody in particular?"

"A guy she met in Al-Anon."

"Maybe they're just friends."

"No, I don't think so." He poured tea for both of us. "You know, I screwed around a lot before I got sober. Whenever I went to a bar I told myself I was looking to meet somebody.

Generally all I got was drunk, but now and then I got lucky. Sometimes I even remembered it."

"And sometimes you'd rather you didn't."

"Well, sure. The point is I didn't give that up completely when I first came into the program. The marriage almost ended during the worst of the drinking, but I bottomed out and sobered up and we worked things out. She started going to Al-Anon, started dealing with her own issues, and we hung together. I would still have something going on the side, you know."

"I didn't know."

"No?" He thought about it. "Well, I guess that was before I knew you, before you got sober. Because I stopped fooling around after a couple of years. It was no great moral decision to reform. I just didn't seem to be doing that anymore. I don't know, the health thing may have been a factor, first herpes and then AIDS, but I don't think I got scared off. I think I lost interest." He took a sip of tea. "And now I'm one of Father Feeney's ninety percent, and she's out there."

"Well, maybe it's her turn. To have a little fling."

"This isn't the first time."

"Oh," I said.

"I don't know how I feel about it."

"Does she know that you know?"

"Who knows what she knows? Who knows what *I* know? I just wanted things to stay the way they were, you know? And they never do."

"I know," I said. "I was with Elaine last night and she said the M word."

"What's that, motherfucker?"

"Marriage."

"Same thing," he said. "Marriage is a motherfucker. She wants to get married?"

"She didn't say that. She said if we were to get married, then she'd stop seeing clients."

"Clients?"

"Johns."

"Oh, right. That's the condition? Marry me and I'll stop?"

"No, nothing like that. Just speaking hypothetically, and then she apologized for saying the word and we both agreed we want things to stay the way they are." I looked down into my teacup the way I used to look into a glass of whiskey. "I don't know if that's going to be possible. It seems to me that when two people want something to stay just the way it is, that's when it changes."

"Well," he said, "you'll have to see how it goes."

"And take it a day at a time, and don't drink."

"I like that," he said. "It has a nice ring to it."

We sat there a long while, talking about one thing and another. I talked about my cases, the legitimate one that I couldn't seem to come to grips with and the other one that I couldn't seem to leave alone. We talked about baseball and how spring training might be delayed by an owners' lockout. We talked about a kid in our home group with a horrendous history of drugs and alcohol who'd gone out after four months of sobriety.

Around eight he said, "What I think I'll do tonight, I think I'll go to some meeting where I won't run into anybody I know. I want to talk about all this shit with Bev at a meeting and I can't do that around here."

"You could."

"Yeah, but I don't want to. I'm an old-timer, I've been sober since the Flood, I wouldn't want the newcomers to realize I'm not a perfect model of serenity." He grinned. "I'll go downtown and give myself permission to sound as confused and fucked-up as I feel. And who knows? Maybe I'll get lucky, find some sweet young thing looking for a father figure."

"That's a good idea," I said. "Find out if she's got a sister."

*   *   *

I went to a meeting myself. There's no meeting at St. Paul's on Sundays, so I went to one at Roosevelt Hospital. A fair number of the people who showed up were in-patients from the detox ward. The speaker had started out as a heroin addict, kicked that in a twenty-eight-day residential program in Minnesota, and devoted the next fifteen years to alcoholic drinking. Now she was almost three years sober.

They went around the room after she was done, and most of the patients just said their names and passed. I decided I'd say something, if just to tell her I enjoyed her story and was glad she was sober, but when it got to me I said, "My name is Matt and I'm an alcoholic. I'll just listen tonight."

Afterward I went back to the hotel. No messages. I sat in my room reading for two hours. Someone had passed along a paperback volume called *The Newgate Calendar*, a case-by-case report on British crimes of the seventeenth and eighteenth centuries. I'd had it around for a month or so, and at night I would read a few pages before I went to sleep.

It was mostly interesting, although some cases were more interesting than others. What got to me some nights, though, was the way nothing changed. People back then killed each other for every reason and for no reason, and they did it with every means at their disposal and all the ingenuity they could bring to bear.

Sometimes it provided a good antidote for the morning paper, with its deadening daily chronicle of contemporary crime. It was easy to read the paper each day and conclude that humanity was infinitely worse than ever, that the world was going to hell and that hell was where we belonged. Then, when I read about men and women killing each other centuries ago for pennies or for love, I could tell myself that we weren't getting worse after all, that we were as good as we'd ever been.

On other nights that same revelation brought not reassurance but despair. We had been ever thus. We were not getting better, we would never get better. Anyone along the way who'd died for our sins had died for nothing. We had more sins in reserve, we had a supply that would last for all eternity.

What I read that night didn't pick me up, and neither did it ready me for sleep. Around midnight I went out. It had turned colder, and there was a raw wind blowing off the Hudson. I walked over to Grogan's Open House, the old Irish saloon Mick owns, although there's another name than his on the license and ownership papers.

The place was almost empty. Two solitary drinkers sat well apart at the long bar, one drinking a bottle of beer, the other nursing a black pint of Guinness. Two old men in long thrift-shop overcoats shared a table along the wall. Burke was behind the bar. Before I could ask he volunteered that Mick hadn't been in all evening. "He could come in any time," he said, "but I don't expect him."

I ordered a Coke and sat at the bar. The TV was tuned to a cable channel that broadcasts old black-and-white films uninterrupted by commercials. They were showing *Little Caesar,* with Edward G. Robinson.

I watched for half an hour or so. Mick didn't come in, and neither did anyone else. I finished my Coke and went home.

10

THE COPS AT THE TWENTIETH PRECINT WEREN'T OVERLY IM-
pressed that I'd been on the job once myself. They were cour-
teous all the same, and would have been happy to fill me in
on the circumstances of Arnold Leveque's death. There was
only one problem. They had never heard of him.

"I don't know the date," I said, "but it happened sometime between April nineteenth and June fourth, and if I were
guessing I'd say early May."

"That's of last year."

"Right."

"That's Arnold Leveque? You want to spell the last name
again, make sure I got it right?"

I did, and supplied the Columbus Avenue address.
"That's here in the Two-oh," he said. "Lemme see if anybody
heard of the guy." No one had. He came back and we puzzled over it for a few minutes, and then he excused himself
again. He came back with a bemused expression on his face.

"Arnold Leveque," he said. "Male Caucasian, died nine
May. Multiple stab wounds. Not in our files because it wasn't
our case. He was killed on the other side of Fifty-ninth Street.
You want Midtown North, that's on West Fifty-fourth."

I told him I knew where it was.

That explained why Herta Eigen got the runaround from the
cops at her local precinct—they hadn't known what she was
talking about. I'd walked up to the Twentieth first thing after

breakfast, and it was mid-morning when I got to Midtown North. Durkin wasn't in, but I didn't need him to run interference for me on this. Anybody could give me the information.

There was a cop named Andreotti whom I'd met a few times over the past year or two. He was at a desk catching up on his paperwork and didn't mind an interruption. "Leveque, Leveque," he said. He frowned and ran a hand through a mop of shaggy black hair. "I think I caught that one, me and Bellamy. A fat guy, right?"

"So they tell me."

"You see so many stiffs in a week you can't keep 'em straight. He musta been murdered. Natural causes, you can't even remember their names."

"No."

"Except if it's the kind of name you can't forget. There was a woman two, three weeks back, Wanda Plainhouse. I thought, yeah, I wouldn't mind playin' house with you." He smiled at the memory, then said, "Of course she was alive, Wanda, but it's an example of how one name'll stick in your mind."

He pulled Leveque's file. The film buff had been found in a narrow alley between two tenements on Forty-ninth Street west of Tenth Avenue. The body had been discovered after an anonymous call to 911 logged in at 6:56 on the morning of May 9th. The medical examiner estimated the time of death at around eleven the previous night. The deceased had been stabbed seven times in the chest and abdomen with a long, narrow-bladed knife. Any of several of the wounds would have been sufficient to cause death.

"Forty-ninth between Tenth and Eleventh," I said.

"Closer to Eleventh. The buildings on either side were scheduled for demolition, X's on the windows and nobody living in 'em. I think they might have come down by now."

"I wonder what he was doing there."

Andreotti shrugged. "Looking for something and unlucky enough to find it. Looking to buy dope, looking for a woman or a man. Everybody's out there looking for something."

I thought of TJ. Everybody's got a jones, he'd said, or what would they be doing on the Deuce?

I asked if Leveque had been a drug user. No outward signs of it, he said, but you never knew. "Maybe he was drunk," he offered. "Staggering around, didn't know where he was. No, that's not it. Blood alcohol's not much more than a trace. Well, whatever he was looking for, he picked the wrong place to look for it."

"You figured robbery?"

"No money in his pockets, no watch and wallet. Sounds like a killer with a crack habit and a switchblade."

"How'd you ID him?"

"The landlady where he lived. She was some piece of work, man. About this high, but she wasn't taking no shit. Let us into his room and stood there watching us like a hawk, like we'll clean the place out if she turns her back. You'd think it was her stuff, which it probably wound up being, because I don't think we ever did turn up any next of kin." He flipped through the few sheets of paper. "No, I don't think we did. Anyway, she ID'd him. She didn't want to go. 'Why I got to look at a dead body? I seen enough in my life, believe me.' But she took a good look and said it was him."

"How did you know to ask her? What gave you his name and address?"

"Oh, I get you. That's a good question. How did we know?" He frowned, paging through the file. "Prints," he said. "His prints were in the computer and that gave us the name and address."

"How did his prints happen to be on file?"

"I don't know. Maybe he was in the service, maybe he had a government job once. You know how many people got their prints on file?"

"Not in the NYPD computer."

"Yeah, you're right." He frowned. "Did we have him or did we have to hook into the main system in Washington? I don't remember. Somebody else probably took care of it. Why?"

"Did you see if he's got a sheet?"

"If he did it must have been jaywalking. There's no notation in his file."

"Could you check?"

He grumbled but did it anyway. "Yeah, just one entry," he said. "Arrested four, almost five years ago. Released OR and charges dropped."

"What charges?"

He squinted at the computer screen. "Violation of Section 235 of the Criminal Code. What the hell is that, it's not a number I'm familiar with." He grabbed up the black looseleaf binder and flipped through it. "Here you go. Obscenity. Maybe he called somebody a bad name. Charges dismissed, and four years later somebody sticks a knife in him. Teach you not to talk nasty, wouldn't it?"

I probably could have learned more about Leveque if Andreotti had felt like jockeying the computer, but he had things of his own to do. I went to the main library on Forty-second Street and checked the *Times Index* on the chance that Arnold Leveque might have made the paper, but he'd managed to be spared publicity when he got arrested and when he got killed.

I took the subway down to Chambers Street and visited a few state and city government offices, where I found several public employees who were willing to do me a favor if I did them favors in return. They checked their records, and I slipped them some money.

I managed to learn that Arnold Leveque had been born thirty-eight years ago in Lowell, Massachusetts. By the time he was twenty-three he was in New York, living at the Sloane House YMCA on West Thirty-fourth and working in the mailroom of a textbook publisher. A year later he had left the publisher and was working for a firm called R & J Merchandise, with an address on Fifth Avenue in the Forties. He was a salesclerk there. I don't know what they sold, and the firm no longer existed. There are a lot of little clip joints on that stretch of Fifth Avenue, salted in among the legitimate stores and having endless Going Out Of Business sales, hawking dubious ivory and jade, cameras and electronic gear. R & J might well have been one of them.

He was still at Sloane House then, and as far as I could tell he stayed there until he moved to Columbus Avenue in the fall of '79. The move may have been prompted by a job switch; a month earlier he had started work at CBS, located a block west of my hotel on Fifty-seventh Street. He'd have been able to walk to work from his new lodgings.

I couldn't tell what he did at CBS, but they only paid him $16,000 a year to do it, so I don't suppose they made him president of the network. He was at CBS a little over three years, and he was up to $18,500 when he left in October of '82.

As far as I could tell he hadn't worked since.

There was mail for me back at the hotel. I could join an international association of retired police officers and attend annual conventions in Fort Lauderdale. The benefits of membership included a membership card, a handsome lapel pin, and a monthly newsletter. What on earth could they run in the newsletter? Obituaries?

There was a message to call Joe Durkin. I caught him at his desk, and he said, "I understand Thurman's not enough for you. You're trying to clear all our open files."

"Just trying to be helpful."

"Arnold Leveque. How does he tie into Thurman?"

"He probably doesn't."

"Oh, I don't know. He got it in May and she got it in

November, almost six months to the day. Looks to me like a definite pattern's shaping up."

"The MO's a little different."

"Well, she was raped and strangled by burglars and he got knifed in an alleyway, but that's just because the killers want to throw us off track. Seriously, you got anything going with Leveque?"

"It's hard to say. I wish I knew what he did the last seven years of his life."

"Hung out in bad neighborhoods, evidently. What else does a man have to do?"

"He didn't work and he wasn't collecting welfare or SSI that I can tell. I saw where he lived and his rent couldn't amount to much, but he had to have money from somewhere."

"Maybe he came into some money. It worked for Amanda Thurman."

"That would give them another point of similarity," I said. "I like your line of reasoning."

"Yeah, well, my mind never stops working. Even when I sleep."

"Especially when you sleep."

"You got it. What's this about he didn't work in seven years? He was working when they arrested him."

"Not according to the state records."

"Well, screw the state records," he said. "That's how he got cracked, he was the clerk when they violated the place for obscenity. Leveque, he's French, I guess they got him for postcards, don't you figure?"

"He was selling pornography?"

"Didn't you get that from Andreotti?"

"Uh-uh. Just the number of the code violation."

"Well, he could have got more than that with a little digging. They did a sweep of Times Square whenever it was, October of '85. Oh, sure, I remember that. It was right before the election; the mayor wanted to look good. I wonder what the new guy's gonna be like."

"I wouldn't want his job."

"Oh, Christ, if it was be mayor or hang myself I'd say, 'Gimme the rope.' Anyway, Leveque. They hit all the stores, bagged all the clerks, hauled off all the dirty magazines and called a press conference. A few guys spent a night in jail and that was the end of it. All charges were dropped."

"And they gave back the dirty books."

He laughed. "There's a stack of them in a warehouse somewhere," he said, "that nobody'll find till the twenty-third century. Of course, a few choice items might have been taken home to spice up some policeman's marriage."

"I'm shocked."

"Yeah, I figured you'd be. No, I don't guess they gave back the confiscated merchandise. But we had a guy just the other day, a street dealer, we locked him up and he walked on a technicality, and he wants to know can he have his dope back."

"Oh, come on, Joe."

"I swear to God. So Nickerson says to him, 'Look, Maurice, if I give you your dope back then I'll have to grab you for possession.' Just shucking him, you know? And the asshole says, 'No, man, you can't do that. Where's your probable cause?' Nick says what do you mean probable cause, my probable cause is I just handed you the fucking dope an' I seen you put it in your pocket. Maurice says no, it'd never stand up, I'd skate. And do you want to know something? I think he's probably right."

Joe gave me the address of the Times Square store where Leveque had taken his brief fall. It was on the block between Eighth and Broadway, right on the Deuce, and since I could tell that from the number I didn't see any reason why I should go down there and look at it. I didn't know if he'd worked there for a day or a year and there was no way I was

going to find out. Even if they wanted to tell me, it was unlikely that anybody knew.

I went over my notes for a few minutes, then leaned back
and put my feet up. When I closed my eyes I got a quick
flash of the man in Maspeth, the perfect father, smoothing
his kid's hair back.

I decided I was reading too much into a gesture. I really
didn't have a clue what the guy in the movie looked like
under all that black rubber. Maybe the boy had looked like
the youth in the film, maybe that was what had triggered my
memory.

And even if it was the right guy? How was I going to
find him by sniffing the fading spoor of some sad bastard
who'd been dead for the better part of a year?

Thursday I'd seen them at the fights. It was Monday now.
If it was his son, if the whole thing was innocent, then I was
just spinning my wheels. If not, then I was too late.

If he'd planned to kill the boy, to spill his blood down
the drain in the floor, it was odds-on he'd done it by now.

But why take him to the fights in the first place? Maybe
he liked to work out an elaborate little psychodrama, maybe
he had a protracted affair with a victim first. That would
explain why the boy in the film had been so unafraid, even
blasé about being tied up on a torture rack.

If the boy was dead already there was nothing I could
do for him. If he was alive there wasn't much I could do,
either, because I was light years from identifying and locating
Rubber Man and I was closing on him at a snail's pace.

All I had was a dead man. And what did I have there?
Leveque died with a tape, and the tape showed Rubber Man
killing a boy. Leveque had died violently, probably but not
necessarily the victim of an ordinary mugging in a part of
town where muggings were commonplace. Leveque had
worked at a porno shop. He'd worked there off the books,
so he could have worked there for years, except that Gus

Giesekind had said that he stayed in most of the time, unlike a man with a regular job.

And his last regular job—

I reached for the phone book and looked up a number. When the machine answered I left a message. Then I grabbed my coat and headed over to Armstrong's.

He was at the bar when I walked in, a slender man with a goatee and a pair of horn-rimmed glasses. He was wearing a brown corduroy jacket with leather elbow patches and smoking a pipe with a curved stem. He would have looked perfectly at home in Paris, sipping an aperitif in a café on the Left Bank. Instead he was drinking Canadian ale in a Fifty-seventh Street saloon, but he didn't look out of place.

"Manny," I said, "I just left you a message."

"I know," he said. "It was still recording when I walked in the door. You said you'd look for me here, so I walked right back out the door again. I didn't have to stop to put my coat on because I hadn't had time to take it off. And, since I live closer to this joint than you do—"

"You got here first."

"So it would appear. Shall we get a table? It's good to see you, Matt. I don't see enough of you."

We used to see each other almost daily when Jimmy's old Ninth Avenue place had been a second home to me. Manny Karesh had been a regular there, dropping in for an hour or so, sometimes hanging around for a whole evening. He was a technician at CBS and lived around the corner. Never a heavy drinker, he came to Jimmy's as much for the food as the beer, and more than either for the company.

We took a table and I ordered coffee and a hamburger and we brought each other up to date. He'd retired, he told me, and I said I'd heard something to that effect.

"I'm working as much as ever," he said. "Free-lancing, sometimes for my former employers and for anyone else who'll hire me. I have all the work I could want, and at the same time I'm collecting my pension."

"Speaking of CBS," I said.

"Were we?"

"Well, we are now. There's a fellow I want to ask you about because you might have known him some years ago. He worked there for three years and left in the fall of '82."

He took his pipe from his mouth and nodded. "Arnie Leveque," he said. "So he called you after all. I had wondered if he would. Why are you looking so puzzled?"

"Why would he call me?"

"You mean he didn't call you? Then why—"

"You first. Why would he have called?"

"Because he wanted a private detective. I ran into him on a shoot. It must have been, oh, six months ago."

Longer than that, I thought.

"And I don't know how it came up, but he wanted to know if I could recommend a detective, although I couldn't swear he used the word. I said that I knew a fellow, an ex-cop who lived right here in the neighborhood, and I gave him your name and said I didn't know your number offhand, but you lived at the Northwestern. You're still there?"

"Yes."

"And you're still doing that sort of work? I hope it was all right to give out your name."

"Of course it was," I said. "I appreciate it. But he never called me."

"Well, I haven't seen him since then, Matt, and I'm sure it's been six months, so if you haven't heard from him by now you probably won't."

"I'm sure I won't," I said, "and I'm pretty sure it's been more than six months. He's been dead since last May."

"You're not serious. He's dead? He was a young man. He carried far too much weight, of course, but even so." He took a sip of beer. "What happened to him?"

"He was killed."

"Oh, for God's sake. How?"

"Stabbed by a mugger. Apparently."

" 'Apparently.' There's a suspicion of foul play?"

"Mugging's reasonably foul play all by itself, but no, there's no official suspicion. Leveque ties into something I'm working on, or at least he may. Why did he want a private detective?"

"He didn't say." He frowned. "I didn't know him all that well. When he started at CBS he was young and eager. He was a technical assistant, part of a camera crew. I don't think he was with us very long."

"Three years."

"I would have said less than that."

"Why did he leave?"

He tugged at his beard. "My sense of it is that we let him go."

"Do you remember why?"

"I doubt that I'd have known in the first place. I don't know that he blotted his copybook, as our British cousins would say, but young Arnold never had what you might call a winning personality. He was a sort of overgrown nerd, which is not a word you'll hear me use often. Still, that's what he was, and he tended to be somewhat casual about matters of personal hygiene. Went a little long between shaves, and wore the same shirt a day or two more than custom dictates. And of course he was fat. Some men are as fat but carry their weight well. Arnold, alas, was not of their number."

"And afterward he got free-lance work?"

"Well, that's what he was doing the last time I ran into him. On the other hand, I've been free-lancing for several years now and I can think of only one other time we were on the same shoot. I guess he must have worked steadily enough, though, because he couldn't have missed many meals."

"He clerked for a while in a Times Square bookstore."

"You know," he said, "I can believe it. It somehow fits

him. There was always something furtive about Arnie, some-thing damp-palmed and out of breath. I can imagine some-one slipping stealthily into one of those places and encountering Arnie behind the counter, rubbing his hands together and giving you a sly look." He winced. "My God, the man's dead, and look how I'm talking about him." He struck a match and got his pipe going again. "I've made him sound like the evil lab assistant in a Frankenstein remake. Well, he'd be a good choice for the part. Always speak ill of the dead, as my sainted mother used to advise me. Because they're in no position to get back at you."

11

"IT'S KIND OF SPOOKY," ELAINE SAID. "HE DIED BEFORE HE could get in touch with you. Then he reached out to you from beyond the grave."

"How do you figure that?"

"Well, what else would you call it? There's a tape in his room when he dies, and his landlady sells it—"

"She's only a super."

"—to a video store, and they rent it out to someone who runs straight to you with it. What are the odds on that?"

"We're all in the neighborhood. Me, Manny, Leveque, Will Haberman, the video place. That puts the needle in a fairly small haystack."

"Uh-huh. What did you tell me coincidence is? God trying to maintain His anonymity?"

"That's what they say."

I'd called her after I left Manny at Armstrong's. She had a cold coming on, she said, and she'd been feeling achy and crummy and sneezy all day. "All those dwarfs," she said, "except Bashful." She was taking a lot of vitamin C and drinking hot water with lemon juice. She said, "What do you really think happened with Leveque? How does he fit in?"

"I think he was the cameraman," I said. "There had to be a fourth person in the room when they made that movie. The camera moved around, zoomed in and out. You can make a home video by positioning the camera and performing in front of it, but that's not what they did, and a lot of the time they were both in the shot at the same time and the camera was moving around to cover the action."

"I never noticed. I was too centered on what was happening."

"You only saw it once. I saw it two more times the other day, don't forget."

"So you could concentrate on the fine points."

"Leveque had a background in video. He worked for three years at a network, admittedly in a menial capacity. He got some work since then on a free-lance basis. And he clerked in a Times Square bookstore and got arrested during one of Koch's cleanup campaigns. If you were going to pick someone to film a dirty movie, he'd be a logical choice."

"But would you let him film you committing murder?"

"Maybe they had enough on him so that they didn't have to worry. Maybe the murder was unplanned, maybe they were just going to hurt the boy a little and they got carried away. It doesn't matter. The boy got killed and the film got made, and if Leveque didn't operate the camcorder somebody else did."

"And he wound up with a tape."

"And he concealed it," I said. "According to Herta Eigen, the only tapes in his apartment were the ones she sold to Fielding. That doesn't figure. Somebody in the trade would be certain to have a lot of noncommercial cassettes around. He was an old film buff, he probably taped things off TV all the time. He probably kept copies of his own camera work, pornographic or otherwise. And he would have had a few blank cassettes around in case he found a use for them."

"You think she was lying?"

"No, what I think is that somebody went to his place on Columbus Avenue while his body temperature was dropping in an alley on West Forty-ninth. His watch and wallet were missing, which suggests robbery, but so were his keys. I think whoever killed him took his keys and went to his apartment and walked out with every cassette except the commercial recordings."

"Why didn't they just take everything?"

"Maybe they didn't want to watch three versions of *The Maltese Falcon*. They probably had enough to carry with the unmarked and homemade material. Why take something that obviously wasn't what they were looking for?"

"And the tape they were looking for is the one we saw?"

"Well, he could have done other work for Rubber Man and he could have kept copies of everything. But he made a particular point of hiding this one. He not only used a commercial film cassette but he let the original movie run for fifteen minutes before he started copying the other one onto the reel. Anybody who gave it a quick check would have seen it was *The Dirty Dozen* and tossed it aside."

"It must have been a real shock to your friend. He and his wife were watching Lee Marvin and the boys, and all of a sudden—"

"I know," I said.

"Why did he conceal the tape so carefully?"

"Because he was scared. That's probably the same reason he asked Manny about a private detective."

"And before he could call you—"

"I don't know that he ever would have called," I said. "I just spoke to Manny again before I called you. He went home and checked his calendar for last year, and he was able to pinpoint his conversation with Leveque because he remembered what job they both worked on. He had that talk with Leveque sometime during the third week in April, and Leveque didn't get killed until the ninth of May. He may have asked other people for recommendations. He may have called somebody else, or he may have decided he could handle it by himself."

"What was he trying to handle? Blackmail?"

"That's certainly a possibility. Maybe he filmed a lot of nasty scenes, maybe Rubber Man wasn't the person he was blackmailing. Maybe somebody else killed him. He may have considered calling me but he never did. He wasn't my client and it's not my job to solve his murder." A couple of lights winked on in the building across the street. I said, "It's not my job to do anything about Rubber Man, either. Thurman's my job and I'm not doing anything about him."

"Wouldn't it be nice if it all tied together?"

"I thought of that," I admitted.

"And?"

"I wouldn't count on it."

She started to say something, sneezed, and said she hoped what she had wasn't the flu. I said I'd see her tomorrow, and to stay with the vitamin C and the lemon juice. She said she would, even though she didn't honestly believe it did you the least bit of good.

I sat there for a while looking out the window. It was supposed to turn colder that night, with snow possible toward morning. I picked up *The Newgate Calendar* and read about a highwayman named Dick Turpin who had been something of a folk hero in his day, although it was hard to figure out why.

Around a quarter to eight I made a couple of calls and managed to reach Ray Galindez, a young police artist who had sat down with me and Elaine and sketched a man who'd threatened to kill us both. I told him I had some work for him if he had an hour or two to spare. He said he could make some time in the morning, and we arranged to meet in the lobby of the Northwestern at ten.

I went to the eight-thirty meeting at St. Paul's and straight home afterward. I thought I'd get to bed early, but instead I wound up sitting up for hours. I would read a paragraph or two about some cutthroat who'd been righteously hanged a couple of centuries ago, then put the book down and stare out the window.

I finally went to bed around three. It never did snow that night.

* * *

Ray Galindez showed up right on time and we went upstairs to my room. He propped his briefcase on the bed and took out a sketch pad and some soft pencils and an Art-Gum eraser. "After I talked with you last night," he said, "I could picture the guy I sketched for you last time. Did you ever catch him?"

"No, but I stopped looking. He killed himself."

"That right? So I guess you never saw him to compare him to the sketch."

I had, but I couldn't say so. "The sketch was right on the money," I said. "I showed it to a lot of people who recognized him on the basis of it."

He was pleased. "You still in touch with that woman? I can picture her apartment, all black and white, that view out over the river. Beautiful place."

"I'm in touch with her," I said. "As a matter of fact I see quite a bit of her."

"Oh yeah? A very nice lady. She still in the same place? She must be, a person'd be crazy to move from a place like that."

I said she was. "And she has the sketch you did."

"The sketch I did. Of that guy? That sketch?"

"Framed on the wall. She says it's a whole category of art the world has overlooked, and after I had the sketch photocopied she got it framed and hung it."

"You're kidding me."

"Swear to God. She had it in the living room but I got her to move it to the bathroom. Otherwise wherever you sat you felt as though he was looking right at you. I'm not putting you on, Ray, she's got it in a nice aluminum frame with non-glare glass and all."

"Jeez," he said. "I never heard of anything like that."

"Well, she's an unusual lady."

"I guess. You know, it's kind of nice to hear that. I mean, she's a woman with good taste. I remember the painting she had on the wall." He described the large abstract oil on the wall near the window, and I told him he had a hell of a memory. "Well, art," he said. "That's, you know, like my thing." He turned away, a little embarrassed. "Well, who've you got for me today? A real bad guy?"

"One very bad guy," I said, "and a couple of kids."

It was easier than I'd thought it would be. I had seen the older of the boys only on videotape and never had a really close look at the younger boy or the man. But I had looked at all three so intently and had thought about them so urgently that all three images were very clear in my mind. The visualization exercise Galindez used was helpful, too, but I think I'd have done as well without it. I didn't have to work to conjure up their faces. All I had to do was close my eyes and they were there.

In less than an hour he'd managed to transfer the images from my mind's eye to three 8 1/2 × 11 sheets of drawing paper. They were all there, the man I'd seen at ringside, the boy who'd been sitting beside him, and the other boy, the one we'd seen murdered.

We worked well together, Galindez and I. There were moments when he seemed to be reading my mind with his pencil, catching something beyond my descriptive abilities. And somehow the three sketches captured the emotional resonance of their subjects. The man looked dangerous, the younger boy blindly vulnerable, the older one doomed.

When we were done he put down his pencil and let out a sigh. "That takes it out of you," he said. "I don't know why, it's just sitting and sketching, I been doing it all my life. But it was like we were hooked up together there."

"Elaine would say we were psychically linked."

"Yeah? I felt something, like maybe I was linked with the three of them, too. Heavy stuff." I told him the sketches were just what I wanted and asked what I owed him. "Oh, I don't know," he said. "What did you give me last time, a hundred? That'd be fine."

"That was for one sketch. You did three this time."

"It was all in one shot, and what did it take me, an hour? A hundred's plenty."

I gave him a pair of hundreds. He started to protest and I told him the bonus was for signing his work. "The originals are for Elaine," I explained. "I'll get them framed and they'll be her Valentine's Day present."

"Jeez, it's time to start thinking about that, isn't it? Valentine's Day." Shyly he pointed to the gold band on his ring finger. "This is new since I saw you," he said.

"Congratulations."

"Thanks. You really want these signed? Because you don't have to pay me extra to sign 'em. I got to say I'm honored."

"Take the money," I said. "Buy something nice for your wife."

He grinned and signed each sketch.

I went downstairs with him. He wanted to catch the subway at Eighth Avenue, and I walked halfway to the corner with him and stopped off at a copy shop where they ran a couple dozen copies of each sketch while I went next door for a cup of coffee and a bagel. I left the originals to be framed at a little graphics gallery on Broadway, then returned to my room and used a rubber stamp to mark my name and address on the back of the copies. I folded a few of each to fit in my inside jacket pocket and went out again, heading on down to Times Square.

The last time I'd hung out on the Deuce was in the middle of a heat wave. Now it was bitter cold. I kept my hands in my pockets and my coat buttoned at the throat and wished I'd had the sense to wear gloves and a muffler. The sky was all shades of gray, and sooner or later we'd get the snow they had predicted.

For all of that, the street didn't look much different. The kids who stood in little bunches on the sidewalk wore somewhat heavier clothing, but you couldn't really say they were dressed for the weather. They tended to move around more, bopping to keep warm, but aside from that they looked pretty much the same.

I walked up one side of the block and down the other, and when a black kid murmured, "Smoke?" I didn't dismiss him with a quick shake of the head. Instead I flicked a finger toward a doorway and walked over to it. He came over right away, and his lips didn't move much when he asked me what I wanted.

I said, "I'm looking for TJ."

"TJ," he said. "Well, if I had some I sure would sell it to you. Give you a real good price on it, too."

"Do you know him?"

"You mean it's a person? I thought it a substance, you know."

"Never mind," I said. I turned from him and he laid a hand on my arm.

"Hey, be cool," he said. "We in the middle of a conversation. Who's this TJ? He a DJ? TJ the DJ, can you dig it?"

"If you don't know him—"

"I hear TJ I think of that old man, pitched for the Yankees. Tommy John? He retired. Anything you want from TJ, man, you do better gettin' it from me."

I gave him one of my cards. "Tell him to call me," I said.

"What I look like, man, his fuckin' beeper?"

I had half a dozen variations of this conversation with half a dozen other pillars of the community. Some of them said they knew TJ and some said they didn't, and I couldn't see any reason to take any of them at their word. Nobody was absolutely certain who I was, but I had to be either a potential exploiter or a prospective victim, someone who would hassle them or someone who could be hustled.

It occurred to me that I might do as well enlisting someone else instead of trying to get in touch with TJ—who was, after all, just another street hustler on the Deuce, and a surprisingly successful one at that, having hustled a streetwise old sonofabitch like me out of five bucks without even trying. If I wanted to give away five-dollar bills, the street was full of kids who would be glad to take my money.

And all of them were easier to find than TJ, who might very well be unavailable. It had been half a year since I'd seen him, and that was a long time on this particular stretch of real estate. He could have moved his act to another part of town. He could have found himself a job. Or he could be on Riker's Island, or doing more serious time upstate.

Or he could be dead. Considering that possibility, I scanned the Deuce and wondered how many of the young men on the street right that minute would ever see thirty-five. Drugs would waste some of them and disease would do for some more, and a fair number of the rest would kill each other. It was a grim thought, and one I didn't care to entertain for long. Forty-second Street was hard enough to bear when you stayed right in present time. When you took the long view it was impossible.

Testament House had gotten its start when an Episcopal priest began allowing runaways to sleep on the floor of his apartment in Chelsea. Before long he had talked a property owner into donating a decaying rooming house a few blocks from Penn Station, and other donors had contributed funds which enabled him to buy the buildings on either side. Two years ago another benefactor had purchased a six-story industrial building and donated that to the cause. I went there after I left Forty-second Street, and a woman with gray hair and unsparing blue eyes told me the institution's history.

"They call this building New Testament House," she said, "and of course the original complex is Old Testament House. Father Joyner has been trying to arrange for the donation of a piece of property in the East Village, and I can't imagine what the kids will call that. All that's left is the Apocrypha, and somehow I don't think that's quite catchy enough for them."

We were in the building's entryway, with a sign running down the building's rules. Anyone under twenty-one was welcome, but no one was allowed on the premises with alcohol or drugs or weapons in his or her possession, and no one would be admitted between the hours of 1:00 and 8:00 A.M.

Mrs. Hillstrom was being charming but cautious, which was understandable; she didn't know yet if I was a prospective donor or someone with a predatory interest in her charges. Whichever I might be, I wasn't going to get past her and into the building proper. I was unarmed and drug-free, but I was clearly over the age limit.

I showed her the sketches of the two boys. Without looking she said, "I'm afraid it's not our policy to disclose who is or isn't staying with us."

"There's nothing to disclose." She looked at me. "Neither of these boys is staying here."

Now she looked at the sketches. "These are drawings," she said. "That's unusual."

"I think one or both of them may have come here. I think they were runaways."

"Lost boys," she said. She peered at each sketch in turn. "They could almost be brothers. Who are they?"

"That's what I'm trying to find out. I don't know their names or where they're from."

"What happened to them?"

"I think this one is dead. I think the younger boy is in danger." I thought for a moment. "Or beyond danger," I said.

" 'Beyond danger.' That means he may be dead also, is that what you're saying?"

"I guess it is."

She cocked her head and searched my eyes. "There's more than you're telling me. Why would you have sketches instead of photographs? How can you be looking for boys if you don't know who they are?"

"There are things you don't want to know about."

"Yes," she said, "and I already know most of them. I'm a paid employee, Mr. Scudder, not an unpaid volunteer. I work twelve hours a day, six days a week, but I don't always take my day off. I get a room of my own and three meals a day and ten dollars a week. That didn't cover cigarettes so I quit smoking, and now I usually give half of my salary away. I've been here for ten months, Mr. Scudder, and I've quit three times. When they train you you agree to stay for a year, so the first time I quit I was afraid I would get yelled at. I told Father Joyner I couldn't take it anymore, that I had to quit, and he said, 'Maggie, I envy you, I wish to God I could quit.' I said, 'I changed my mind, I'm staying.' 'Welcome back,' he said.

"Another time I quit screaming and another time I quit crying. I don't mean I ceased to scream or cry. I was angry, so I quit, and I was weeping, so I quit, but then each time I calmed down and decided to stay. Every day I see something that makes me want to walk down the street and grab every person I meet and shake them all and tell them what's going on. Every day I learn another of the things you say I don't want to know about. One of the three buildings at the Old Testament House is our HIV wing now, did you know that? All the boys there have tested positive for the virus. They're all under twenty-one. You have to leave here when you're twenty-one. Most of them will never have to leave because they'll be dead by then. You think there's something you can't tell me? You think you know something worse than that?"

I said, "The reason I think the older boy is dead is I saw a film he was in with a man and a woman. At the end of the film they killed him. I think the younger boy is either dead or in danger because last week I saw him with a man who I think was one of the performers in the film."

"And you drew these sketches."

"I couldn't draw water. A police artist did these."

"I see." She looked off to one side. "Are there many movies like that? Is it very profitable to make them?"

"I don't know how many there are. And no, I don't think it's particularly profitable. I think these people made the film for their own amusement."

" 'For their own amusement.' " She shook her head. "There was a figure in Greek mythology who devoured his own children. Cronus. I forget why. I'm sure he had a reason." Her eyes flashed at me. "We are devouring our children, a whole generation of them. Wasting them, trashing them, throwing them away. Literally devouring them, in some cases. Devil worshipers sacrificing newborns and . . . and . . . cooking them, eating them. Men buying children on the street and having sex with them and then killing them. You say you saw this man, you saw him with the younger boy? You actually saw him?"

"I think it was the same man."

"Was he normal? Did he look human?" I showed her the sketch. "He looks ordinary," she said. "I hate that. I hate the thought that ordinary people perform such awful acts. I want them to look like monsters. They act like monsters, why shouldn't they look like monsters? Do you understand why people do such things?"

"No."

" 'I envy you,' Father Joyner said. 'I envy you, I wish to God I could quit myself.' Afterward I thought, well, Buster, that was a pretty well calculated way to get me to stay. That was pretty crafty. But I don't think so. I think he meant it, I think it was the literal truth. Because it's true for me. I wish to God I could quit."

"I know what you mean."

"Do you?" She looked at the sketches again. "I could have seen them here, the boys. I don't recognize them but it's possible."

"You wouldn't have seen the older one. You said you've

been here ten months, and I think they'd already made their picture by then."

She asked me if I'd wait for a moment and disappeared into the building. I stood there while a couple of kids entered the building and a few others left. They just looked like ordinary kids, not streetwise like the ones on Forty-second, not as woebegone as their circumstances would warrant. I wondered what had driven them out of their homes and into this crumbling city. Maggie Hillstrom probably could have told me, but I didn't much want to hear it.

Brutal fathers, negligent mothers. Drunken violence. Incest. I didn't have to hear it, I could figure it all out for myself. Nobody walked out of *The Brady Bunch* and wound up here.

I was reading the rules again when she returned. No one recognized either of the sketches. She offered to keep them and show them around later. I told her that would be good, and gave her extra copies of both. "My number's on the back," I said. "Call anytime. And let me give you some copies of the third sketch, the older man. You might want to show those around and tell your kids not to go anywhere with a man who looks like that."

"We tell them not to go with any men," she said. "But they don't listen."

12

"FATHER MICHAEL JOYNER," GORDIE KELTNER SAID. "I GET mail from him, I suppose most of the free world gets mail from him, but I'll receive his newsletters forever because I sent him money once. 'I can save a boy for twenty-five dollars'—that was the headline of one of his fund-raisers. 'Here's fifty,' I wrote. 'Save two of them for me, won't you?' And I sent it back with my check for fifty dollars. Have you met the good father?"

"No."

"Neither have I, but I caught his act on the tube. He was telling Phil or Geraldo or Oprah all about the danger of adult males who prey on lost youth, and the nasty role of pornography in inflaming all concerned and creating an industry that exploits the kids. All of which may well be true, but I thought, Oh, Michael, aren't you playing it the least bit heavy? Because I swear the good padre's as gay as a jay."

"Really?"

"Well, you know what Tallulah Bankhead said. 'All I know is he never sucked *my* cock, dahling.' I haven't heard any stories and I haven't seen him around the bars, and he may be perfectly celibate, although you don't have to be when you're Episcopalian, do you? But he looks gay and his energy is gay. It must be hell for him, living among all those hot kids and making sure he keeps his pants zipped. No wonder he doesn't have too many kind words for those of us who aren't such good little boys."

I first met Gordie years ago when I was a detective attached to the Sixth Precinct in the Village. The station house was on Charles Street then—it's long since moved to West Tenth—and Gordie was working part time behind the bar at Sinthia's. Sinthia's was gone now—Kenny Banks, who'd owned it, had sold out and moved to Key West. Before that happened, Gordie and a partner had moved to my neighborhood and opened Kid Gloves in the room on Ninth Avenue where Skip Devoe and John Kasabian had had Miss Kitty's. Kid Gloves didn't last too long, and now Gordie was working in a joint that had been warehouse space back when I was carrying a gold shield. It was down in the southwest corner of the Village at Clarkson and Greenwich, and it had called itself Uncle Bill's when it opened a few years ago. Since then it had been reborn as Calamity Jack's, with a western motif.

It was late afternoon and Gordie had plenty of time to spend with me. I was one of three customers in the place. An older man in a suit was drinking Irish coffee and reading a newspaper at the end of the bar, and a stocky man in jeans and square-toed black boots was playing bumper pool. I showed Gordie my sketches, as I'd shown them in other Village bars, and he shook his head.

"They're cute, though," he said. "But I never had a taste for chicken, my campy remarks to Father Mike notwithstanding."

"Kenny liked them young," I remembered.

"Kenny was incorrigible. I was a sweet young thing myself when I worked for him, and I was already too old to catch his eye. But you won't find much chicken around the bars, Matt. Not the way you used to, not since the drinking age went from eighteen to twenty-one. A fourteen-year-old could pass for eighteen in dim lighting, especially if he was tall for his age or could show some convincing fake ID. But you'd have to be seventeen to pass for twenty-one, and by that time you're past your prime."

"What a world."

"I know. I decided years ago not to be judgmental, and I know most young boys are eager participants in their own seduction. Sometimes they even initiate it. But I don't care. I'm turning into a moralist in my old age. I think it's wrong for a grown-up to have sex with a child. I don't care if the kid wants it. I think it's wrong."

"I don't know what's right and wrong anymore."

"I thought cops always know."

"They're supposed to. And that might have been one of the reasons I stopped being a cop."

"I certainly hope this doesn't mean I'm going to have to stop being a faggot," he said. "It's all I know." He picked up one of the sketches and tugged his lower lip as he looked at it. "The boys who hustle older men are mostly on the street these days, from what I hear. Lexington Avenue in the low Fifties. Times Square, of course. And the Hudson piers from Morton Street on up. The kids hang out on the river side of West Street and the johns drive up in their cars."

"I was in a few of the West Street bars before I came here."

He shook his head. "They don't let the young stuff in those places. And the hawks don't gather there, either. They're mostly bridge and tunnel types, cruising in their cars, then going home to their wives and kiddies." He put a fresh squirt of seltzer in my glass. "There is one bar you should try, but not until later on in the day. Not before nine-thirty or ten, I wouldn't think. You won't find boys there, but you might run into some dirty old men with an interest in them. That's at the Eighth Square. On Tenth Street just off Greenwich Avenue."

"I know it," I said. "I've passed it, but I never knew it was gay."

"You wouldn't necessarily know from the outside. But it's where all the most dedicated chickenhawks do their drinking. The name says it all, doesn't it?" I must have looked puzzled. "Chess," he explained. "The Eighth Square. That's where a pawn becomes a queen."

I had called Elaine earlier and she'd begged out of our dinner date. She had either flu or the worst cold ever and it had knocked out her energy, her appetite, and her ability to make sense out of what she was reading. All she could manage was naps in front of the TV. I stayed downtown and had spinach pie and a baked potato at a Sheridan Square coffee shop and went to a meeting at a storefront clubhouse on Perry Street. I ran into a woman I'd known at St. Paul's. She'd sobered up there, then moved in with her boyfriend on Bleecker Street. She was married now, and visibly pregnant.

After the meeting I walked over to the Eighth Square. The bartender wore a tanktop with a German eagle on it and looked as though he spent a lot of time at the gym. I told him Gordie at Calamity Jack's had suggested I ask him for help, and I showed him the sketches of the boys.

"Look around," he said. "See anyone like that here? You won't, either. Didn't you see the sign? 'Be twenty-one or be gone.' It's not purely decorative. It means what it says."

"Julius's used to have a sign," I said. " 'If you're gay please stay away.' "

"I remember!" he said, brightening. "As if anyone who *wasn't* a little light on his feet would ever darken their door. But what would you expect from those Ivy League queens?" He leaned on an elbow. "But you're going way back. Before Gay Pride, before Stonewall."

"True."

"Let me have another look. Are they brothers? No, they don't really look alike, it's more attitude, isn't it? You look at them and you think of wholesome things, Scout hikes and skinny-dipping. A paper route. Playing catch on the back lawn with Dad. Listen to me, will you, I sound like *The Donna Reed Show*."

He didn't recognize the boys, and neither did the few

customers he showed the sketches to. "We really don't allow the sandbox set in here," he said. "We come here to complain about how cruel they are, or how much it costs to keep them happy. Wait a minute, now. Who's this?" He was studying the third sketch, the one of Rubber Man. "I think I've seen him," he said. "I can't swear to it, but I think I've seen him."

A couple of other men came over and leaned over me to examine the sketch. "Of course you've seen him," one said. "You've seen him in the movies. It's Gene Hackman."

"It does look like him," another said.

"On the worst day of his life," the bartender said. "I see what you mean, but it's not him, is it?" I said it wasn't. "Why use drawings, though? Isn't it easier to identify someone with a photograph?"

"Photographs are so common," one of the others said. "I'm all for drawings, I think they're a very fresh idea."

"We're not thinking of redecorating, Jon. This is about identification, not redoing the breakfast nook."

Another man, his face wasted with AIDS, said, "I've seen this man. I've seen him in here and I've seen him on West Street. Maybe half a dozen times over the past two years. On a couple of occasions he was with a woman."

"What did she look like?"

"Like a Doberman pinscher. Black leather from the toes up, high-heeled boots, and I think she was wearing spiked cuffs on her wrists."

"Probably his mother," someone said.

"They were definitely hunting," the man with AIDS said. "They were on the prowl for a playmate. Did he kill those boys? Is that why you're looking for him?"

The question startled me into an unguarded response. "One of them," I said. "How did you know?"

"They looked like killers," he said simply. "I had that thought the first time I saw them together. She was Diana, goddess of the hunt. I don't know who he was."

"Cronus," I suggested.

"Cronus? Well, that would fit, wouldn't it, but it's not the thought I had. I remember he was wearing a floor-length leather coat and he looked like a Gestapo agent, somebody who'd come knocking on your door at three in the morning. You know what I mean, you've seen those movies."

"Yes."

"I thought, these two are killers, they're looking for someone to take home and kill. You're being silly, I told myself, but I was right, wasn't I?"

"Yes," I said. "You were right."

I took the subway to Columbus Circle and picked up the early edition of the *Times* on my way home. There were no messages at the desk and nothing interesting in the mail. I turned the TV on and watched the news on CNN and read the paper during the commercials. Somewhere along the way I got interested in a long article on drug gangs in Los Angeles and reached to switch off the television set.

It was past midnight when the phone rang. A soft voice said, "Matt, it's Gary at Paris Green. I don't know if you care, but the fellow you asked about the other night just walked in and took a seat at the bar. He might drink up and walk out the minute I hang up, but if I were guessing I'd say he'll stay put for a while."

I'd taken my shoes off, but other than that I was ready to roll. I was tired, I'd had a late night last night, but to hell with that.

I said I'd be right over.

The cab ride couldn't have taken more than five minutes, but before it was half over I was wondering what the hell I was doing. What was I going to do, watch the man drink and figure out if he was a killer?

The absurdity of the whole thing became still more evident when I opened the door and went in. There were just two people in the whole place, Gary behind the bar and Richard Thurman in front of it. The kitchen was closed, and before they'd left the waiters had put the chairs on top of the tables. Paris Green wasn't a late joint, and Gary usually closed down the bar around the time the waiters finished and went home. I had the feeling he was staying open tonight on my account, and I only wished there was more sense in it.

Thurman turned at my approach. Some people barely show their drink. Mick Ballou is like that. He can take on a heavy load and the only outward sign of it is a slight hardening in the gaze of his green eyes. Richard Thurman was just the opposite. One look at him and I knew he'd been making a night of it. It showed in the glassiness of the hard blue eyes, the suggestion of bloat in the lower part of the face, the softening around the pouty mouth.

He nodded shortly and went back to his own drink. I couldn't see what it was. Something on the rocks, neither his usual light beer nor his pre-dinner martini. I picked a spot eight or ten feet down the bar from him and Gary brought me a glass of club soda without asking.

"Double vodka tonic," he said. "Want this on your tab, Matt?"

It wasn't vodka and I didn't have a tab there. Gary was one of the few bartenders in the neighborhood who wasn't trying to make it as an actor or writer, but he had a head for drama all the same. "That'll be fine," I told him, and I took a long drink of my soda water.

"That's a summer drink," Thurman said.

"I guess it is," I agreed. "I got in the habit of drinking it year round."

"The Brits invented tonic. They colonized the tropics and started drinking it. You know why?"

"To keep cool?"

"As a malaria preventive. Preventative. You know what tonic is? What's another name for it?"

"Quinine water?"

"Very good. And you take quinine to prevent malaria. You worried about malaria? You see any mosquitoes?"

"No."

"Then you're drinking the wrong drink." He raised his own glass. " 'Claret for boys, port for men, and for heroes it's nothing but brandy.' You know who said that?"

"Some drunk, it sounds like."

"Samuel Johnson, but you probably think he plays right field for the Mets."

"You're talking about Darryl Strawberry now. He a brandy drinker?"

"Jesus Christ," Thurman said. "What am I doing here? What the hell is the matter with me?"

He put his head in his hands. I said, "Hey, cheer up. Is that brandy you're drinking?"

"Brandy and crème de menthe. It's a stinger."

No wonder he was shitfaced. "A hero's drink," I said. "Gary, give my father here another hero's drink."

"I don't know," Thurman said.

"Oh, come on," I said. "You can handle one more."

Gary brought him another stinger and set up another glass of soda for me, whisking away the one I'd barely touched. Thurman and I raised our glasses at each other, and I said, "Absent friends."

"Jesus," he said. "Not that one."

"How's this, then? 'Here's to crime.' "

His shoulders drooped and he looked at me. His full lips were slightly parted. He looked as though he was about to say something, but then he changed his mind and took a long swallow of his drink. He made a face and shuddered a little as it went down.

He said, "You know me, don't you?"

"Hell, we're practically old friends."

"I'm serious. Don't you know who I am?"

I looked at him. "Wait a minute," I said.

He was waiting for me to recognize him from his picture

in the papers. I let him wait another beat. Then I said, "Maspeth Arena. The Thursday night fights. Am I right?"

"I don't believe this."

"You were the cameraman. No, I'm wrong. You were in the ring telling the cameraman what to do."

"I produce the telecast."

"On cable."

"Five Borough Cable, right. I don't believe this. We give the seats away and we can't get people to sit in them. Nobody even knows where Maspeth is. The only subway anywhere near there is the M and nobody in Manhattan can figure out where you go to catch it. If you saw me there, it's no wonder you recognized me. We were just about the only people there."

"Pretty good job," I said.

"You think so, huh?"

"You get to watch the fights. Get to grab a pretty girl by the ass."

"Who, Chelsea? Just a tramp, my friend. Take my word for it." He downed some more of his stinger. "What brought you out there? You a big fight fan, never miss a bout?"

"I was working."

"You too, huh? What are you, a reporter? I thought I knew all the press guys."

I gave him one of my cards, and when he pointed out that it had only my name and address I showed him the card I used when I worked for Wally, a business card for Reliable Investigations with their address and phone number and my name.

"You're a detective," he said.

"That's right."

"And you were working the other night when you came out to Maspeth." I nodded. "What are you doing now? This all part of the job?"

"This? Drinking and bullshitting? No, they don't pay me for this. I wish they did, I'll tell you."

I had put the card from Reliable away, but I'd let him keep the other and he was looking at it now. He read my name aloud and looked at me. He asked me if I knew his name.

"No," I said. "How would I?"

"It's Richard Thurman. Does that ring a bell?"

"Just the obvious. Thurman Munson."

"I get that a lot."

"Yankees haven't been the same since the plane crash."

"Yeah, well, I haven't been the same myself. Since the crash."

"I don't follow you."

"Never mind. It's not important." He was silent for a moment. Then he said, "You were starting to tell me what you were doing in Maspeth."

"Oh, you know."

"No, I don't know. That's why I'm asking."

"You wouldn't be interested."

"Are you kidding? A private detective, everybody's fantasy job, of course I'd be interested." He dropped a friendly hand onto my shoulder. "What's the bartender's name?"

"Gary."

"Hey, Gary, another stinger, another double vee-tee. So what brought you to Maspeth, Matt?"

"You know," I said, "the funny thing is you might be able to help."

"How's that?"

"Well, you were there," I said. "You might have seen him. He was right at ringside."

"What are you talking about?"

"The guy I was supposed to follow." I got out a copy of a sketch and made sure it was the right one. "Here we go. He was sitting up front, had his son with him. I picked him up there the way I was supposed to and then I lost him. You happen to know who he is?"

He looked at the sketch and I looked at him. "This is a

drawing," he said after a moment. I agreed that it was. "You do this? 'Raymond Galindez.' That's not you."

"No."

"Where'd you get this?"

"They gave it to me," I said. "So I would recognize him."

"And you were supposed to follow him?"

"Right. And I went to take a leak and when I got back he was gone. Him and the boy both, like they disappeared while my back was turned."

"Why were you following him?"

"They don't tell me everything. Do you recognize him? Do you know who he is? He was right in the front row, you must have seen him."

"Who's your client? Who told you to follow him?"

"I couldn't tell you that even if I knew. Confidentiality, it's everything in this business, you know."

"Hey, c'mon," he said winningly. "We're all alone here. Who'm I gonna tell?"

"I don't even know who the client is," I said, "or why I was supposed to follow him. I caught hell for losing the son-ofabitch, believe me."

"I can imagine."

"So do you recognize him? Do you know who he is?"

"No," he said. "I never saw him before."

He left shortly thereafter. I slipped out myself and crossed to the downtown side of the intersection so I could watch him walking toward Eighth Avenue. When he had a good lead I tagged along after him, just keeping him in sight. He went into his own building, and a few minutes later I saw the lights go on in the fourth-floor windows.

I went back to Paris Green. Gary had locked up, but he opened the door for me. "That was a nice touch," I said. "Vodka and tonic."

"*Double* vodka tonic."

"And on my tab at that."

"Well, I couldn't charge you six dollars for club soda, could I? Much simpler this way. There's still some coffee left. Want a cup before I shut down for the night?"

I had a cup and Gary uncapped a bottle of Dos Equis for himself. I tried to give him some money but he wouldn't hear of it. "I'd rather keep my efforts as a Ninth Avenue Irregular strictly pro bono," he said. "I wouldn't enjoy it half as much if I took money for it, as the actress said to the bishop. Well, have you reached a verdict? Did he do it?"

"I'm sure he's guilty," I said. "But I was sure before, and I don't have any more evidence now than I did then."

"I overheard a little of the conversation. It was fascinating the way you became another person. All of a sudden you were a saloon character and about half lit in the bargain. For a second there you had me worried that I'd put vodka in your drink by mistake."

"Well, I put in enough time in ginmills. It's not hard to remember the moves." And it wouldn't be hard to be that person again. Just add alcohol and stir. I said, "He was this close to talking about it. I don't know that there was any way to crack him open tonight, but there were things he wanted to say. I don't know, it may have been a mistake showing him the sketch."

"Is that what it was, that sheet of paper you handed him? He took it with him."

"Did he? I see he left my card." I picked it up. "Of course my name and number are on the back of the sketch. He recognized it, too. That was obvious, and his denial wasn't terribly convincing. He knows the guy."

"I wonder if I do."

"I think I've got another copy," I said. I checked my pocket, unfolded sketches until I got the right one. I handed it to Gary and he tilted it to catch the light.

He said, "Mean-looking bastard, isn't he? Looks like Gene Hackman."

"You're not the first person to point that out."

"Really? I never noticed it before." I looked at him. "When he was here. I told you Thurman and his wife had dinner here with another couple. This was the male half of the couple."

"You're sure?"

"I'm sure this chap and a woman had dinner at least once with the Thurmans. It may have been more than once. If he said he didn't know him, he was lying."

"You also said he was here with another man sometime after his wife's death. Same guy?"

"No. That was a blond fellow around his own age. This man"—he tapped the drawing—"was closer to your age."

"And he was here with Thurman and his wife."

"I'm sure of it."

"And another woman. What did she look like, do you happen to remember?"

"Haven't a clue. I couldn't have told you what he looked like if I hadn't seen a picture of him. That brought it all back. If you've got a picture of her—"

I didn't. I had thought of trying to work with Galindez on a sketch of the placard girl but her facial features were too imperfectly defined in my memory, and I wasn't at all certain she was the same woman I'd seen in the movie.

I let him look at the pictures of the two boys, but he hadn't seen either of them before. "Nuts," he said. "I was doing so well, and now my average is down to one in three. Do you want more coffee? I can make another pot."

That made a good exit cue, and I said I had to be getting home. "And thanks again," I said. "I owe you a big one. Anything I can do, anytime at all—"

"Don't be silly," he said. He looked embarrassed. In a bad Cockney accent he said, "Just doin' me duty, guvnor. Let a man get by wiv killin' 'is wife and there's no tellin' what narsty thing 'e'll do next."

*   *   *

I swear I meant to go home. But my feet had other ideas. They took me south instead of north, and west on Fiftieth to Tenth Avenue.

Grogan's was dark, but the steel gates were drawn only part of the way across the front and there was one light lit inside. I walked over to the entrance and peered through the glass. Mick saw me before I could knock. He opened up for me, locked the door once I was inside.

"Good man," he said. "I knew you'd be here."

"How could you? I didn't know it myself."

"But I did. I told Burke to put on a pot of strong coffee, I was that sure you'd be by to drink it. Then I sent him home an hour ago, I sent them all home and sat down to wait for you. Will it be coffee then? Or will you have Coca-Cola, or soda water?"

"Coffee's fine. I'll get it."

"You will not. Sit down." A smile played lightly on his thin lips. "Ah, Jesus," he said. "I'm glad you're here."

13

WE SAT AT A TABLE OFF TO THE SIDE. I HAD A MUG OF STRONG black coffee and he had a bottle of the twelve-year-old Irish that is his regular drink. The bottle had a cork stopper, a rarity these days; stripped of its label it would make a pretty decent decanter. Mick was drinking his whiskey out of a small cut-glass tumbler that may have been Waterford. Whatever it was it stood a cut above the regular bar glassware, and like the whiskey it was reserved for his private use.

"I was here the night before last," I said.

"Burke told me you came by."

"I watched an old movie and waited for you. *Little Caesar*, Edward G. Robinson. 'Mother of Mercy, is this the end of Rico?' "

"You'd have had a long wait," he said. "I worked that night." He picked up his glass and held it to catch the light. "Tell me something, man. Do you always need money?"

"I can't go very far without it. I have to spend it and that means I have to earn it."

"But are you scratching for it all the fucking time?"

I had to think about it. "No," I said at length. "Not really. I don't earn a lot, but I don't seem to need much. My rent's cheap, I don't have a car, I don't carry any insurance, and I've got no one to support except myself. I couldn't last long without working, but some work always seems to come along before the money runs out."

"I always need money," he said. "And I go out and get

it, and I turn around and it's gone. I don't know where it goes."

"That's what everyone says."

"I swear it melts away like snow in the sun. Of course you know Andy Buckley."

"The best dart player I ever saw."

"He's a fair hand. A good lad, too."

"I like Andy."

"You'd have to like him. Did you know he still lives at home with his mother? God bless the Irish, what a strange fucking race of men we are." He drank. "Andy doesn't make a living throwing darts in a board, you know."

"I thought he might do more than that."

"Sometimes he'll do something for me. He's a grand driver, Andy is. He can drive anything. A car, a truck, anything you could ask him to drive. He could likely fly a plane if you gave him the keys." The smile was there for an instant. "Or if you didn't. If you misplaced the keys and needed someone to drive without them, Andy's your man."

"I see."

"So he went off to drive a truck for me. The truck was full of men's suits. Botany 500, a good line of clothing. The driver knew what he was supposed to do. Just let himself be tied up and take his time working himself loose and then tell how a couple of niggers jumped him. He was getting well paid for his troubles, you can be sure of that."

"What happened?"

"Ah, 'twas the wrong driver," he said, disgusted. "Your man woke up with a bad head and called in sick, entirely forgetting he was to be hijacked that day, and Andy went to tie up the wrong man and had to knock him on the head to get the job done. And of course the fellow got loose as quick as he could, and of course he called the police at once and they spotted the truck and followed it. By the grace of God Andy saw he was being followed and so he didn't drive to the warehouse, or there would have been more men than himself arrested. He parked the truck on the street and tried to walk away from it, hoping they'd wait for him to come back to it, but they outguessed him and took him right down, and the fucking driver came down and picked him out of a lineup."

"Where's Andy now?"

"Home in bed, I shouldn't doubt. He was in earlier and said he had a touch of the flu."

"I think that's what Elaine's got."

"Has she? It's a nasty thing. I sent him home. Get in bed with a hot whiskey, I told him, and ye'll be a new man in the morning."

"He's out on bail?"

"My bondsman had him out in an hour, but now he's been released altogether. Do you know a lawyer named Mark Rosenstein? A very soft-spoken Jewish lad, I'm forever asking him to speak up. Don't ask how much money I handed him."

"I won't."

"I'll tell you anyway. Fifty thousand dollars. I don't know where it all went, I just put it into his hands and left it to him. Some went to the driver, and your man changed his story and swore it wasn't Andy at all, it was someone else entirely, someone taller and thinner and darker and with a Russian accent, I shouldn't wonder. Oh, he's very good, Rosenstein is. He'd make no impression in court, you could never hear what he was saying, but you do better if you stay out of court entirely, wouldn't you say?" He freshened his drink. "I wonder how much of the money stayed with the little Jew. What would you guess? Half?"

"That sounds about right."

"Ah, well. He earned it, didn't he? You can't let your men rot in prison cells." He sighed. "But when you spend money like that you have to go out and get more."

"You mean they wouldn't let Andy keep the suits?" I went on to tell him Joe Durkin's story of Maurice, the dope dealer who'd demanded the return of his confiscated cocaine. Mick put his head back and laughed.

"Ah, that's grand," he said. "I ought to tell that one to Rosenstein. 'If you were any good at all,' I'll tell him, 'ye'd have arranged it so that we got to keep the suits.'" He shook his head. "The fucking dope dealers," he said. "Did you ever try any of that shit yourself, Matt? Cocaine, I mean."

"Never."

"I tried it once."

"You didn't like it?"

He looked at me. "The hell I didn't," he said. "By God it was lovely! I was with a girl and she wouldn't rest until I tried some. And then she got no rest at all, let me tell you. I never felt so fine in my life. I knew I was the grandest fellow that ever lived and I could take charge of the world and solve all its problems. But before I did that it might be nice to have a little more of the cocaine, don't you know. And the next thing you knew it was the middle of the afternoon, and the cocaine was all gone, and the girl and I had fucked our silly brains out, and she was rubbing up against me like a cat and telling me she knew where to get more.

"'Get your clothes on,' I told her, 'and buy yourself some more cocaine if you want it, but don't bring it back here because I never want to see it again, or you either.' She didn't know what was wrong but she knew not to stay around to find out. And she took the money. They always take the money."

I thought of Durkin and the hundred dollars I'd given him. "I shouldn't take this from you," he'd said. But he hadn't given it back.

"I never touched cocaine again," Mick said. "And do you know why? Because it was too fucking good. I don't ever want to feel that good again." He brandished the bottle. "This lets me feel as good as I need to feel. Anything more than that is unnatural. It's worse than that, it's fucking dangerous. I hate the stuff. I hate the rich bastards with their jade snuff bottles and gold spoons and silver straws. I hate the ones who smoke it on the streetcorners. My God, what it's doing to the city. There was a cop on television tonight saying you should lock your doors when you're riding in a taxi. Because when your cab stops for a light they'll come in after you and rob you. Can you imagine?"

"It keeps getting worse out there."

"It does," he said. He took a drink and I watched him savor the whiskey in his mouth before he swallowed it. I knew what the JJ&S twelve-year-old tasted like. I used to drink it with Billie Keegan years ago when he tended bar for Jimmy. I could taste it now, but somehow the sense-memory didn't make me crave a drink, nor did it make me fear the dormant thirst within me.

A drink was the last thing I wanted on nights like this. I had tried to explain it to Jim Faber, who was understandably uncertain of the wisdom of my spending long nights in a saloon watching another man drink. The best I could do was to suggest that somehow Ballou was drinking for both of us, that the whiskey that went down his throat quenched my thirst as well as his own, and left me sober in the process.

He said, "I went to Queens again Sunday night."

"Not to Maspeth."

"No, not to Maspeth. Another part entirely. Jamaica Estates. Do you know it?"

"I have a vague idea of where it is."

"You go out Grand Central Parkway and get off at Utopia. The house we were looking for was on a little street off Croydon Road. I couldn't tell you what the neighborhood looked like. It was full dark when we went out there. Three of us, and Andy driving. He's a grand driver, did I tell you?"

"You told me."

"They were expecting us, but they didn't expect we'd have guns in our hands. Spanish they were, from somewhere in South America. A man and his wife and the wife's mother. They were dope dealers, they sold cocaine by the kilo.

"We asked him where his money was. No money, he said. They had cocaine to sell, they didn't have any cash. Now I knew they had money in the house. They'd had a big sale the day before and they still had some of the money around."

"How did you know?"

"From the lad who gave me the address and told me how to get through the door. Well, I took the man in a bedroom and tried to talk sense to him. Talked with my hands, you might say. He stuck fast to his story, the little greaseball.

"And then one of the lads comes in with a baby. 'Get up off the money,' he tells the man, 'or I'll cut the wee bastard's throat.' And the babe's screaming through all this. No one's hurting him, you understand, but he's hungry or he wants his mother. You know how it is with babies."

"What happened?"

"If you can believe this," he said, "the father as much as says we can go to hell. 'I don't think you do thees,' he says, looking me right in the eye.

" 'You're right,' I told him. 'I don't kill babies.' And I told my man to take the babe to its mother and have her change his diaper or give him a bottle, whatever would stop his crying." He straightened up in his chair. "And then I took the father," he said, "and I put him in a chair, and I left the room and came back wearing my father's apron. One of the lads— Tom it was, you know Tom, behind the bar most afternoons."

"Yes."

"Tom had a gun to his head, and I had the big cleaver that was my father's also. I went over and tried it out on the bedside table, just took a good whack at it and it collapsed into a pile of kindling. Then I took hold of his arm just above the wrist, pinning it to the arm of the chair, and with my other hand I raised up the cleaver.

" 'Now, you spic bastard,' I said, 'where's your money,

or don't you theenk I'll take your fucking hand off?' " He smiled with satisfaction at the memory. "The money was in the laundry room, in the vent pipe for the dryer. You could have turned the house upside down and never found it. We were out of there in no time, and Andy had us safely home. I'd have been lost out there, but he knew all the turns."

I got up and went behind the bar to pour myself another cup of coffee. When I got back to the table Mick was gazing off to one side. I sat down and waited for the coffee to cool and we both let the silence stretch for a while.

Then he said, "We left them alive, the whole household. I don't know, that could have been a bad idea."

"They wouldn't call the police."

"They couldn't do that, and they weren't well connected, so I didn't think they'd come back at us. And we left the cocaine. There was ten kilos of it that we found, shaped like little footballs. 'I'm leaving you your coca,' I told him, 'and I'm leaving you alive. But if you ever come back at me,' I said, 'then I'll come back here. And I'll wear this'—pointing to the apron—'and I'll carry this'—the cleaver—'and I'll lop off your hands and feet and whatever else I can think of.' I'd do no such thing, of course. I'd just kill him and be done with it. But you can't scare a drug dealer by telling him you'll kill him. They all know somebody will kill them sooner or later. Tell them you'll leave them with some pieces missing, though, and the picture sticks in their mind."

He filled his glass and took a drink. "I didn't want to kill him," he said, "because I'd have had to kill the wife too, and the old woman. I'd leave the baby because a baby can't pick you out of a lineup, but what kind of a life would I be leaving it? It's got a bad enough life already, with that for a father.

"Because look how he called my bluff. 'I don't think you do thees.' The bastard didn't *care* if I did it. Go ahead, kill the baby, he can always start another one. But when it was a question of his hand winding up on the floor, why, he wasn't so fucking tough then, was he?"

A little later he said, "Sometimes you have to kill them. One runs for the door and you drop him, and then you have to take out all the rest of them. Or you know they're not people who will let it go, and it's kill them or watch your back for the rest of your life. What you do then is scatter the drugs all over the place. Grind the bricks to powder, pour it on the bodies, tread it into the rug. Let it look like dealers killing each other. The cops don't break their necks to solve that kind of killing."

"Don't you ever take the drugs along?"

"I don't," he said, "and I'm giving up a fortune, and I just don't care. There's so much money in it. You wouldn't have to deal in it, you could sell the lot to someone. It wouldn't be hard to find someone who wanted to buy it."

"No, I don't suppose it would."

"But I'll have no part of it, and I won't work with anyone who'll use it or traffic in it. The cocaine I left behind the other night, I could have got more for it than I took in cash from the dryer vent. There was only eighty thousand there." He lifted his glass, set it down again. "There should have been more. I know he had another stash somewhere in the fucking house, but I'd have had to chop off his hand to get it. And that would have meant killing him after, and killing the lot of them. And calling the police later, telling them there was a baby crying in a house on such-and-such a street."

"Better to take the eighty thousand."

"That's what I thought," he said. "But there's four thousand right off the top for the lad who told us where to go and how to get in. A finder's fee, you call it. Five percent, and I shouldn't wonder he thought we got more and were cheating him. Four thousand for him, and a good night's pay for Tom and Andy and the fourth fellow, whom you don't know. And what's left for myself is a little less than what I paid to get Andy off the hook for the hijacking." He shook his head. "I always need money," he said. "I don't understand it."

*   *   *

I talked some about Richard Thurman and his dead wife, and about the man we'd seen at the fights in Maspeth. I took out the sketch and he looked at it. "It's very like him," he said. "And the man who drew it never saw the man he was drawing? You wouldn't think it could be done."

I put the sketch away and he said, "Do you believe in hell?"

"I don't think so."

"Ah, you're fortunate. I believe in it. I believe there's a place reserved for me there, a chair by the fire."

"Do you really believe that, Mick?"

"I don't know about the fire, or little devils with fucking pitchforks. I believe there's something for you after you die, and if you lead a bad life you've got a bad lot ahead of you. And I don't lead the life of a saint."

"No."

"I kill people. I only do it out of need, but I lead a life that makes killing a requirement." He looked hard at me. "And I don't mind the killing," he said. "There are times I have a taste for it. Can you understand that?"

"Yes."

"But to kill a wife for the insurance money, or to kill a child for pleasure." He frowned. "Or taking a woman against her will. There's more men than you'd think who'll do that last. You'd think it was just the twisted ones but sometimes I think it's half the human race. Half the male sex, anyway."

"I know," I said. "When I was at the Academy they taught us that rape was a crime of anger toward women, that it wasn't sexual at all. But over the years I stopped believing that. Half the time nowadays it seems to be a crime of opportunity, a way to have sex without taking her to dinner first. You're committing a robbery or a burglary, there's a woman there, she looks good to you, so why not?"

He nodded. "Another time," he said. "Like last night, but over the river in Jersey. Dope dealers in a fine house out in the country, and we were going to have to kill everybody in the house. We knew that before we went in." He drank whiskey and sighed. "I'll go to hell for sure. Oh, they were killers themselves, but that's no excuse, is it?"

"Maybe it is," I said. "I don't know."

"It's not." He put the glass down and wrapped his hand around the bottle but didn't lift it from the table. "I'd just shot the man," he said, "and one of the lads was searching for more cash, and I heard cries coming from another room. So I went in there, and there's one of the boys on top of the woman, with her skirt up and her clothes ripped, and she's fighting him and crying out."

" 'Get off her,' I told him, and he looked at me like I was mad. She was choice, he said, and we were going to kill her anyway, so why shouldn't he have her before she was no use to anybody?"

"What did you do?"

"I kicked him," he said. "I kicked him hard enough to break three ribs, and then before I did anything else I shot her between the eyes, because she shouldn't have to put up with more of it. And then I picked him up and threw him against the wall, and when he came stumbling off it I hit him in the face. I wanted to kill him, but there were people who knew he'd worked for me and it would be like leaving a calling card behind. I took him away from there and paid him his share and got a closemouthed doctor to bandage his ribs, and then I packed him off. He was from Philadelphia, and I told him to go back there, that he was finished in New York. I'm sure he doesn't know to this day what he did that was wrong. She was going to die anyway, so why not have the use of her first? And why not roast her liver and eat it, why let the flesh go to waste?"

"There's a pretty thought."

"In the name of Jesus," he said, "we're all going to die, aren't we? So why not do any bloody thing we please with each other? Is that it? Is that how the world works?"

"I don't know how the world works."

"No, and neither do I. And I don't know how you get through it on fucking coffee, I swear I don't. If I didn't have this—"

He filled his glass.

Later we were talking about black men. He had little use for them and I let him tell me why. "Now there's some who are all right," he said. "I'll grant you that. What was the name of that fellow we met at the fights?"

"Chance."

"I liked him," he said, "but you'd have to say he's another type entirely from the usual run. He's educated, he's a gentleman, he's a professional man."

"Do you know how I got to know him?"

"At his place of business, I would suppose. Or didn't you say you met him at the fights?"

"That's where we met, but there was a business reason for the meeting. That was before Chance was an art dealer. He was a pimp then. One of his whores got killed by a lunatic with a machete, and he hired me to look into it."

"He's a pimp, then."

"Not anymore. Now he's an art dealer."

"And a friend of yours."

"And a friend of mine."

"You have an odd taste in friends. What's so funny?"

" 'An odd taste in friends.' A cop I know said that to me."

"So?"

"He was talking about you."

"Was he now." He laughed. "Ah, well. Hard to argue with that, isn't it?"

On a night like that the stories come easy, and the silences between the stories are easy, too. He talked about his father and mother, both long gone, and about his brother Dennis who had died in Vietnam. There were two other brothers, one a lawyer and real estate broker in White Plains, the other selling cars in Medford, Oregon.

"At least he was the last I heard of him," he said. "He was going to be a priest, Francis was, but he lasted less than a year at the seminary. 'I learned I liked the girls and the gargle too much.' Hell, there's priests that have their share of both. He tried one thing and another and two years ago he was in Oregon selling Plymouths. 'It's great here, Mickey, come out and see me.' But I never did, and he's likely gone somewhere else by now. I think the poor bastard still wishes he was a priest, even though his faith's long since lost. Can you understand that?"

"I think so."

"Were you raised Catholic? You weren't, were you?"

"No. There were Catholics and Protestants in the family but nobody worked at it very hard. I grew up not going to church and wouldn't have known which one to go to. I even had one grandparent who was half-Jewish."

"Is that so? You could have been a lawyer like Rosenstein."

He told the story he'd started Thursday night, about the man who owned the factory in Maspeth where they assembled staple removers. The man had incurred gambling debts and wanted Mick to burn the place so he could collect the insurance. The arsonist Mick used had made a mistake and torched the place directly across the street instead. When Mick told the arsonist of his error the man insisted it was no problem, he'd go back the next night and do it right. And he'd include an extra for goodwill, he offered. He'd burn the man's house down and not charge him for it.

I told a story I hadn't thought of in years. "I was fresh out of the Academy," I said, "and they teamed me up with an old hairbag named Vince Mahaffey. He must have had thirty years in and he never made plainclothes and never wanted to. He taught me plenty, including things they probably didn't want me to learn, like the difference between clean graft and dirty graft and how to get as much of the first kind as you can. He drank like a fish and ate like a pig and he smoked those little Italian cigars. Guinea stinkers, he called them. I thought you had to be in one of the five families to smoke those things. He was a hell of a role model, Vince was.

"One night we caught one, a domestic disturbance, the neighbors called it in. This was in Brooklyn, in Park Slope. It's all gentrified there now, but this was before any of that got started. It was an ordinary white working-class neighborhood then.

"The apartment was a fifth-floor walk-up, and Mahaffey had to stop a couple of times along the way. Finally we're standing in front of the door and you can't hear a thing. 'Ah, shit,' Vince said. 'What do you bet he killed her? Now he'll be crying and yanking his hair out and we'll have to take him in.'

"But we rang the bell and they both answered it, a man and a woman. He was a big guy around thirty-five, a construction worker, and she looked like a girl who'd been pretty in high school and let herself go. And they were surprised to hear that we'd had a complaint. Oh, had they been making too much noise? Well, maybe they'd been playing the TV a little loud. It wasn't even on now, the whole place was silent as a grave. Mahaffey pushed it the least little bit, said we'd had a report of sounds of a struggle and a loud argument, and they looked at each other and said, well, yeah, they'd had a discussion that turned into a little bit of an argument, maybe they shouted at each other some, and maybe he'd pounded on the kitchen table to make a point, and they'd be careful to keep it down for the rest of the evening, because they certainly didn't want to disturb anybody.

"He'd been drinking but I wouldn't have said he was drunk, and they were both calm and anxious to please, and I was ready to wish 'em goodnight and get on to something else. But Vince had been to hundreds of domestics and this one smelled and he could tell. I might have picked up on it myself if I hadn't been so new. Because they were hiding something. Otherwise they'd have said there was no fight and no problem and told us to go to hell.

"So he stalled, talking about this and that, and I'm wondering what's the matter with him, is he waiting for the husband to break out the bottle and offer us drinks. And then we both heard a noise, like a cat but not like a cat. 'Oh, it's nothing,' they said, but Mahaffey pushed them out of the way and opened a door, and we found a little girl there, seven years old but small for her age, and now you could see why the domestic disturbance hadn't left any marks on the wife. All of the marks were on the girl.

"The father had beaten the shit out of her. Bruises all over her, one eye closed, and marks on one arm where they burned her with cigarettes. 'She fell down,' the mother insisted. 'He never touched her, she fell down.'

"We took them to the station house and parked them in a holding cell. Then we took the kid to a hospital, but first Mahaffey dragged her into an empty office and borrowed somebody's camera. He undressed the kid except for her underpants and took a dozen pictures of her. 'I'm a shit photographer,' he said. 'If I take enough shots maybe something'll come out.'

"We had to let the parents go. The doctors at the hospital confirmed what we already knew, that the child's injuries could only have been the result of a beating, but the husband was swearing he didn't do it and the wife was backing him up, and you weren't going to get testimony out of the kid. And they were very reluctant to prosecute child abuse in those days anyway. It's a little better now. At least I think it is. But we had no choice but to cut the parents loose."

"You must have wanted to kill the bastard," Mick said.

"I wanted to put him away. I couldn't believe that he could do something like that and get away with it. Mahaffey told me it happened all the time. You hardly ever got a case like that to court, not unless the child died and sometimes not then. Then why, I asked, had he bothered taking the pictures? He patted me on the shoulder and told me the pictures were worth a thousand words apiece. I didn't know what he was talking about.

"Middle of the next week we're in the car. 'It's a nice day,' he said. 'Let's go for a ride, let's go to Manhattan.' I didn't know where the hell he was taking me. We wound up on Third Avenue in the Eighties. It was a construction site, they'd knocked down a batch of small buildings and were putting up a big one. 'I found out where he drinks,' Mahaffey said, and we went into this neighborhood tavern, Carney's or Carty's or something, it's long gone now. The place was full of guys with work shoes and hard hats, construction workers on their break or at the end of their shift, having a ball and a beer and unwinding.

"Well, we were both in uniform, and the conversation stopped when we walked in. The father was at the bar in the middle of a knot of his buddies. It's funny, I don't remember his name."

"Why should you? As many years ago as it was."

"You would think I would remember. Anyway, Mahaffey walked right through them all and went up to the guy, and he turned to the men standing around and asked them if they knew him. 'You think he's all right? You think he's a decent sort of a guy?' And they all said sure, he's a good man. What else are they going to say?

"So Mahaffey opens his blouse, his blue shirt, and he takes out a brown envelope, and it's got all the pictures he took of the kid. He had them blow them up to eight-by-ten, and they all came out perfect. 'This is what he did to his own fucking child,' Mahaffey says, and he passes the pictures around. 'Take a good look, this is what the bastard does to a defenseless child.' And, when they've all had a good look, he tells them we're cops, we can't put this man in jail, we can't lay a finger on this man. But, he says, *they* aren't cops, and once we're out the door we can't stop them from doing whatever they think they have to do. 'And I know you're good American working men,' he tells them, 'and I know you'll do the right thing.' "

"What did they do?"

"We didn't hang around to watch. Driving back to Brooklyn Mahaffey said, 'Matt, there's a lesson for you. Never do something when you can get somebody else to do it for you.' Because he knew they'd do it, and we found out later that they damn near killed the sonofabitch in the process. Lundy, that was his name. Jim Lundy, or maybe it was John.

"He wound up in the hospital and he stayed a full week. Wouldn't make a complaint, wouldn't say who did it to him. Swore he fell down and it was his own clumsiness.

"He couldn't go back to that job when he got out of the hospital because there was no way those men would work with him again. But I guess he stayed in construction and was able to get jobs, because a few years later I heard he went in the hole. That's what they call it when you're working high steel and you fall off a building, they call it going in the hole."

"Did someone push him?"

"I don't know. He could have been drunk and lost his balance, or he could have done the same thing cold sober, as far as that goes. Or maybe he gave somebody a reason to throw him off the building. I don't know. I don't know what happened to the kid, or to the mother. Probably nothing good, but that would just give them something in common with most of the rest of the world."

"And Mahaffey? I suppose he's gone by now."

I nodded. "He died in harness. They kept trying to retire him and he kept fighting it, and one day—I wasn't partnered with him by then, I had just made detective on the strength of a terrific collar that was ninety-eight percent luck—anyway, one day he was climbing the stairs of another tenement and his heart cut out on him. He was DOA at Kings County.

At his wake everybody said that was the way he would have wanted it, but they got that wrong. I knew what he wanted. What he wanted was to live forever."

Not long before dawn he said, "Matt, would you say that I'm an alcoholic?"

"Oh, Jesus," I said. "How many years did it take me to say I was one myself? I'm not in a hurry to take anybody else's inventory."

I got up and went to the men's room, and when I came back he said, "God knows I like the drink. It'd be a bad bastard of a world without it."

"It's that kind of world either way."

"Ah, but sometimes this stuff lets you lose sight of it for a while. Or at least it softens the focus." He lifted his glass, gazed into it. "They say you can't stare at an eclipse of the sun with your naked eye. You have to look through a piece of smoked glass to save your vision. Isn't it as dangerous to see life straight on? And don't you need this smoky stuff to make it safe to look at?"

"That's a good way to put it."

"Well, bullshit and poetry, that's the Irish stock in trade. But let me tell you something. Do you know what's the best thing about drinking?"

"Nights like this."

"Nights like this, but it's not just the booze makes nights like this. It's one of us drinking and one of us not, and something else I couldn't lay my finger on." He leaned forward and put his elbows on the table. "No," he said, "the best thing about drinking is a certain kind of moment that only happens once in a while. I don't know that it happens for everyone, either.

"It happens for me on nights when I'm sitting up alone with a glass and a bottle. I'll be drunk but not too drunk, you know, and I'll be looking off into the distance, thinking but not thinking—do you know what I mean?"

"Yes."

"And there'll be a moment when it all comes clear, a moment when I can just about see the whole of it. My mind reaches out and wraps itself around all of creation, and I'm this close to having hold of it. And then"—he snapped his fingers—"it's gone. Do you know what I mean?"

"Yes."

"When you drank, did you—"

"Yes," I said. "Once in a while. But do you want to know something? I've had the same thing happen sober."

"Have you now!"

"Yes. Not often, and not at all the first two years or so. But every now and then I'll be sitting in my hotel room with a book, reading a few pages and then looking out the window and thinking about what I've just read, or of something else, or of nothing at all."

"Ah."

"And then I'll have that experience just about as you described it. It's a kind of knowing, isn't it?"

"It is."

"But knowing what? I can't explain it. I always took it for granted it was the booze that allowed it to happen, but then it happened sober and I realized it couldn't be that."

"Now you've given me something to think about. I never thought for a moment it could happen sober."

"It can, though. And it's just as you described it. But I'll tell you something, Mick. When it happens to you sober, and you're seeing it without that piece of smoked glass—"

"Ah."

"—and you have it, you just about have it, and then it's gone." I looked into his eyes. "It can break your heart."

"It will do that," he said. "Drunk or sober, it will break your heart."

It was light out when he looked at his watch and got to his feet. He went into his office and came back wearing his butcher's apron. It was white cotton, frayed here and there from years of laundering, and it covered him from the neck to below the knees. Bloodstains the color of rust patterned it like an abstract canvas. Some had faded almost to invisibility. Others looked fresh.

"Come on," he said. "It's time."

We hadn't discussed it once throughout the long night but I knew where we were going and had no objections. We walked to the garage where he kept his car and rode down Ninth Avenue to Fourteenth Street. We turned left, and partway down the block he left the big car in a no-parking zone in front of a funeral parlor. The proprietor, Twomey, knew him and knew the car. It wouldn't be towed or ticketed.

St. Bernard's stood just east of Twomey's. I followed Mick up the steps and down the left-hand aisle. There is a seven o'clock mass weekdays in the main sanctuary, which he had missed, but there is a smaller mass an hour later in a small chamber to the left of the altar, generally attended by a handful of nuns and various others who stopped in on their way to work. Mick's father had done so virtually every day, and there were always butchers in attendance, though I don't know if anyone else called it the butchers' mass.

Mick attended sporadically, coming every day for a week or two, then staying away for a month. I had joined him a handful of times since I'd come to know him. I wasn't sure why he went, and I certainly didn't know why I sometimes tagged along.

This occasion was like all the others. I followed the service in the book and picked up my cues from the others, standing when they stood, kneeling when they knelt, mouthing the appropriate responses. When the young priest handed out the Communion wafers Mick and I stayed where we were. As far as I could tell, everybody else approached the altar and received the Host.

Outside again Mick said, "Will you look at that?"

It was snowing. Big soft flakes floated slowly down. It

must have started just after we entered the old church. There was already a light dusting of snow on the church steps, and on the sidewalk.

"Come on," he said. "I'll run you home."

14

I WOKE UP AROUND TWO AFTER FIVE HOURS OF A RESTLESS, dream-ridden sleep, most of it suspended just a degree or two below the horizon of consciousness. All that coffee may have had something to do with it, much of it on a stomach unsupplied with food since the spinach pie at Tiffany's.

I rang downstairs and told the desk clerk he could put through my calls again. The phone rang while I was in the shower. I called down again to see who it was, and the clerk said there was no message. "You had a few calls during the morning," he said, "but no messages."

I shaved and dressed and went out for breakfast. The snow had stopped falling but it was still fresh and white where human and vehicular traffic hadn't yet turned it to slush. I bought a paper and carried it back to the room. I read the paper and looked out the window at the snow on roof-tops and window ledges. We'd had about three inches of it, enough to muffle some of the noise of the city. It was something pretty to look at while I waited for the phone to ring.

The first to get through was Elaine, and I asked her if she'd tried earlier. She hadn't. I asked her how she was feeling.

"Not great," she said. "I'm a little feverish and I've got diarrhea, which is just the body trying to get rid of everything it doesn't need. That seems to include everything but bones and blood vessels."

"Do you think you ought to see a doctor?"

"What for? He'll tell me I've got this crud that's going around, and I already know that. 'Keep warm, drink lots of fluids.' Right. The thing is, see, I'm reading this book by Borges, he's this Argentinian writer who's blind. He's also dead, but—"

"But he wasn't when he wrote it."

"Right. And his work is kind of surreal and spacy, and I don't know where the writing leaves off and the fever starts, if you know what I mean. Part of the time it seems to me that this is not the best condition to be in while I read this stuff, and other times I think it's the only way to do it."

I filled her in on some of what happened since our last conversation. I told her about the run-in with Thurman at Paris Green, and that I'd spent a long night with Mick Ballou.

"Oh, well," she said. "Boys will be boys."

I went back to the paper. There were two stories that particularly struck me. One reported that a jury had acquitted an alleged mob boss charged with ordering an assault on a union official. The acquittal had been expected, especially in view of the fact that the victim, shot several times in both legs, had seen fit to testify for the defense, and there was a photo of the dapper defendant surrounded by well-wishers and fans on his way out of the courthouse. This was the third time he'd been brought to trial in the past four years, and the third time he'd skated. He was, the reporter said, something of a folk hero.

The other story concerned a workingman who'd been leaving the subway station with his four-year-old daughter when a homeless person, apparently deranged, attacked the pair and spat at them. In the course of defending himself the father pounded the lunatic's head against the ground, and when it was over the homeless man was dead. A spokesman for the DA's Office had announced the decision to prosecute the father for manslaughter. They ran a photo of him, looking confused and besieged. He wasn't dapper, and seemed an unlikely folk hero.

I put the paper down and the phone rang again. I picked it up and a voice said, "Is this where it's at?"

It took me a moment. Then I said, "TJ?"

"Where it's at, Matt. Everybody want to know who's this dude, hangin' loose on the Deuce, passin' out cards an' askin' everybody where's TJ. I was at the movies, man, watchin' this kung fu shit. You know how to do that shit?"

"No."

"That is some wild shit, man. Like to learn me some of that sometime."

I gave him my address and asked him if he could come up. "I don't know," he said. "What kind of hotel? One of them big fancy ones?"

"Not fancy at all. They won't give you a hard time downstairs. If they do, just tell them to call me on the house phone."

"I guess that be all right."

I hung up, and it rang again almost immediately. It was Maggie Hillstrom, the woman from Testament House. She had shown my sketches to kids and staff members at both Old Testament House and New Testament House. No one could identify the younger boy or the man, although some of the kids had said that either or both of them looked familiar.

"But I don't know how much stock to place in that," she said. "More to the point, we were able to identify the older boy. He never actually lived here but he did stay overnight on several occasions."

"Did you manage to come up with a name for him?"

"Happy," she said. "That's what he called himself. It seems ironic, doesn't it, and in a shabby way. I don't know if that was a long-standing nickname or if he acquired it here on the street. The consensus is that he was from the South or Southwest. A staff member seems to recall that he said he was from Texas, but a boy who knew him is just as certain he came from North Carolina. Of course he may have said different things to different people."

He was a hustler, she said. He went with men for money and took drugs when he could afford them. No one could recall having seen him within the past year.

"They are forever disappearing," she said. "It's normal not to see them for a few days, and then suddenly you'll realize you haven't seen someone for a week or two weeks or a month. And sometimes they come back and sometimes they don't, and you never know if the next place they went to was better or worse for them." She sighed. "One boy told me he thought Happy had most likely gone home. And, in a manner of speaking, perhaps he has."

The next call was from the desk, announcing TJ's arrival. I told them to send him on up and met him at the elevator. I took him to my room and he moved around it like a dancer, checking it out. "Hey, this is cool," he said. "See the Trade Center from here, can't you? An' you got your own bathroom. Must be nice."

As far as I could tell he was wearing the same outfit I'd seen him in before. The denim jacket that had looked too warm for the summer now appeared unequal to the winter's cold. His high-top sneakers looked new, and he had added a royal-blue watch cap.

I handed him the sketches. He glanced at the top one and looked up at me, his eyes wary. He said, "You want to draw my picture? Why you laughin'?"

"I'm sure you'd make a fine model," I said, "but I'm no artist."

"You didn't draw these here?" He looked at each in turn, examined the signature. "Raymond something. What do you say, Ray? What's happenin'?"

"Do you recognize any of them?"

He said he didn't, and I ran it down for him. "The older boy's name is Happy," I said. "I think he's dead."

"You think they both be dead. Don't you?"

"I'm afraid so."

"What you want to know about them?"

"Their names. Where they're from."

"You already know his name, you said. Happy, you said."

"I figure his name is Happy like your name is TJ."

He gave me a look. "You say TJ," he said, "everybody gone know who you be referrin' to." He looked at the sketch again. "You sayin' Happy's his street name."

"That's right."

"If that's his name on the street, that the only name the street gone know. Who give you that name, Testament House?"

I nodded. "They said he didn't live there but he stayed there a couple of nights."

"Yeah, well, they be good people, but not everybody can handle the rules an' shit, you know what I'm sayin'?"

"Did you ever stay there, TJ?"

"Shit, why'd I do that? I don't need no place like that. I got a place where I live, man."

"Where?"

"Never mind where. Long as I can find it, that's all that matters." He shuffled through the sketches. Casually he said, "I seen this man."

"Where?"

"I dunno. On the Deuce, but don't be askin' me where or when." He sat down on the edge of the bed, yanked his cap off, turned it over in his hands. He said, "What you want from me, man?"

I took a twenty from my wallet and held it out to him. He didn't move to take it, and his eyes repeated his question. What did I want from him?

I said, "You know the Deuce and the bus terminal and the kids on the street. You could go places I don't know about and talk to people who wouldn't talk to me."

"Tha's a lot for twenty dollars." He grinned. "Other time I seen you, you gimme fi' dollars and I didn't do nothin'."

"You haven't done anything this time either," I said.

"Could take a lot of time, though. Jivin' with the people, goin' here an' there." I started to take back the twenty and his hand moved to snatch it from me. "Don't be doin' that," he said. "I didn't say no, did I? Just tuggin' you 'round some is all." He looked around the room. "But I don't guess you's rich, huh?"

I had to laugh. "No," I said. "Not quite."

Chance called. He had asked a few people in the fight crowd, and some had recalled an apparent father and son at ringside Thursday. No one remembered having seen the pair before, in Maspeth or elsewhere. I said the man would probably not have had the boy along on other occasions, and he said it was the two of them that people remembered. "So it's not like the people I talked to recognized him," he said. "Are you going back out there tomorrow night?"

"I don't know."

"Or you could watch it on television. You might see him if he's in the first row again."

We didn't stay on the phone long because I wanted to keep the line open. I hung up and waited, and Danny Boy Bell was the next to call. "I'll be having dinner at Poogan's," he said. "Why don't you join me? You know how I hate to eat alone."

"You've got something?"

"Nothing remarkable," he said, "but you have to eat dinner sometime, don't you? Eight o'clock."

I hung up and checked the time. It was five o'clock. I turned on the TV and watched the opening of the news and turned it off when I realized I wasn't paying attention. I picked up the phone and dialed Thurman's number. When the machine picked up I didn't say anything but I didn't hang up, either. I sat there with the line open for thirty seconds or so before I finally broke the connection.

I picked up *The Newgate Calendar* and the phone rang almost immediately. I grabbed it and said hello and it was Jim Faber.

"Oh, hi," I said.

"You sound disappointed."

"I've been waiting on a call all afternoon," I said.

"Well, I won't keep you," he said. "It's not important. Will you be going to St. Paul's tonight?"

"I don't think so. I have to meet somebody at eight on Seventy-second Street and I don't know how long that'll last. Anyway, I went last night."

"That's funny, I looked for you and didn't see you there."

"I was downtown, I went to Perry Street."

"Oh, did you? That's where I wound up Sunday night. The perfect choice, you can say anything there and nobody gives a rat's ass. I said terrible things about Bev and felt a hundred percent better for it. Was Helen there last night? Did she tell you about the holdup?"

"What holdup?"

"At Perry Street. Look, you're expecting a call, I don't want to keep you."

"That's all right," I said. "Somebody held up Perry Street? What could they get? They don't even have coffee there anymore."

"Well, it wasn't a brilliantly conceived crime. It was their Friday night step meeting a week or two ago. A fellow named Bruce was speaking. I don't know if you know him and it's not important. Anyway, he gave his qualification for twenty minutes, and then some wacko stood up and announced that he had come to that meeting a year earlier and put forty dollars in the basket by mistake, and he had a gun in his pocket, and if he didn't get his forty dollars back he was going to start blowing people away."

"Jesus."

"Wait, here's the good part. Bruce told him, 'I'm sorry, you're out of order, we can't interrupt the meeting for something like that. You'll have to wait until the break at a quarter of nine.' The guy starts to say something and Bruce bangs the gavel on that sort of podium they have there and tells him to sit down and calls on somebody else, and the meeting goes on."

"And the nut just sits there?"

"I guess he figured he had no choice. Rules are rules, right? Then another fellow, a guy named Harry, went over to him and asked him if he wanted some coffee or some cigarettes, and the nut allowed as to how coffee would be nice. 'I'll just slip out and get you some,' Harry whispered, and he slipped out and around the corner to the police station, I think there's one fairly close—"

"The Sixth Precinct's just a couple blocks away on West Tenth."

"Then that's where he went, and he came back with a couple of New York's Finest, and they bundled up the lunatic and took him away. 'Wait a minute,' he said. 'Where's my forty dollars? Where's my coffee?' Only at Perry Street."

"Oh, that could happen anywhere, don't you think?"

"I'm not so sure of that. I can think of an Upper East Side meeting where they would have taken up a collection for the sonofabitch and then tried to see if they could find him an apartment. Well, I won't keep you, I know you're expecting a call. But I had to pass that on."

"Thanks for sharing," I said.

Just sitting still can drive you crazy. But I didn't want to go anywhere. I knew he was going to call and I didn't want to miss it.

The phone rang at six-thirty. I grabbed it and said hello and there was no answer. I said hello again and waited. I could tell the line was open. I said hello a third time and the connection was broken.

I picked up my book and put it down again, and then I looked in my notebook and dialed Lyman Warriner in Cambridge. "I know I told you I wouldn't be filing any progress reports," I said, "but I wanted to let you know that there's been some progress. I have a pretty good idea at this point of what happened."

"He's guilty, isn't he?"

"I don't think there's any question of that," I said. "Not in my mind and not in his."

"In his?"

"Something's working on him, guilt or fear or both. He called here a minute ago. He didn't say a word. He's scared to talk but he's also scared not to talk and that's why he called. I'm positive he'll call again."

"You sound as though you expect him to confess."

"I think he wants to. At the same time I'm sure he's afraid to. I'm not sure why I called you, Lyman. I probably should have waited until everything's resolved."

"No, I'm glad you called."

"I have a feeling once things start to move they're going to move fast." I hesitated. "Your sister's murder is only part of it."

"Really."

"That's how it looks at this stage. I'll let you know when I have something more concrete. But in the meantime I wanted to keep you in the picture."

There was another call at seven. I picked it up and said hello and there was a click right away as he hung up. I called back right away, dialing the number of the phone at his apartment. It rang four times and his machine picked up. I hung up.

At seven-thirty he called again. I said hello and when there was no reply I said, "I know who you are. You can go ahead and talk, it's all right."

Silence.

"I have to go out now," I said. "I'll be back here at ten o'clock. Call me at ten."

I could hear him breathing.

"Ten o'clock," I said, and broke the connection. I waited for ten minutes on the off chance that he'd call back right away and be ready to spill it, but no, that was it for now. I grabbed my coat and went to keep my dinner date with Danny Boy.

15

"FIVE BOROUGH CABLE," DANNY BOY SAID. "A GOOD IDEA, based on the premise that New Yorkers might go for sports programming with a little more local interest than celebrity bass fishing and Australian rules football. But they had a slow start and they made a very common mistake. They were undercapitalized.

"Just about a year ago they solved that problem by selling a substantial share to a pair of brothers with a last name I can't pronounce, but which I've been assured is Iranian. That's all anyone knows about them, aside from the fact that they live in Los Angeles, and are represented by an attorney in that city.

"For Five Borough, it's business as usual. They're not making money but they're not getting killed, and the new investors are willing to lose money for a few years. In fact they might be willing to lose money forever."

"I see."

"Do you? Interestingly enough, the new investors seem content to play a very passive role. You'd think they might make changes in the company's management, but they kept all the old people on and didn't bring in anybody new. Except that there's someone now who's around a lot. He doesn't work for Five Borough, he doesn't draw a salary, but if you look at the company you'll always see him out of the corner of your eye."

"Who is he?"

"Now that," he said, "is an interesting question. His name is Bergen Stettner, which sounds German, or at least Teutonic, but I don't think that's the name he was born with. He lives with his wife in an apartment on a high floor in that hotel of Trump's on Central Park South. Keeps an office in the Graybar Building on Lexington. He deals in foreign currencies, and he also buys and sells precious metals. What does this begin to suggest to you?"

"That he's a laundryman."

"And that Five Borough is functioning as some sort of laundry. How or why or for whom or to what extent are questions I wouldn't presume to answer." He poured himself some vodka. "So I don't know if this does you any good at all, Matthew. I couldn't find out anything at all about young Richard Thurman. If he hired some street scum to tie him up and savage his wife, either he picked a remarkably close-mouthed pair or their fee included passage to New Zealand, because the word on the street is no word at all."

"That figures."

"Does it?" He knocked back the Stoly. "I hope the news about Five Borough isn't completely useless to you. I didn't want to say anything over the phone. That's never something I like to do, and your calls go through the hotel switchboard, don't they? Isn't that a nuisance?"

"I can dial out direct," I said. "And they take messages."

"I'm sure they do, although I don't like to leave them if I can help it. I'd offer to find out more about Stettner, but I might have a hard time doing that. He keeps a low profile. What have you got there?"

"I think it's his picture," I said, and unfolded the sketch. Danny Boy looked at it, then at me.

"You already knew about him," he said.

"No."

"You just happened to have his pencil portrait tucked in your jacket pocket. It's *signed*, for God's sake. Who, pray tell, is Raymond Galindez?"

"The next Norman Rockwell. Is that Stettner?"

"I don't know, Matthew. I never set eyes on the man."

"Well, I'm ahead of you there. I had a good look at him. I just didn't happen to know who I was looking at." I folded the sketch and put it away. "Keep this to yourself for now," I said, "but if things break right, he's going to go away for a long long time."

"For running a laundry?"

"No," I said. "That's what he does for a living. What's going to put him away is what he does for a hobby."

My walk home took me past St. Paul's. It was nine-thirty when I got there, and I stopped in for the last half hour of the meeting. I got a cup of coffee and dropped into a chair in the back row. I noticed Will Haberman a few rows in front of me and imagined bringing him up to date. *In that version of* The Dirty Dozen *you lent me, Will, we've so far learned that the part of Rubber Man was played by Bergen Stettner. A young fellow with no previous acting experience played the male ingenue. He was using the stage name of Happy. We're not sure yet about Leather Woman, but there's a possibility her name is Chelsea.*

That was the name Thurman had dropped last night. "Who, Chelsea? Just a tramp, my friend. Take my word for it." I was willing enough to take his word, but I was less and less persuaded that the girl who'd strutted around the ring with the numbered cards was the masked woman in leather.

I couldn't pay any real attention to the meeting. The discussion went on around me while my mind spun off in circles of its own. I'd come down into the church basement not for what I might hear but just to be in a safe place for a few minutes.

I ducked out early and got back to my room with two minutes to spare. Ten o'clock came and went, and at five minutes after the hour the phone rang and I grabbed it. "Scudder," I said.

"You know who this is?"

"Yes."

"Don't say my name. Just say where you know me from."

"Paris Green," I said. "Among other places."

"Yeah, right. I didn't know how much you were drinking last night, how much you'd remember."

"I have a pretty good memory."

"So do I, and I'll tell you something, there's times I wish I didn't. You're a detective."

"That's right."

"Is that straight? I couldn't find you in the book."

"I'm not listed."

"You work for some agency. You showed me a card but I didn't get the name."

"I just free-lance for them. Mostly I'm on my own."

"So I could hire you directly."

"Yes," I said. "You could do that."

There was a pause while he thought it over. "The thing is," he said, "I think I'm in trouble."

"I can see where you'd think that."

"What do you know about me, Scudder?"

"What everybody knows."

"Last night you didn't recognize my name."

"That was then."

"And this is now, huh? Look, I think we ought to talk."

"I think so, too."

"Where, though? That's the question. Not Paris Green."

"How about your place?"

"No. No, I don't think that's a good idea. Someplace public, but not where somebody might recognize me. All the places that come to my mind are out, because they're the places I go all the time."

"I know a place," I said.

He said, "You know this is perfect, and I never would have thought of a place like this. This is what you'd call your basic Irish neighborhood tavern, isn't it?"

"You could."

"Just a few blocks from where I live and I never knew it existed, but then I could walk past it every day and never notice it, never pay any attention, you know? Different worlds. Here you got your decent working-class people, honest as the day is long, real salt-of-the-earth types. And look, you got your tin ceiling, tile floor, dart board on the wall. This is perfect."

We were in Grogan's, of course, and I wondered if anyone had ever described its owner as the salt of the earth, or honest as the day was long. Still, it seemed to suit our purpose. It was quiet and nearly empty, and no one who knew Thurman was likely to put in an appearance.

I asked him what he wanted to drink. He said he guessed a beer would be good, and I went to the bar for a bottle of Harp and a glass of Coke. "You missed the big fellow," Burke told me. "He was in an hour ago, said you kept him up all night."

I went back to the table and Thurman noticed my Coke. "That's not what you were drinking last night," he said.

"You were drinking stingers."

"Don't remind me. The thing is, I'm not that much of a drinker ordinarily. A martini before dinner, and maybe a couple of beers. Last night I was hitting it. Matter of fact, I'm not sure how much I said to you. Or how much you know."

"I know more than I did last night."

"And you knew more then than you let on."

"Maybe you'd better just tell me what's bothering you."

He thought about it, then nodded shortly. He patted his pockets and found the sketch I'd given him the night before. He unfolded it and looked from it to me. He asked if I knew who it was.

"Why don't you tell me?"

"His name is Bergen Stettner."

Good, I thought.

"I'm afraid he's going to kill me."

"Why? Has he ever killed anyone before?"

"God," he said. "I don't know where to start."

He said, "I never met anyone like Bergen before. He started to come around after the buy-in and we hit it off right away. I thought he was fantastic. Very strong, very sure of himself, and when you're with him it's very easy to believe that the ordinary rules don't apply. The first time I met him he took me back to his apartment. We drank champagne on the terrace with all of Central Park spread out below us like our private backyard.

"The next time I was over there I met his wife. Olga. Beautiful woman, and there was so much sexual energy around her it was dizzying. He went to the bathroom and she sat down next to me and put her hand in my lap and started stroking me through my pants. 'I want to suck your cock,' she said. 'I want you to fuck me in the ass. I want to sit on your face.' I couldn't believe what was happening. I was sure he'd walk in and catch us like that, but by the time he came back she was sitting in a chair on the other side of the room, talking about one of the paintings.

"The next day he kept telling me how much Olga liked me, how she said they should see more of me. A few days later we went out to dinner with them, my wife and I. It was awkward, because there was this whole thing going on between me and Olga. At the end of the evening Bergen kissed Amanda's hand, very Continental, but with a self-mocking quality to it at the same time. And Olga gave me her hand to kiss, and it smelled of, well, it smelled of pussy. She must have touched herself. And I looked up at her, you know, and there was this expression on her face, it got to me as much as the smell did.

"Of course he knew everything that was going on, they planned it together, I know all that now. The next time I was over at their apartment he said he had something to show me, it wasn't something I'd be likely to see on cable but he thought it would interest me. He put on a videocassette, and it was porno, an amateur video. Two men sharing a woman. Halfway through Olga came in and sat down next to me. I hadn't even known she was in the apartment, I'd thought Bergen and I were there alone.

"When the cassette ended Bergen took it off and put on another one. This one featured two women, one black and one white. The black woman was a slave. It took me a minute to realize that the white woman was Olga. I couldn't take my eyes off the screen.

"After it ended I looked around and Bergen had left the room. Olga and I tore our clothes off and got on the couch. At some point I realized Bergen was in the room, watching us. Then we all got up and went into the bedroom together."

Along with the sex Stettner fed him a steady diet of philosophy. Rules were for those who lacked the imagination to break them. Superior men and women made their own rules, or lived with none at all. He quoted Nietzsche often, and Olga put a New Age gloss on the old German. There were truly no victims when you claimed your power, because their fate was just a manifestation of their own desire for subjugation. They created their destiny even as you created yours.

One day Stettner called him at the office. "Stop what you're doing," he said. "Go downstairs, wait on the corner, I'll pick you up in fifteen minutes." Stettner took him for a long drive, telling him only that he had a gift for him. He parked in an unfamiliar neighborhood and led Thurman down a flight of stairs into a basement chamber. There he beheld a naked woman manacled to a metal frame, her mouth stopped with a gag. "She's yours," Stettner told him. "Do whatever you want with her."

He had sex with the woman. It would have been discourteous to refuse, like turning down a drink or a meal or any other offer of hospitality. Besides, the woman's utter helplessness was fiercely exciting to him. When he had finished having intercourse with her Stettner asked him if there was anything else he wanted to do to the woman. He said there wasn't.

They left the building and got back into Stettner's car. The older man told him to wait a minute, that there was something he had forgotten to do. He was back shortly and began driving. He asked Thurman if he'd ever been a woman's first lover. Thurman said that he had.

"But not your wife."

No, Thurman acknowledged. Amanda had not been a virgin when they met.

"Well, I have given you a gift," Stettner said. "You have already been a woman's first lover, and now you have been this one's last. That girl you were just with, no one will ever have her again, no one but the worms. Do you know what I did when I went back? I killed her for you. I took the gag out of her mouth, and I said, 'Goodbye, darling,' and I cut her throat."

Thurman didn't know what to say.

"You don't know if you should believe me. Maybe I just went back to take a piss, or to cut her loose. Do you want to go back and see for yourself?"

"No."

"Good. Because you know I always tell the truth. You're confused, you don't know how to feel about this. Relax. You didn't do anything. I did it. And she would have died anyway. No one lives forever." He reached over and took Thurman's hand in his. "We are closer than close, you and I. We are brothers in blood and semen."

It had taken him a long time to pour the beer and now it was taking him longer to drink it. He would pick up the glass and have it halfway to his lips and set it down and resume talking. He didn't really care about the beer. He wanted to talk.

He said, "I don't know if he killed that woman. She could

have been some whore hired for the occasion and he went back to pay her and let her free. Or he could have cut her throat the way he said. There's no way to know."

From that point on he was leading two lives. On the surface he was a young executive on the way up. He had a great apartment and a rich wife and a rosy future. At the same time he was living a secret life with Bergen and Olga Stettner.

"I learned to turn it on and off," he said. "Like you leave your job at the office, I left that whole side of myself for when I was with them. I saw them once, twice a week. We didn't always do anything. Sometimes we would just sit around and talk. But there was always that edge, that current flowing among us. And then I'd shut it off and go home and be a husband."

After he'd known the two of them for several months, Stettner needed his help.

"He was being blackmailed. There was a tape they had made. I don't know what was on it but it must have been bad because the cameraman kept a copy and he wanted fifty thousand dollars for it."

"Arnold Leveque," I said.

His eyes widened. "How did you know that? How much do you know?"

"I know what happened to Leveque. Did you help kill him?"

This time he got the glass to his lips. He wiped his mouth with the back of his hand and said, "I swear I didn't know that was how it was going to go. He said he would pay the fifty thousand but he couldn't meet with Leveque, the man was afraid of him. It's not hard to guess why. He said it would be one payment and that would be the end of it, because the man would not be fool enough to try the same stunt twice.

"There's a Thai restaurant on the corner of Tenth Avenue and Forty-ninth Street. I met Leveque there. He was this comical fat man who waddled like a windup toy. He kept telling me that he was sorry to be doing this but he really needed the money. The more he said it the more despicable he seemed.

"I gave him the briefcase full of money and let him open it. He seemed more frightened when he saw the money. I was supposed to be a lawyer, that was the story, and I was wearing a Brooks pinstripe and trying to slip legal terms into my conversation. As if it mattered.

"We made the exchange, and I told him he could retain the briefcase but I couldn't allow him to go off with it until I was assured that the cassette was the one my client wanted. 'My car's parked nearby,' I said, 'and we're just minutes from my office, and as soon as I've seen five minutes of the tape you can be on your way with the money."

He shook his head. "He could have just stood up and walked out of there," he said. "What was I going to do? But I guess he trusted me. We walked halfway to Eleventh Avenue and Bergen was waiting at the mouth of an alleyway. He was going to hit Leveque over the head and then we were going to get out of there with the money and the tape."

"But that's not what happened."

"No," he said. "Before Leveque could even react Bergen was punching him. At least that's what it looked like, but then I saw that he had a knife in his hand. He stabbed him right there on the street, then grabbed him and dragged him into the alley and told me to get the briefcase. I got it and went into the alley and he had Leveque against the brick wall and he was stabbing him. Leveque was just staring. Maybe he was already dead, I don't know. He never made a sound."

Afterward they took Leveque's keys and searched his apartment, carrying off two bags full of homemade tapes. Stettner had thought Leveque would have kept a backup tape of the one he was using for blackmail, but it turned out he hadn't.

"Most of them were movies he taped off the TV," Thurman said. "Old black-and-white classics, mostly. A few were porn, and some were old TV shows." Stettner screened them himself and wound up throwing just about everything out. Thurman had never seen the tape he helped recover, the one that had cost Arnold Leveque his life.

"I saw it," I said. "It shows the two of them committing murder. Killing a boy."

"I figured that's what it was, or why would they pay that kind of money for it? But how could you have seen it?"

"Leveque had a copy that you missed. It was dubbed onto a commercial cassette."

"He had a whole lot of those," he remembered. "We didn't bother with them, we left them there. That was clever of him." He picked up his glass, put it down untouched. "Not that it did him much good."

Boys were a part of Stettner's life, and one Thurman was never interested in sharing. "I don't like homosexuals," he said flatly. "Don't care for them, never did. Amanda's brother is a homosexual. He never liked me and I never liked him, it was right out there from the jump. Stettner said he was the same way, he thought faggots were weaklings and that AIDS was the planet's way of grinding them under its heel. 'It's not a homosexual act to use these boys,' he would say. 'You take them as you take a woman, that's all. And they're so easy to get, they're all over the place begging to be taken. And no one cares. You can do as you please with them and no one cares.' "

"How did he get them?"

"I don't know. I told you, that was an area of his life I made it my business to stay out of. Sometimes I would see him with a boy. He would take up with one sometimes, the way he did with the one you saw at the fights last week. He would treat him like a son, and then one day you wouldn't see the boy anymore. And I would never ask what happened to the boy."

"But you would know."

"I wouldn't even think about it. It was none of my business, so why should I think about it?"

"But you had to know, Richard."

I hadn't called him by his first name before. Maybe that helped the words get through his armor. Something did, because he winced as if he'd taken a hard right to the heart.

"I guess he killed them," he said.

I didn't say anything.

"I guess he killed a lot of people."

"What about you?"

"I never killed anyone," he said quickly.

"You were an accessory to Leveque's murder. According to the law, you were as guilty as if you'd used the knife yourself."

"I didn't even know he was going to kill him!"

He knew, just as he had known what happened to the boys. I let it pass. "You knew he was going to commit assault and robbery," I said. "That made you a participant in felony, and that's enough to make you fully culpable if the felony results in a death. You'd be guilty of murder if Leveque had died of a heart attack. As far as the law is concerned, you're guilty."

He took a couple of deep breaths. Dully he said, "All right, I know that. You could say the same thing about the girl he went back and killed, if he killed her. I suppose I was guilty of rape. She didn't resist, but I didn't exactly have her consent." He looked at me. "I can't defend what I did. I can't justify it. I'm not going to try to say that he hypnotized me, although it was like that, it really was, the way the two of them set me up and . . . and just got me to do what they wanted."

"How did they do that, Richard?"

"They just—"

"How did they get you to kill your wife?"

"Oh, God," he said, and put his face in his hands.

*   *   *

Maybe they had planned it from the beginning. Maybe it had been part of a secret agenda all along.

"You'd better take a shower," Olga would say. "It's time for you to go home to your little wife." Your little wife, your darling wife, your charming wife—always said with a hint of irony, a touch of mockery. You have spent an hour in the world of the brave, the bold, the reckless, the daring, she was telling him, and now you may return to the black-and-white humdrum world and the Barbie doll who shares it with you.

"A shame she has all the money," Stettner said early on. "You give all your power away when your woman has more money than you do."

At first he'd been afraid that Stettner would want Amanda sexually. He had allowed Thurman to share Olga, and would want a quid pro quo. Thurman hadn't liked the idea. He wanted to keep the two lives separate, and was relieved when the Stettners did not seem to want Amanda included in their relationship. The first meeting of all four had not been a success, and, on the two subsequent occasions when both couples had drinks and dinner together, the conversation was stilted.

It was Stettner who first suggested he increase his insurance coverage. "You have a child coming, you want to protect that child. And you should have the mother covered as well. If anything happened to her you'd have a nurse, you'd have a governess, you'd have expenses for years." And then, when the policies were in force: "You know, Richard, you're a man with a rich wife. If she died you'd be a rich man. There's an interesting distinction, don't you think?"

The idea grew gradually, little by little.

"I don't know how to explain this," he said. "It wasn't real. We would joke about it, we would think up impossibly farfetched ways to do it. 'It's a shame microwave ovens are so small,' he said. 'We could stuff Amanda in with an apple in her mouth and cook her from the inside out.' It's sickening to think of now, but then it was funny because there was no reality to it, it was a harmless joke. And, because we went on joking about it, it began to have a kind of reality.

" 'We'll do it next Thursday,' Bergen would say, and we'd plan some ridiculous black-comedy scenario, and that would be the end of it. And then when Thursday came Olga would say, 'Oh, we forgot, today was the day we were supposed to kill little Amanda.' It was a joke, a running gag.

"When I was with Amanda, when they weren't around, I was a normal happily married man. That sounds impossible, doesn't it? But it was true. I guess I must have had this idea that someday Bergen and Olga would just disappear. I don't know how I expected this to happen, whether they would get caught for some of the things they had done or whether they would just drop me or move out of the country or, I don't know. Maybe I expected them to die. And then the whole dark side of life that I was leading with them would vanish and Amanda and I would live happily ever after.

"One time, though, I was lying in bed and she was asleep next to me and I started having images of different ways of killing her. I didn't want to have those thoughts but I couldn't get them out of my head. Smothering her with a pillow, stabbing her, all sorts of murderous images. I had to go into the other room and have a couple of drinks. I wasn't afraid I would do anything, I was just upset by the thoughts.

"Right around the first of November I mentioned that our downstairs neighbors would be spending the next six months in Florida. 'Good,' Bergen said. 'That's where we'll kill Amanda. It's a natural site for a burglary, with the owners in Florida. And it's convenient, she won't have to travel far, and it's better than doing it in your apartment because you wouldn't want police parading in and out of your place. They make a mess, sometimes they even steal things.'

"I thought it was a joke. 'Oh, you're going to a party? When you come home we'll be waiting in the Jews' apartment downstairs. You'll walk right in on a burglary in progress. I hope I can still remember how to break in. I'm sure it's like swimming, once you learn it you never forget it.'

"The night of the party I didn't know if it was a joke or not. This is hard to explain. I knew but I didn't know. The two sides of my life were so far apart it's as if I didn't really believe something on one side could touch something on the other. It's like I knew they would be waiting there for us but I couldn't really believe it.

"When we left the party I wanted to walk home because I wanted to delay getting there for fear that they'd be there, that it would be real this time. And on the way home she started talking about her brother, how she was worried about his health, and I made a nasty crack. So we had an argument, and I thought, all right, bitch, in an hour you'll be history. And the thought was exciting.

"Walking up the stairs I saw the door to the Gottschalks' apartment was closed and I felt relieved, and then I saw that the doorframe was splintered and there were jimmy marks around the lock so I knew they were there. But I thought if we were quiet we could get past the closed door and upstairs to our own apartment and we'd be safe. Of course we could have turned around and gone back down the stairs, but I didn't even think of that at the time.

"Then we got to the top of the flight of stairs and the door opened and they were waiting for us. Olga had on a leather outfit she wears sometimes and Bergen was wearing a long leather coat. They looked as though they'd stepped out of a comic book. Amanda didn't recognize them at first. She was just staring at them, not knowing what to make of it, and before she could say anything Bergen said, 'You're dead, bitch,' and punched her in the face. He was wearing thin leather driving gloves. He made a fist and hit her full force in the jaw.

"Bergen grabbed her and dragged her inside with his hand clamped over her mouth. Olga got Amanda's hands behind her back and handcuffed her. They taped her mouth and Olga tripped her and kicked her in the face when she fell.

"They stripped her and dragged her into the bedroom and threw her on the bed. Bergen raped her and turned her over and raped her again. Olga hit her in the face with a crowbar and I think that may have knocked her out. I don't think she was conscious for most of it.

"I hope not.

"They told me I had to have sex with her. And this is the worst part. I thought I was going to be sick to my stomach, I thought I was going to puke, but get this, I was excited. I was hard. I didn't want to have sex, *I* didn't want to, but my cock wanted to. God, it makes me sick to think about it. I couldn't finish. I was on top of her and I couldn't finish and I just wanted to come so I could stop but I couldn't.

"Then I was standing over her and Bergen had her panty hose wrapped around her neck and he made me take an end in each hand. He told me I had to do it and I just stood there. Olga was on her knees blowing me and Bergen's gloved hands were holding my hands, and I was holding the ends of the panty hose, I couldn't let go because of his grip. And he pulled his hands apart, and that pulled *my* hands apart, and her eyes were staring up at me, staring, you know. And Olga was doing what she was doing, you know, and Bergen was holding me very tight, and there was the smell of the blood and the leather and the sex.

"And I had an orgasm.

"And Amanda was dead."

16

"THE REST WAS PRETTY MUCH THE WAY WE FIGURED," I TOLD Durkin. "They tied him up and knocked him around a little to make it look good, set the stage so it fit the profile of a bungled burglary. They walked out and went home, and he called it in an hour or so later, whenever it was. He had his story all ready. He'd had days to work it out, all the while he was telling himself it was a joke."

"And now he wants to hire you."

"He did hire me," I said. "Last night, before we parted company."

"What for?"

"He's afraid of the Stettners. Afraid they'll kill him."

"Why would they do that?"

"To cover their asses. His conscience has been bothering him."

"I should fucking hope so."

"Well, according to him, it has. He keeps having the thought that she really loved him and she was the only person who ever did or ever will."

"Only person damn fool enough."

"And he wants to believe that she died without realizing he was a part of her murder. That she was unconscious when he had sex with her, that she was either unconscious or already dead when Stettner made him strangle her."

"He wants the answer to that one, he doesn't need a detective, he needs a medium."

It was midmorning, Thursday. I had gone to Midtown North after breakfast and waited for Joe to show, and we were at his desk now. He had a cigarette going. He must have quit smoking a dozen times that I knew about. He couldn't seem to stay off it.

I said, "He thinks his conscience is showing. And he thinks Stettner doesn't need him anymore."

"How did Stettner need him in the first place, Matt? It sounds to me like he's making Stettner the heavy when he was the one using Stettner instead of the other way around. Way I figure it he got a mil and a half out of the deal, and what did Stettner get? A quick piece of ass with a woman who's half-dead?"

"So far," I said, "Stettner got four hundred thousand dollars."

"I must have missed that part."

"I was just getting to it. After it was all over, after she was buried and the press coverage had died down, Stettner had a talk with him. He said their little joint venture had been a great success, but of course if it was indeed a joint venture it was only fair that the proceeds be shared jointly."

"In other words, come up with half the dough."

"That's the idea. Not the money he inherited from his wife, Stettner was willing to overlook that, but certainly the insurance proceeds. As soon as the insurance company paid up, he wanted half. It was a million with the double indemnity, since murder is accidental death—"

"Which I never understood."

"Neither did I, but I guess it's an accident from the point of view of the victim. Anyway, it came to a million tax-free, and Stettner wanted half of it. The insurance company paid up late last month, which seems pretty quick in a case like this."

"They had a guy over here," he said. "Wanted to know if Thurman was a suspect. Officially he wasn't, which is what I had to tell him. I was convinced he did it, I told you that—"

"Yes."

"—but the only motive we had was the money, and we couldn't establish any need for the money, or anybody else he was mixed up with, or any reason to kill her." He frowned. "What you've been telling me is he really didn't have a reason."

"Not the way he tells it. But the insurance company paid, and Stettner wanted his, and the way they worked it was that Thurman would turn over cash to Stettner in increments of a hundred thousand dollars that would ostensibly be used to purchase foreign currencies. The money would just go in Stettner's pocket, but Thurman would get memos of nonexistent transactions and they'd be structured in such a way that he would ultimately be able to write off most of it as losses for tax purposes. I think that may be my favorite part, Joe. Split the proceeds with your partner in crime and write it off on your taxes."

"It's not bad. He's made four of these payments?"

"At one-week intervals. The final payment's due tonight. He'll be meeting Stettner in Maspeth, he's producing a telecast at a boxing arena out there. He'll turn over a briefcase with a hundred grand in it and that'll be that."

"And then he thinks Stettner'll kill him. Because he'll have the money and he won't need Thurman anymore, and Thurman's just a loose end and is starting to develop a conscience, so why not close the account."

"Right."

"And he wants you to protect him," he said. "Did he happen to say how?"

"We left it open. I'm meeting him this afternoon to figure all that out."

"And then you go out to whatchacallit, Maspeth?"

"Probably."

He stubbed out his cigarette. "Why you?"

"He knows me."

"He knows you? How does he know you?"

"We met in a bar."

"So you said, last night in that shithole your friend Ballou owns. Incidentally, I don't know what the hell you're doing keeping company with a guy like that."

"He's a friend of mine."

"One of these days he's gonna step on his cock and you don't want to be there when it happens. He's a good dancer, he's slippery as a fucking eel, but one of these days the Feds'll put a RICO case together and he's got free room and board in Atlanta."

" 'Mother of mercy, is this the end of RICO?' "

"Huh?"

"Nothing," I said. "It's not important. We met at Grogan's last night because we needed a quiet place to talk. The reason he called me is we ran into each other the night before in another bar, a place in his neighborhood."

"You ran into him because you're on his case. Did he know that?"

"No. He thought I was on Stettner's case."

"Why would you be on Stettner's case?"

I hadn't told him anything about the tape of Happy's murder, or about the killing of Arnold Leveque. All of that seemed extraneous. The case in Joe's open file was the murder of Amanda Thurman, and that was the case I'd been hired for and the one that looked to be breaking.

"It was a way to hook him," I said. "I'd managed to connect him with Stettner, and that turned out to be the shoe in the door. If he can hang it all on Bergen and Olga, maybe he can get off the hook himself."

"You think you can get him to come in, Matt?"

"That's what I'm hoping. That's what I'll be working on when I see him this afternoon."

"I want you wearing a wire when you see him."

"Fine."

" 'Fine.' I wish to God you'd been wearing a wire when you saw him last night. You can get lucky, a guy feels like talking, he spills his guts and feels better. Then he gets up the next morning and wonders what got into him, and for the rest of his life he never gets the urge to open up again. Why the hell didn't you come in and get a wire before you saw him?"

"Come on," I said. "He called out of the blue at ten and wanted to meet me right away. Were you even here last night?"

"There's other people could have fitted you with a wire."

"Sure, and it only would have taken two hours and ten phone calls to clear it, and I had no realistic reason to think he was going to open up like that in the first place."

"Yeah, you're right."

"I think I can get him to come in," I said. "I think that's what he wants to do."

"That'd be nice," he said. "But if not at least he'll talk to you, and you'll be wearing a wire. You're meeting him at four? I wish it was earlier."

"He's got appointments until then."

"And business is business, right? I'll see you here at three." He stood up. "Meantime I got appointments myself."

I walked across town to Elaine's, stopping en route for flowers and a bag of Jaffa oranges. She put the flowers in water and the oranges in a large blue glass bowl and told me she was feeling a lot better. "Weak," she said, "but definitely on the mend. What about you? Are you all right?"

"Why?"

"You look drawn. Were you up again last night?"

"No, but I didn't sleep very well. The case is breaking. It ought to wrap up in a couple more hours."

"How did all that happen? It's Wednesday, isn't it? Or did I get delirious and miss a couple of days?"

"Thurman needed a confidant and I managed to be it. He was feeling pressured, partly by me, I suppose, but mostly by Stettner."

"Who's Stettner?"

"Rubber Man," I said. I gave her an abridged version of our conversation last night at Grogan's. "I was in the right place at the right time," I said. "I was lucky."

"Unlike Amanda Thurman."

"And a whole lot of other people, from the sound of it. But Amanda's the one they'll all go away for. Between Thurman's testimony and whatever physical evidence they can put together, they ought to be able to build a nice solid case."

"Then why so glum, chum? Shouldn't you be strutting around like a bantam rooster? Whatever happened to enjoying the moment of triumph?"

"I guess I'm tired."

"And what else?"

I shrugged. "I don't know," I said. "I spent a couple of hours with Thurman last night. It didn't make me like the little prick but it didn't leave me ready to rejoice in his downfall, either. A week ago he looked to be some kind of cold criminal genius, and now it turns out he's just a dimwit. A couple of manipulative perverts led him around by his cock."

"You feel sorry for him."

"I don't feel sorry for him. I think he's a manipulative bastard himself, he just ran into a better one in Stettner. And I'm not buying everything he told me last night. I don't think he fed me any outright lies, but I think he made himself look better than he had any right to. For one thing, I'll bet anything Amanda wasn't the first person he killed."

"What makes you say that?"

"Because Stettner's not stupid. He knew the cops would grill Thurman up one side and down the other if his wife was murdered under that sort of circumstances. Even if they didn't suspect he was involved, they'd question him repeatedly in order to get a line on the killers and not overlook any possible clue. So Stettner would have tempered him first by getting him accustomed to killing. He was there when Leveque was killed, he was an accessory, and I think there must have been times when he and one or both of the Stettners did a number on a woman and she wound up dead. That's what I would have done if I were Stettner."

"I'm glad you're not."

"And I'm not sure how much I buy of his attack of conscience," I said. "I think he's scared, I think that part's true enough. Once Stettner gets the last hundred grand from him he's got no reason to keep him alive. Unless he wants to try for the rest of the money, which is always a possibility. Maybe that's Thurman's real fear. He doesn't want to give up the rest of the money."

"He can't keep it anyway, can he? If he confesses?"

"He doesn't intend to confess."

"But I thought you said you were going to bring him in."

"I'm going to try. I'm hoping I can manipulate him the way Stettner did."

"You want me to come along and blow him?"

"I don't think that'll be necessary."

"Good."

"See," I said, "I think he's trying to manipulate me. Maybe he wants me to kill Stettner for him. That seems far-fetched, but it's not out of the question. He may want my help in arranging some sort of Mexican standoff, whereby he leaves evidence and testimony that will nail Stettner in the event of his own death. If he sets that up right and Stettner knows it, then he's home free."

"But any evidence he gives you—"

"Goes straight to Joe Durkin. Damn it."

"What's the matter?"

"It's eleven-thirty and I'm not seeing him until four. I should have kept pressing him last night instead of giving him time to think it over. The problem was that he was exhausted and so was I. I thought we'd do it this morning but he went into this song and dance about his business appointments. I wanted to tell him he could afford to cancel, that he was out of business, but I couldn't do that. You know, he called me a few times yesterday afternoon and wouldn't talk."

"You told me."

"If I could have got together with him then it might be wrapped up by now. Of course I wouldn't have talked to Danny Boy and I wouldn't have gone in knowing about Stettner." I sighed. "I guess it'll all work out."

"It always does, baby. Why don't you lie down for an hour or two. Take the bed, or I'll make up the couch for you."

"I don't think so."

"It won't hurt you. And I'll wake you in plenty of time to go see Joe and get wired."

"I'm already wired. In a manner of speaking."

"That's my point."

I caught a noon meeting and walked back to my hotel, stopping for a stand-up lunch at a pizza parlor. I had pepperoni on it to make sure I covered the four basic food groups.

Maybe the meeting relaxed me, or maybe it was the result of good nutrition, but when I got back to my room I felt tired enough to lie down for an hour. I set my alarm for two-thirty and left a call at the desk for that time as a backup. I kicked my shoes off and stretched out in my clothes, and I must have been out before my eyes were completely shut.

The next thing I knew the phone was ringing. I sat up and looked at my clock and it was only two, and I picked up the phone prepared to snarl at the desk clerk. TJ said, "Man, why is it you ain't never home? How I gone tell you what I find if I can't even find where you at?"

"What did you find out?"

"The boy's name. The young one. I met this kid who knows him, says his name be Bobby."

"Did you learn his last name?"

"There ain't a lot of last names on the Deuce, Matt. Ain't too many first names, either. Mostly it's street names, you know? Cool Fool and Hats and Dagwood. Bobby, he too new on the block to have hisself a street name. Kid I talked to say he just got here around Christmastime."

He hadn't lasted long. I wanted to tell TJ that it didn't matter, that the man who'd been with Bobby was about to go away for something else, something that would keep him away from kids for a long time.

"Don't know where he came from," TJ was saying. "Got off a bus one day is all. Musta come from some place where they had men who liked young boys, 'cause that what he was lookin' for from the jump. 'Fore he knew it one of the pimps scooped him up an' started sellin' his white ass."

"What pimp?"

"You want for me to find out? I most likely could, but the meter already run to the twenty-dollar mark."

Was there any point? The easy case against Stettner was the murder of Amanda Thurman. There was a body and a witness and, in all likelihood, some kind of physical evidence, all of them lacking in the disappearance and probably murder of the boy called Bobby. Why bother to chase some pimp?

"See what you can find out," I heard myself say. "I'll cover the meter."

At three I presented myself at Midtown North and took off my jacket and shirt. A police officer named Westerberg wired me for sound. "You've worn one of these before," Durkin said. "With that landlady, one the papers called the Angel of Death."

"That's right."

"So you know how it works. You shouldn't have any trouble with Thurman. If he wants you to go to bed with him just make sure you keep your shirt on."

"He won't want me to. He doesn't like homosexuals."

"Right, nothing queer about Richard. You want a vest? I think you ought to wear one."

"On top of the wire?"

"It's Kevlar, it shouldn't interfere with the pickup. The only thing it's supposed to stop is a bullet."

"There won't be any bullets, Joe. Nobody's used a gun in this so far. The vest won't stop a blade."

"Sometimes it will."

"Or a pair of panty hose around the neck."

"I guess," he said. "I just don't like the idea of sending you in without backup."

"You're not sending me in. I'm not under your command. I'm a private citizen wearing a wire out of a sense of civic responsibility. I'm cooperating with you, but you're not responsible for my safety."

"I'll remember to tell them that at the hearing after you wind up in a body bag."

"That's not going to happen," I said.

"Say Thurman woke up this morning and realized he talked too much, and now you're the loose end he has to get rid of."

I shook my head. "I'm his ace in the hole," I said. "I'm his backup, I'm the man who can make sure Stettner won't take a chance on killing him. Hell, he hired me, Joe. He's not going to kill me."

"He hired you?"

"Last night. He gave me a retainer, insisted I take it."

"What did he give you?"

"A hundred dollars. A nice crisp hundred-dollar bill."

"Hey, every little bit helps."

"I didn't keep it."

"What do you mean, you didn't keep it? You gave it back to him, how's he gonna trust you?"

"I didn't give it back to him. I got rid of it."

"Why? Money's money. It doesn't know where it came from."

"Maybe not."

"Money knows no owner. Basic principle of law. How'd you get rid of it?"

"Walking home," I said. "We walked as far as Ninth Avenue and Fifty-second Street and then he went one way and I went the other. The first guy who staggered out of a doorway looking for a handout, I wadded up Thurman's money and stuck it in his cup. They all have cups now, Styrofoam coffee cups that they hold out at you."

"That's so people won't have to touch them. You gave some bum on the street a hundred-dollar bill? How's he gonna spend it? Who's gonna change it for him?"

"Well," I said, "that's not my problem, is it?"

17

I WALKED OVER TO WHERE RICHARD THURMAN LIVED AND stood in a doorway across from his building. I got there ten minutes early for our four o'clock appointment and I spent the time watching the sidewalk traffic. I couldn't tell whether or not there was a light on in his apartment. His building was on the uptown side of the block and the windows on the upper floors caught the sunlight and reflected it back at me.

I waited until four, and then I waited another two minutes or so before I crossed the street and entered the vestibule next door to Radicchio's entrance. I pressed the button for Thurman and waited to be buzzed in. Nothing happened. I rang again and waited and again nothing happened. I went next door and checked the restaurant bar. He wasn't there. I went back to my station across the street, and after ten more minutes I walked to the corner and found a working pay phone. I called his apartment and the machine answered, and at the tone I said, "Richard, are you there? Pick up the phone if you are." He didn't pick up.

I called my hotel to see if there had been any calls. There hadn't. I got Five Borough's number from Information and got a secretary who would tell me only that he was not in the office. She didn't know where he was or when he was expected back.

I went back to Thurman's building and rang the bell of the travel agent on the second floor. The buzzer sounded immediately and I walked up a flight, waiting for someone to come out on the landing and challenge me. No one did. I went on up the stairs. The Gottschalks' door had been secured since the break-in, with the doorframe reinforced and the locks replaced. I climbed another flight to the fifth floor and listened at Thurman's door. I couldn't hear anything. I rang the bell and heard it sound within the apartment. I knocked on the door anyway. There was no response.

I tried the door and it didn't budge. There were three locks, although there was no way to tell how many of them were engaged. Two had pickproof Medeco cylinders, and all were secured by escutcheon plates. An angle iron installed at the juncture of door and frame rendered the door secure against jimmying.

I stopped at the two second-floor offices, the travel agent and the ticket broker, and asked if they'd seen Richard Thurman that day, if by any chance he'd left any sort of message with them. They hadn't and he hadn't. I asked the same question in Radicchio's and got the same answer. I went back to my post across the street, and at five o'clock I called the Northwestern again and learned that I hadn't had any calls, from Thurman or from anyone else. I hung up and spent another quarter to call Durkin.

"He never showed," I said.

"Shit. What is he, an hour late?"

"He hasn't tried to call me, either."

"The cocksucker's probably on his way to Brazil."

"No, that doesn't figure," I said. "He's probably stuck in traffic or hung up with some client or sports promoter or sponsor."

"Or giving Mrs. Stettner a farewell hump."

"An hour's nothing. Remember, he hired me. I'm working for him, so I suppose he can stand me up or run late without worrying that I'm going to throw a fit. I know where he's going to be this evening. I was supposed to go out to Maspeth with him for the boxing telecast. I'll give him another hour or so and if he still doesn't show I'll look for him at the arena."

"You'll keep on wearing the wire."

"Sure. It won't start recording until I turn it on and I haven't done that yet."

He thought it over. "I guess that's okay," he said.

"Except there's one thing."

"What's that?"

"I was wondering if you could send somebody over to open his apartment."

"Now?"

"Why not? I don't think he's going to show in the next hour. If he does I'll cut him off downstairs, drag him someplace for a drink."

"What do you expect to find?"

"I don't know."

After a short silence he said, "No, I couldn't get a court order. What am I gonna tell a judge? He had an appointment with a guy and he didn't show so I wanta kick his door in? Besides, time it took to get a court order you'd be out in Maspeth."

"Suppose you forget to get a court order."

"No way. Worst thing in the world. Say we find something, it's fruit of the poisoned tree. Could be a signed confession plus an eight-by-ten glossy of him strangling her and we couldn't do shit with it. It's not admissible because we got it through an unauthorized search and seizure." He sighed. "Now if you were to go in on your own and I didn't know about it—"

"I haven't got the skills. He's got pickproof cylinders. I could spend a week and not get in the door."

"Then forget it. It's his confession's gonna hang the bunch of them, not any evidence sitting in his apartment."

I said what I'd been thinking about. "Suppose he's in there."

"Dead, you mean. Well, dead's dead, you know? If he's

dead now he'll be just as dead tomorrow, and if you still haven't heard from him by then I'll have enough grounds to hunt up a judge and get in legally. Matt, if he's already dead he can't say anything to you that he can't say tomorrow." When I was silent he said, "Tell me straight out. You were standing in front of his door. Did you get the sense that he was dead on the other side of it?"

"Come on," I said. "I'm not a psychic."

"No, but you got cop instincts. How would you call it? Was he in there?"

"No," I said. "No, the place felt empty to me."

By six he still hadn't shown and I was tired of lurking in doorways. I called my hotel again, and while I was at it I wasted two more quarters on calls to Paris Green and Grogan's. Not surprisingly, he wasn't at either of those places.

Three cabdrivers in a row made it clear that they weren't going to Maspeth. I went into the subway station at Fiftieth and Eighth and studied the map. The M would get me to Maspeth, but it seemed enormously complicated to get to it and I wouldn't know which way to walk when I got off it. Instead I took the E train two stops into Queens, getting off at Queens Plaza where I figured there would be taxis waiting. I got a driver who not only knew how to get to Maspeth but was able to find the arena. He pulled up in front of the entrance and I could see the FBCS vans parked where I'd seen them a week ago.

The sight was reassuring. I paid my cabby and walked over to the vans but didn't see Thurman. I bought a ticket and went through the turnstile and found a seat in the same spot where Mick and I had sat a week earlier. The first prelims were under way and a couple of listless middleweights were swinging at each other in the middle of the ring. I scanned the ringside seats of the center section, where I'd seen Bergen Stettner. I didn't see him now, or the boy either.

The four-rounder went to a decision. While the official

was collecting the scorecards from the judges I went over to ringside and got the cameraman's attention. I asked him where Richard Thurman was.

"I don't know where the hell he is," he said. "He supposed to be here tonight? Maybe he's in the truck."

I went outside and nobody knew where Thurman was. One man watching the telecast on a monitor said he heard the producer was going to show up late, and another man said he had the impression Thurman wasn't coming in at all. Nobody seemed greatly concerned over his absence.

I showed my stub and went through the turnstile again and returned to my seat. The next bout matched two local featherweights, a pair of scrappy young Hispanics. One was from nearby Woodside, and he got a big hand. They both threw a lot of punches but neither of them seemed capable of doing much damage, and the fight went six rounds to a decision. It went to the kid from Brooklyn, which seemed fair to me, but the crowd didn't like it.

There were two eight-rounders scheduled before the ten-round main event. The first one didn't go any distance at all; the fighters were heavyweights, both carrying far too much flab, both given to telegraphing their punches. About a minute into the first round one of them missed with a roundhouse right, spun around full circle, and caught a left hook right on the button. He went down like a felled ox and they had to throw water on him to revive him. The crowd loved it.

The fighters on the top of the undercard were in the ring waiting for the introduction when I glanced up the aisle toward the entrance. And there was Bergen Stettner.

He wasn't wearing the Gestapo coat a few people had described, or the blazer I'd seen him in last week. His jacket was suede, light brown in color, and beneath it he wore a dark brown shirt and a paisley ascot.

He didn't have the boy with him.

I watched as he chatted with another man a few yards

from the turnstile. They finished the introductions, rang the opening bell. I went on watching Stettner. After another minute or two he clapped the other man on the shoulder and left the arena.

I walked out after him, but when I got outside I didn't see him anywhere. I drifted over to where the FBCS vans were parked and looked around for Richard Thurman, but he wasn't there to be seen and I didn't really think he was coming. I stood in the shadows and saw Bergen Stettner come around the side of the building and approach the vans. He talked with someone inside the van for a minute, then returned in the direction he'd come from.

I waited a few minutes before approaching the van. I stuck my head in the back and said, "Where the hell is Stettner? I can't find him anywhere."

"He was just here," the man said without turning around. "You just missed him, he was here not five minutes ago."

"Shit," I said. "Say, did he happen to say where Thurman went to?"

Now he turned. "Oh, right," he said. "You were looking for him earlier. No, Stettner wanted to know where he was, too. Looks like Thurman's gonna catch hell."

"You don't know the half of it," I said.

I showed my stub and went through the turnstile again. They were in the fourth round now. I didn't know anything about the fighters, I'd missed the introductions, and I didn't bother to reclaim my seat. I went over to the refreshment stand and got a Coke in a paper cup and stood in back drinking it. I looked around for Stettner but couldn't find him. I turned toward the entrance again and saw a woman, and for a second or two I thought she was Chelsea, the placard girl. I looked again and realized I was looking at Olga Stettner.

She had her long hair pulled back off her face and done up in a sort of bun on the back of her head. I think it's called a chignon. The style accented her prominent cheekbones and gave her a severe look, but she probably would have looked fairly stern anyway. She was wearing a short jacket of some dark fur and a pair of suede boots that reached to the tops of her calves. I watched as she scanned the room. I didn't know who she was looking for, her husband or Thurman. She wasn't looking for me; her eyes passed right over me with no flicker of recognition.

I wonder how I'd have reacted to her if I hadn't known who she was. She was an attractive woman, certainly, but there was something about her, some magnetism, that may have owed a lot to what I already knew about her. And I knew too goddamned much about her. What I knew made it impossible to look at her, and impossible not to.

By the end of the fight they were both standing there, Bergen and Olga, looking out over the big room as if they owned it. The ring announcer gave the decision and each fighter in turn, along with a three- or four-man retinue, made his way from the ring to the stairwell off to the left of the entrance doors. After they'd dropped from sight two other fighters emerged via the same set of basement stairs, fresh where the outgoing fighters had been spent, making their way in turn down the main aisle to the ring. They were middleweights and they had both had a good number of fights in the area. I knew them from the Garden. They were both black, both had won almost all of their bouts, and the shorter and darker of the two had knockout power in either hand. The other kid wasn't as strong a puncher but he was very quick and had a reach advantage. It figured to be a very good matchup.

Like the previous week, they introduced a handful of boxing figures, including both scheduled participants in next week's main bout. A politician, the deputy borough president of Queens, got introduced and received a chorus of boos, which in turn sparked some laughter. Then they cleared the ring and introduced the fighters, and I glanced over at the Stettners and saw them making their way toward the stairs.

I gave them a minute's head start. Then they rang the

bell for the start of the fight and I walked down the stairs to the basement.

At the foot of the stairs was a broad hallway with walls on either side of unfinished concrete block. The first door I came to was open, and inside I could see the winner of the previous bout. He had a pint bottle of Smirnoff in his hand and he was pouring drinks for his friends and taking quick nips from the bottle for himself.

I walked a little further and listened at a closed door, tried the knob. It was locked. The next door was open but the light was out and the room empty. It had the same interior walls as the hallway, the same floor of black and white tiles. I walked on, and a male voice called, "Hey!"

I turned around. It was Stettner, with his wife a few steps behind him. He was fifteen or twenty yards behind me and he walked slowly toward me, a slight smile on his lips. "Can I help you?" he asked. "Are you looking for something?"

"Yeah," I said. "The men's room. Where the hell is it?"

"Upstairs."

"Then why did that clown send me down here?"

"I don't know," he said, "but this is a private area down here. Go upstairs, the men's room is right next door to the refreshment stand."

"Oh, sure," I said. "I know where that is."

I moved past him and mounted the stairs. I could feel his eyes on my back all the way to the top.

I went back to my seat and tried to watch the fight. They were mixing it up and the crowd loved it but after two rounds I realized I wasn't paying any attention. I got up and left.

Outside, the air was colder and a wind had blown up. I walked a block and tried to get my bearings. I didn't know the neighborhood and there was no one to ask. I wanted a taxi or a telephone and had no idea where to find either.

I wound up flagging down a gypsy cab on Grand Avenue. He didn't have a meter or a city medallion and wasn't supposed to pick up fares on the street, but once you get outside of Manhattan nobody pays too much attention to that rule. He wanted a flat twenty dollars to take me anywhere in Manhattan. We settled on fifteen and I gave him Thurman's address, then changed my mind at the thought of spending another hour in a doorway. I told him to take me to my hotel.

The cab was a wreck, with exhaust fumes coming up through the floorboards. I cranked down both rear windows as far as they would go. The driver had the radio tuned to a broadcast of polka music, with a disc jockey who chattered away gaily in what I took to be Polish. We got onto Metropolitan Avenue and went over the Williamsburg Bridge to the Lower East Side, which struck me as the long way around, but I kept my mouth shut. There was no meter ticking away so it wasn't costing me extra, and for all I knew his way was shorter.

The only message waiting for me was from Joe Durkin. He'd left his home phone number. I went upstairs and tried Thurman first and hung up when the machine answered. I called Joe and his wife answered and called him to the phone, and when he came on the line I said, "He didn't show in Maspeth but Stettner did. Both Stettners. They were looking for him the same as I was, so I guess I wasn't the only person who got stood up tonight. Nobody on the TV crew had a clue where he went to. I think he flew the coop."

"He tried. His wings fell off."

"Huh?"

"There's a restaurant downstairs. I forget the name, it means radish in Italian."

"Radicchio's not radish. It's a kind of lettuce."

"Well, whatever it is. Six-thirty or so, you must of just got on your way to Maspeth, guy goes out back with a load of kitchen garbage. Way in the back behind two of the cans there's a body. Guess who."

"Oh, no."

"I'm afraid so. No question about the ID. He went out a fifth-floor window so he's not as pretty as he used to be, but there's enough of his face left so you know right away who you're looking at. Are you sure it doesn't mean radish? It was Antonelli told me. You'd think he'd know, wouldn't you?"

18

THE PAPERS LOVED IT. RICHARD THURMAN HAD FALLEN TO HIS death just a matter of yards from where his wife had been brutally raped and murdered less than three months previously. One potential Pulitzer Prize-winner theorized that his last sight in this life might have been a glimpse of the Gottschalk apartment as he sailed past its window on the way down. That seemed unlikely, since you generally draw the blinds when you leave town for six months and a day, but I didn't have strong enough feelings on the subject to write a letter to the editor.

Nobody was questioning the suicide, although opinion seemed to be divided on the motive. Either he was despondent over the loss of his wife and unborn child or he was guilt-ridden over having caused their deaths. An editorial page columnist in the *News* saw the case as epitomizing the failure of the greed of the eighties. "You used to hear a lot of talk about Having It All," he wrote. "Well, three months ago Richard Thurman had it all—money in the bank, a great apartment, a beautiful wife, a glamorous job in the booming cable TV industry, and a baby on the way. In no time at all it turned to ashes, and the job and the money weren't enough to fill the void in Richard Thurman's heart. You may think he was a villain, that he engineered the unholy scenario enacted in November at that house on West Fifty-second Street. Or you may see him as a victim. Either way, he turned out to be a man who had had it all—and who had nothing left to cling to when he lost it."

"Your instincts were on target," Durkin told me. "You were afraid something happened to him and you wanted to get into the apartment. Same time, you didn't really think he was in there. Well, he wasn't. The ME's guess on time of death is seven to nine A.M., which would figure, because from ten in the morning you had kitchen staff in the joint downstairs and they probably would have heard the impact when he landed. Why nobody noticed the body during lunch hour is hard to figure, except that it was way over at one end of the court-yard and their service door was at the other end, and nobody got close enough to notice anything. You got your arms full of leftover eggplant, I guess you just want to dump it and get back inside, especially on a cold day."

It was Friday morning now and we were in Thurman's apartment. The lab crew had been all through the place the previous evening, while I was chasing shadows in Maspeth. I walked around the place, moving from room to room, not knowing what I was looking for. Maybe not looking for any-thing at all.

"Nice place," Joe said. "Modern furniture, looks stylish but a person could live with it. Everything overstuffed, built for comfort. You usually hear them say that about a woman, don't you? 'Built for comfort, not for speed.' Where does speed come into it, do you happen to know?"

"I think they once said it about horses."

"Yeah? Makes sense. Assuming you get a more comfort-able ride on a fat horse. I'll have to ask one of the guys in TPF. When I was a kid, first wanted to be a cop, that's what I wanted to do, you know. I'd see the cops on horseback and that's what I wanted to be. Of course I got over it by the time I got to the Academy. Still, you know, it's not a bad life."

"If you like horses."

"Well, sure. If you didn't like 'em in the first place—"

"Thurman didn't kill himself," I said.

"Hard to be sure of that. Guy spills his guts, comes home, wakes up early, realizes what he's done. Sees he's got no way out, which he didn't, because you were gonna bag him for doing his wife. Maybe his conscience starts working for real. Maybe he just happens to realize he's looking at some real time upstate, and he knows what it's gonna be like in the joint, a pretty boy like him. Out the window and your troubles are over."

"He wasn't the type. And he wasn't afraid of the law, he was afraid of Stettner."

"Only his prints on the window, Matt."

"Stettner wore gloves when he did Amanda. He could put them on again to throw Richard out the window. Thurman lived here, his prints would already be there. Or Stettner gets him to open the window. 'Richard, it's roasting in here, could we have a little air?' "

"He left a note."

"Typewritten, you said."

"Yeah, I know, but some bona fide suicides type their notes. It was pretty much your generic suicide note. 'God forgive me, I can't take it anymore.' Didn't say he did it, didn't say he didn't."

"That's because Stettner wouldn't have known how much we already knew."

"Or because Thurman wasn't taking any chances. Suppose he falls four stories and lives? He's in the hospital with twenty bones broken, last thing he wants is to face murder charges on the basis of his fucking suicide note." He put out a cigarette in a souvenir ashtray. "It so happens I agree with you," he said. "I think the odds are he had help going out the window. That's one reason I had the lab boys do a real thorough job last night and it's why we're looking for a witness who saw anybody going in or out of here yesterday morning. It'd be nice to turn one up, and it'd be nice if you could put Stettner at the scene, but I can tell you now it ain't gonna happen. And even if it did there's no case against him. So he was here, so what? Thurman was alive when he left. He was despondent, he seemed upset, but who ever thought the poor man would take his own life? Horseshit on the half shell, but let's see you go and prove it."

I didn't say anything.

"Besides," he said, "is it so bad this way? We know Thurman killed his wife and we know he didn't get away with it. True, he had help, and maybe it was Stettner—"

"Of course it was Stettner."

"What of course? All we got for that is Thurman's word, which he said to you in a private unrecorded conversation a few hours before he fell to his death. Maybe he was jerking you around, did you stop to think of that?"

"I know he was jerking me around, Joe. He was trying to make himself look as good as possible and trying to make Stettner look like a combination of Svengali and Jack the Ripper. So what?"

"So maybe it wasn't Stettner. Maybe Thurman had some other accomplices, maybe he had some business reason to do a number on Stettner. Look, I'm not saying that's what happened. I know its farfetched. The whole fucking case is farfetched. What I'm saying is that Thurman set up his wife's killing and he's dead now, and if every murder case I ever had worked out this well I wouldn't sit around eating my heart out, you know what I mean? If Stettner did it and he skates, well, I live with worse than that every day of my life. If he was as bad as Thurman made him out to be he would have got his dick in the wringer somewhere along the line, and it never once happened. Man's never been arrested, hasn't got a sheet on him anywhere. Far as I can tell he never even got a speeding ticket."

"You checked around."

"Of course I checked around, for Christ's sake. What do you expect me to do? If he's a bad guy I'd love to put him away. But he doesn't look so bad, not on the record."

"He's another Albert Schweitzer."

"No," he said, "he's probably a real prick, I'll grant you that. But that's not a crime."

I called Lyman Warriner in Cambridge. I didn't have to break the news to him. Some sharp-witted reporter had done that for me, calling Amanda's brother for his reaction. "Of course I declined to comment," he said. "I didn't even know if it was true. He killed himself?"

"That's what it looks like."

"I see. That's not quite the same thing as yes, is it?"

"There's a possibility that he was murdered by an accomplice. The police are pursuing that possibility, but they don't expect to get anywhere. At the present time there's no evidence that contradicts a verdict of suicide."

"But you don't believe that's what happened."

"I don't, but what I believe's not terribly important. I spent a couple of hours with Thurman last night and I got what you were hoping I'd get. He admitted murdering your sister."

"He actually admitted it."

"Yes, he did. He tried to make his accomplice the heavy, but he admitted his own role in what happened." I decided to stretch a point. "He said she was unconscious for virtually all of it, Lyman. She got a blow on the head early on and never knew what happened to her."

"I'd like to believe that."

"I was scheduled to meet with him yesterday afternoon," I went on. "I was hoping to talk him into a full confession, but failing that I was prepared to record our conversation and turn it over to the police. But before I could do that—"

"He killed himself. Well, I'll say one thing. I'm certainly glad I hired you."

"Oh?"

"Wouldn't you say your investigation precipitated his actions?"

I thought about it. "I guess you could say that," I said.

"And I'm just as glad it ended as it did. It's quicker and cleaner than suffering through a court trial, and a lot of the time they walk away, don't they? Even when everybody knows they're guilty."

"It happens."

"And even when it doesn't the sentences are never long enough, or they behave themselves, they're model prisoners and after four or five years they're out on parole. No, I'm more than satisfied, Matthew. Do I owe you any money?"

"You probably have a refund coming."

"Don't be ridiculous. Don't you dare send me anything. I wouldn't accept it if you did."

Speaking of money, I told him he might be able to institute proceedings to recover his sister's estate and the insurance payment. "You're not legally entitled to profit from the commission of a crime," I explained. "If Thurman murdered your sister, he can't inherit and he can't collect the insurance money. I'm not familiar with the terms of your sister's will, but I assume everything comes to you in the event that he's out of the picture."

"I believe it does."

"He hasn't been legally implicated in her death," I said, "and there won't be charges brought against him now because he's dead. But I think you can institute civil proceedings, and the rules are different from criminal court. For instance, I might be able to testify to the substance of my conversation with him the night before he died. That's hearsay, but it's not necessarily inadmissible. You would want to talk to your attorney. In a case like this I don't think you have to prove guilt to the same degree as in a criminal trial, beyond a reasonable doubt. I think there's a different standard that applies. As I said, you'll want to talk to your lawyer."

He was silent for a moment. Then he said, "I don't think I will. Where would the money go if I don't? I doubt that he's redrawn his will since Amanda's death. He would have left everything to her, and to his own relatives in the event she predecease him." He coughed, got control of himself. "I don't want to fight with his sisters and his cousins and his aunts. I don't care if they get the money. What difference does it make?"

"I don't know."

"I have more money than I'll ever have time to spend. Time is worth more to me than money, and I don't want to spend it in courtrooms and lawyers' offices. You can understand that, can't you?"

"Of course I can."

"It may seem cavalier of me, but—"

"No," I said. "I don't think so."

At five-thirty that afternoon I went to a meeting in a Franciscan church around the corner from Penn Station. The crowd was an interesting mix of commuters in suits and low-bottom drunks in the early stages of recovery. Neither element seemed at all uncomfortable with the other.

During the discussion I raised my hand and said, "I've felt like drinking all day today. I'm in a situation that I can't do anything about and it feels as though I ought to be able to. I already did everything I could and everybody else is perfectly happy with the results, but I'm an alcoholic and I want everything to be perfect and it never is."

I went back to the hotel and there were two messages, both that TJ had called. I didn't have a number for him. I walked over to Armstrong's and had a bowl of the black bean chili, then caught the eight-thirty step meeting at St. Paul's. We were on the Second Step, the one about coming to believe in the capacity of a power greater than ourselves to restore us to sanity. When it was my turn to say something I said, "My name is Matt and I'm an alcoholic, and all I know about my Higher Power is he works in mysterious ways his wonders to perform." I was sitting next to Jim Faber, and he whispered to me that if the detective business went to hell I could always get a job writing fortune cookies.

Another member, a woman named Jane, said, "If a normal person gets up in the morning and his car's got a flat tire, he calls Triple A. An alcoholic calls Suicide Prevention League."

Jim nudged me significantly in the ribs.

"It can't possibly apply to me," I told him. "I haven't even got a car."

When I got back to the hotel there was another message from TJ and still no way to get in touch with him. I showered and went to bed, and I was starting to doze off when the phone rang.

"You hard to reach," he said.

"You're the one who's hard to reach. You left all these messages."

"That's 'cause last time you said I didn't leave no message."

"This time you did, but I didn't have any way to get in touch with you."

"You mean like a number to call."

"Something like that."

"Well, I ain't got no phone."

"I didn't figure you did."

"Yeah," he said. "Well, we work it out one of these days. Thing is, I found out what I supposed to find out."

"The pimp."

"Yeah, I learned a whole bunch of shit."

"Let's hear it."

"On the phone, Joan? I mean I will if that be what you want, but—"

"No."

"Because it don't seem too cool."

"No, probably not." I sat up. "There's a coffee shop called the Flame, corner of Fifty-eighth and Ninth, it would be the southwest corner—"

"It be anywhere on that corner, I gone find it."

"Yeah, I guess you will," I said. "Half an hour."

He met me outside the place and we went in and got a booth. He sniffed the air theatrically and announced that something smelled good, and I laughed and handed him the menu and told him to have whatever he wanted. He ordered a cheese-burger with bacon and an order of fries and a double-rich chocolate shake. I had a cup of coffee and a toasted English.

"Found this chick," he said, "livin' way over in Alphabet City. Say she used to be with this pimp name of Juke. Prob'ly his pimpin' name. Man, she was scared shit! She cut out on Juke last summer, like she 'scaped from where he had her livin', an' she still lookin' over her shoulder for him to catch up with her. Told her once she ever pulled any shit on him he be cuttin' her nose off, and whole time I'm there with her she be touchin' her nose, like she want to make sure it still there."

"If she left him last summer she wouldn't have known Bobby."

"Yeah, right," he said. "But what it is, this kid I found who knew Bobby, all he knew about the pimp was it was the dude used to pimp—" He caught himself and said, "I told her I wouldn't say her name. I guess it be all right to tell you, but—"

"No, I don't have to know her name. They both had the same pimp but not at the same time, so if you found out who her pimp was, then you knew who was pimping Bobby."

"Yeah, right."

"And it was somebody named Juke."

"Yeah. She don't know his last name. Box, most likely." He laughed. "Don't know where he lived, either. Had her livin' up in Washington Heights, but she said how he got a few different apartments, got kids stashed here an' there." He picked up a French fry, dipped it in ketchup. "He always lookin' for new kids, Juke is."

"Business is that good, huh?"

"What she say, he always lookin' for new kids 'cause the old ones don't last long." He cocked his head, trying to look on top of what he was telling me, unaffected by it. He didn't quite bring it off. "He tell her, tell everybody, there two ways they can go on a date. Date can be a round trip or a one-way rental. You know what that means?"

"Tell me."

"Round trip is you come back. One-way is you don't. Like if the john buys you one-way, he don't have to return you. He can, like, do what he want." He looked down at his plate. "He can kill you, that be what he want, an' everything be cool with Juke. She say he tell her, 'You be good or I send you out on a one-way ticket.' An' she say the thing is you don't never know you goin' out one-way. He say, 'Oh, this john, he a easy trick, he prob'ly buy you some nice clothes, treat you fine.' Then she out the door an' he say to the other kids, 'Now you ain't never gone see that bitch again, 'cause I done sent her out on a one-way ticket.' An' they cry some, you know, if she be a good friend of theirs, but they never see her again."

When he had finished his meal I gave him three twenties and told him I hoped that would cover the meter. He said, "Yeah, that be cool. 'Cause I know you ain't rich, man."

Outside I said, "Don't take it any further, TJ. Don't try to find out anything more about Juke."

"I could just ask a few dudes, see what they say."

"No, don't."

"Wouldn't cost you nothing."

"That's not what I'm worried about. I wouldn't want Juke to know somebody was looking for him. He might turn around and start looking for you."

He rolled his eyes. "Don't want that," he said. "Girl say he a mean motherfucker. Say he be big, too, but everybody be lookin' big to that girl."

"How old is she?"

"She twelve," he said. "But she small for her age."

19

I STAYED CLOSE TO HOME ON SATURDAY, LEAVING DURING THE day only to eat a sandwich and drink a cup of coffee and catch a noon meeting across the street from Phil Fielding's video store. At ten to eight I met Elaine in front of the Carnegie Recital Hall on Fifty-seventh. She had tickets from a series of chamber music concerts and felt well enough to use them. The group that night was a string quartet. The cellist was a black woman with a shaved head. The other three were Chinese-American males, all of them dressed and groomed like management trainees.

At intermission we made plans to go to Paris Green afterward, with maybe a quick stop at Grogan's, but by the time the second half ended we were less energetic. We went back to her apartment and ordered in Chinese food. I stayed over, and in the morning we went out for brunch.

Sunday I had dinner with Jim and went to the eight-thirty meeting at Roosevelt.

Monday morning I walked over to Midtown North. I had called ahead, so Durkin was expecting me. I had my notebook with me, as I almost always do. I had the videocassette of *The Dirty Dozen*, too. I had taken it with me when I left Elaine's the day before.

He said, "Sit down. You want some coffee?"

"I just had some."

"I wish I could say the same. What's on your mind?"

"Bergen Stettner."

238 | LAWRENCE BLOCK

"Yeah, well, I can't say I'm surprised. You're like a dog with a bone. What have you got?"

I handed him the cassette.

"Great picture," he said. "So?"

"This version is a little different from the way you may remember it. The highlight comes when Bergen and Olga Stettner commit murder on-camera."

"What are you talking about?"

"Someone dubbed another tape onto this cassette. After fifteen minutes of Lee Marvin we cut to amateur home video. Bergen and Olga and a friend, but by the time the movie is over the friend is dead."

He picked up the cassette, weighed it in his hand. "You're saying you've got a snuff film here."

"A snuff tape, anyway."

"And it's the Stettners? How in hell—"

"It's a long story."

"I got time."

"It's complicated, too."

"Well, it's good you caught me early in the day," he said. "While my mind's still fresh."

I must have talked for an hour. I told it from the beginning, with Will Haberman's panicky request that I scan the tape, and I went through the whole thing and didn't leave out anything important. Durkin had a spiral notebook on his desk, and early on he flipped it open to a clean page and began jotting things down. He would interrupt me from time to time to clarify a point, but for the most part he just let me tell it my way.

When I was done he said, "It's funny how it all fits together. If your friend doesn't happen to be the one who rents the tape, and if he doesn't happen to run to you with it, then there's never anything ties Thurman and Stettner together."

"And I probably don't have a wedge into Thurman," I agreed, "and he doesn't pick me to spill his guts to. The night

I met him in Paris Green I was just fishing, I didn't really seem to be getting anywhere with him. I thought he might know Stettner because of the connection through Five Borough Cable, and because I'd seen them both at the New Maspeth Arena. I showed him the sketch just to shove him off-balance a little, and that was what got things going."

"And sent him out a window."

"But it was a coincidence that was trying to happen," I said. "I was almost involved in the whole thing before Haberman rented the tape. A friend of mine mentioned my name when Leveque was looking for a private detective. If he'd called me then he might never have been killed."

"Or you might have been killed with him." He passed the cassette from one hand to the other as if he wished someone would take it away from him. "I guess I have to look at this," he said. "There's a VCR in the lounge, if we can pry it away from the old hairbags who sit around all day watching Debbie do Dallas." He stood up. "Watch it with me, okay? I miss any of the subtleties, you can point 'em out to me."

The lounge was empty, and he hung a sign on the door to keep anybody from walking in on us. We fast-forwarded through the opening of *The Dirty Dozen,* and then the Stettners' home movie came on. At first he made cop comments, remarking on the costumes and on Olga's figure, but once the action was under way he fell silent. The movie had that effect. Nothing you could say was a match for what you were seeing.

While it was rewinding he said, "Jesus."

"Yeah."

"Tell me one more time about the kid they did. You said his name was Bobby?"

"Happy," I said. "Bobby was the younger one, the other sketch I gave you."

"Bobby's the one you saw at the fight. You never saw Happy?"

"No."

"No, of course not. How could you? He's already dead before you see the cassette, before Leveque gets killed, even. This is complicated, but you said it was, didn't you?" He got out a cigarette and tapped the end against the back of his hand. "I got to run this past some people. Upstairs, and most likely at the Manhattan DA's Office. This is very tricky."

"I know."

"Let me keep all of this, Matt. You'll be at the same number? The hotel?"

"I should be in and out the rest of the day."

"Yeah, well, don't be surprised if you don't hear anything today. Tomorrow's more likely, or it could even be Wednesday. I got other cases I'm supposed to be working, far as that goes, but I'm gonna move on this right away." He retrieved the cassette from the machine. "This is something," he said. "You ever see anything like this before?"

"No."

"I hate the shit you have to look at. When I was a kid, looking at the TPF guys up on top of their horses, you know, I had no idea."

"I know."

"No fucking idea at all," he said. "None."

I didn't hear from him until Wednesday evening. I was at St. Paul's until ten o'clock, and when I got back to the hotel there were two messages. The first one, logged in at a quarter to nine, requested that I call him at the station house. He'd called again three-quarters of an hour later to leave a number I didn't recognize.

I made the call and asked the man who answered for Joe Durkin. He covered the mouthpiece with his hand but I could hear him call the name: "Joe Durkin? There a Joe Durkin here?" There was a pause, and then Joe came on the line.

"You keep late hours," I said.

"Yeah, well, I'm not on the city's time now. Listen, you got a few minutes? I want to talk with you."

"Sure."

"Come over here, huh? Where the hell is this place, anyway? Hold on a minute." He came back and said, "Name of the place is Pete's All-American, it's on—"

"I know where it is. Jesus."

"What's the matter?"

"Nothing at all," I said. "Is a sport jacket and tie all right or will I need a suit?"

"Don't be a wiseass."

"All right."

"The place is a little lowdown. You got a problem with that?"

"No problem."

"I'm in a lowdown mood. Where am I gonna go, the Carlyle? The Rainbow Room?"

"I'll be right over," I said.

Pete's All-American is on the west side of Tenth Avenue a block up from Grogan's. It's been there for generations but remains an unlikely candidate for the National Register of Historic Places. It has never been anything but a bucket of blood.

It smelled of stale beer and bad plumbing. The bartender looked up without interest when I came in the door. The half-dozen old lags at the bar didn't bother to turn around. I walked past them to a table in back where Joe was sitting with his back to the wall. There was an overflowing ashtray on the table, along with a rocks glass and a bottle of Hiram Walker Ten High. They aren't supposed to bring the bottle to the table like that, it's a violation of an SLA rule, but a lot of people will bend the rules for somebody who shows them a gold shield.

"You found the joint," he said. "Get yourself a glass."

"That's all right."

"Oh, right, you don't drink. Never touch the dirty stuff." He picked up his glass, drank some, made a face. "You want a Coke or something? You gotta get it yourself, they're not big on service here."

"Maybe later."

"Sit down then." He ground out his cigarette. "Jesus Christ, Matt. Jesus Christ."

"What's the matter?"

"Ah, shit," he said. He reached down beside him, came up with the videocassette and tossed it onto the table. It skidded off and landed in my lap. "Don't drop that," he said. "I had a hell of a time getting it back. They didn't want to give it to me. They wanted to keep it."

"What happened?"

"But I pitched a bitch," he went on. "I said, hey, you ain't gonna play the game, you can give back the bat and ball. They didn't like it but it was easier to give it to me than to put up with all the hell I was raising." He drained his glass and banged it down on the tabletop. "You can forget about Stettner. There's no case."

"What do you mean?"

"I mean there's no case. I talked to cops, I talked to an ADA. You got a whole batch of different things and they don't add up to dick."

"One thing you've got," I said, "is a visual record of two people committing murder."

"Yeah," he said. "Right. That's what I saw and that's what I can't get out of my fucking head and that's why I'm drinking bad whiskey in the worst shithole in town. But what does it really amount to? He's got a hood covers most of his face and she's got a fucking mask. Who are they? You say it's Bergen and Olga and I say you're probably right, but can you imagine putting the two of them in the dock and making a jury watch this and trying to make an identification on that basis? 'Bailiff, will you please remove the female defendant's dress so the jury can get a good look at her tits, see if they match the set in the movie?' Because the tits are all you really get a good look at."

"You get to see her mouth."

"Yeah, and there's generally something in it. Look, here's the point. Odds are you could never get the tape seen by a jury. Any defense attorney's gonna try and get it disallowed, and they most likely could, because it's inflammatory. I'll fucking well say it's inflammatory. It inflamed the shit out of me, it made me want to jail those two fuckers and weld the cell door shut."

"But a jury can't see it."

"Probably not, but before it gets that far they tell me you can't even get an indictment, because what have you got to present to a grand jury? First off, who was murdered?"

"A kid."

"A kid we don't know zip about. Maybe his name is Happy and maybe he comes from Texas or South Carolina or some state where they play a lot of high school football. Where's the body? Nobody knows. When did the alleged homicide take place? Nobody knows. Did he really get killed? Nobody knows."

"You saw it, Joe."

"I see stuff on TV and in the movies all the time. Special effects, they call it. They got these hero killers, Jason, Freddie, they're in one movie after another, wasting people left and right. I'll tell you, they make it look as good as Bergen and Olga."

"There were no special effects in what we saw. That was home video."

"I know that. I also know that the tape doesn't amount to evidentiary proof that a murder was committed, and that without the where and the when and some proof that some-body actually got killed, you got next to nothing to walk into a courtroom with."

"What about Leveque?"

"What about him?"

"His murder's a matter of record."

"So? There is nothing anywhere to link Arnold Leveque

to either of the Stettners. The only tie is the unsupported testimony of Richard Thurman, who's conveniently dead himself and who told you this in a private conversation with no witnesses present, and it's all hearsay and almost certainly not allowable. And not even Thurman could connect the Stettners to the film. He said Leveque was trying to blackmail Stettner with a film, but he also said Stettner got that film and that was the end of it. You can be positive in your own mind that we're talking about the same film here, and you can work it out that Leveque was the cameraman and was there when the kid's blood went down the drain, but that's not proof. You couldn't even say it in court without some lawyer jumping straight down your throat."

"What about the other boy? Bobby, the younger one."

"Jesus," he said. "What have you got? You've got a sketch based on a look you got at him sitting next to Stettner at a boxing match. You got some kid somebody hunted up who says he recognizes the kid and his name's Bobby, but he doesn't know his last name or where he's from or what happened to him. You got somebody else who says Bobby used to be with a pimp who used to threaten kids that he'd send them out and they wouldn't come back."

"His name's Juke," I said. "He shouldn't be too hard to trace."

"He was a cinch, as a matter of fact. People complain a lot about the computer system but it makes some things easy. Juke is a guy named Walter Nicholson. A/k/a Juke, a/k/a Juke Box. First bit he did was for breaking into coin-operated vending machines, which is where the nickname came from. Arrested for statutory rape, contributing to the delinquency of a minor, and immoral solicitation. In other words a lot of pimping arrests, a whole profile of pimping kids. A class act."

"Can't you pick him up? He could tie Bobby to Stettner."

"You got to get him to talk, which would be hard without having something to hold over his head, which I don't see here. And then you'd have to get somebody to believe anything a scumbag like Juke might say. But you can't do any of that because the prick happens to be dead."

"Stettner got him."

"No, Stettner didn't get him. He—"

"The same as he got Thurman, to get rid of a witness before anybody could get to him. Dammit, if I'd come in right away, if I hadn't waited over the weekend—"

"Matt, Juke got killed a week ago. And Stettner didn't have anything to do with it and probably doesn't even know it happened. Juke and another of Nature's noblemen shot each other in a social club on Lenox Avenue. They were fighting over a ten-year-old girl. Must be some hot broad, got two grown men shooting each other over her, don't you think?"

I didn't say anything.

"Look," he said, "I fucking hate this. I got the word last night and I went in this morning and carried on, and they're right. They're wrong but they're right. And I waited until tonight to call you because I wasn't looking forward to this conversation, believe it or not. Much as I like your company under other circumstances." He poured more whiskey into his glass. I got a whiff of it, but it didn't make me want it. Nor was it the worst smell in Pete's All-American.

I said, "I think I understand, Joe. I knew it was thin with Thurman dead."

"With Thurman alive I think we probably would have had them. But once he's dead there's no case."

"But if you mount a full-scale investigation—"

"Jesus," he said, "don't you get it? There's no grounds for an investigation. There's no complaint to act on, there's no probable cause for a warrant, there's a whole lot of nothing is what there is. The man's not a criminal, for openers. Never been arrested. You say mob connections, but his name's not in any files, never came up in any RICO investigations. Man's clean as a whistle. Lives on Central Park South, makes a good living trading in foreign currencies—"

"That's money laundering."

"So you say, but can you prove it? He pays his taxes, he gives to charities, he's made substantial political contributions—"

"Oh?"

"Don't give me that. It's not any clout that makes it impossible to take him down. Nobody ordered us off it because the prick's untouchable, he's got a hook with somebody important. No such thing. But he's not some street kid you can push around and never hear about it. You gotta have something'll stand up in court, and you want to know what stands up in court? Let me just say two words. You wanna hear two words? Warren Madison."

"Oh."

"Yeah, 'Oh.' Warren Madison, terror of the Bronx. Deals dope, kills four other dealers we know for sure and is listed as probable for five others, and when they finally corner this wanted fugitive in his mother's apartment he shoots six cops before they get the cuffs on him. He shoots six cops!"

"I remember."

"And that cocksucker Gruliow defends him, and what does he do, what he always does, he puts the cops on trial. Spins out all this shit about how the Bronx cops were using Madison as a snitch, and they were giving him confiscated cocaine to sell, and then they tried to murder him to keep him from talking. Do you fucking believe it? Six police officers with bullets in 'em, not a single bullet in Warren fucking Madison, and that means it was all a police department plot to kill the fuck."

"The jury bought it."

"Fucking Bronx jury, they would have cut Hitler loose, sent him home in a cab. And that's with a piece of shit of a dope dealer that everybody knew was guilty. You imagine what you'd get bringing a shaky case against a solid citizen like Stettner? Look, Matt, do you see what I mean? Do you want me to go over it again?"

I saw, but we went over it anyway. Somewhere in the

course of it the Ten High began to get the upper hand. His eyes lost their sharp focus and he started slurring his words. Pretty soon he began repeating himself, losing track of his own arguments.

"Let's get out of this dive," I said. "Are you hungry? Let's get something to eat, maybe some coffee."

"What's that supposed to mean?"

"Just that I wouldn't mind some food."

"Horseshit. Don't patronize me, you son of a bitch."

"I wasn't doing that."

"Fuck you weren't. That what they teach you at those meetings? How to be a pain in the ass when another man wants to have a quiet couple of drinks?"

"No."

"Just because you're some kind of candyass who can't handle it anymore doesn't mean God appointed you to sober up the rest of the fucking world."

"You're right."

"Sit down. Where you going? For Christ's sake sit down."

"I think I'll get on home now," I said.

"Matt? I'm sorry. I was out of line there, okay? I didn't mean anything by it."

"No problem."

He apologized again and I told him it was fine, and then the booze took him back in the other direction and he decided he didn't like the tone of what I'd said. "Hang on one second," I told him. "Stay right where you are, I'll be back in a minute." And I walked out of there and headed home.

He was drunk, with the better part of a bottle still sitting there in front of him. He had his service revolver on his hip and I thought I recognized his car parked at the curb alongside a fire hydrant. It was a dangerous combination, but God hadn't appointed me to sober up the rest of the fucking world, or to make sure everybody got home safe, either.

20

WHEN I WENT TO SLEEP THAT NIGHT THE VIDEOCASSETTE WAS on the table next to the clock, and it was the first thing my eyes happened to hit the next morning. I left it there and went out to meet the day. That was Thursday, and while I didn't chase out to Maspeth to watch the fights that night, I did get home in time to catch the main event on television. Somehow it wasn't the same.

Another day passed before it occurred to me that the cassette belonged in my safety-deposit box, and by then it was Saturday and the bank was closed. I saw Elaine Saturday; we spent the late afternoon browsing through art galleries in SoHo, ate at an Italian place in the Village, and listened to a piano trio at Sweet Basil. It was a day of long silences of the sort possible only for people who have grown very comfortable together. In the cab home we held hands and didn't say a word.

I had told her earlier about my conversation with Joe, and neither of us returned to the topic that afternoon or evening. The following night Jim Faber and I had our standing Sunday dinner date, and I didn't discuss the case with him at all. It crossed my mind once or twice in the course of our conversation but it wasn't something I felt the need to talk about.

It seems odd now, but I didn't even spend that much time thinking about it for those several days. It's not as though I had a great deal of other things on my mind. I didn't, nor did sports provide much in the way of diversion, not in that stretch of frozen desert that extends from the Super Bowl to the start of spring training.

The mind, from what I know of it, has various levels or chambers, and deals with matters in many other ways than conscious thought. When I was a police detective, and since then in my private work, there have not been that many occasions when I sat down and consciously figured something out. Most of the time the accretion of detail ultimately made a solution obvious, but, when some insight on my part was required, it more often than not simply came to me. Some unconscious portion of the mind evidently processed the available data and allowed me to see the puzzle in a new light.

So I can only suppose that I made an unconscious decision to shelve the whole subject of the Stettners for the time being, to put it out of my mind (or, perhaps, into my mind, into some deeper recess of self) until I knew what to do about it.

It didn't take all that long. As to how well it worked, well, that's harder to say.

Tuesday morning I dialed 411 and asked for the number for Bergen Stettner on Central Park South. The operator told me she could not give out that number, but volunteered that she had a business listing for the same party on Lexington Avenue. I thanked her and broke the connection. I called back and got a different operator, a man, and identified myself as a police officer, supplying a name and shield number. I said I needed an unlisted number and gave him the name and address. He gave me the number and I thanked him and dialed it.

A woman answered and I asked for Mr. Stettner. She said he was out and I asked if she was Mrs. Stettner. She took an extra second or two to decide, then allowed that she was.

I said, "Mrs. Stettner, I have something that belongs to you and your husband, and I'm hoping that you're offering a substantial reward for its return."

"Who is this?"

"My name is Scudder," I said. "Matthew Scudder."

"I don't believe I know you."

"We met," I said, "but I wouldn't expect you to remember me. I'm a friend of Richard Thurman's."

There was a pronounced pause this time, while I suppose she tried to work out whether her friendship with Thurman was a matter of record. Evidently she decided that it was.

"Such a tragic affair," she said. "It was a great shock."

"It must have been."

"And you say you were a friend of his?"

"That's right. I was also a close friend of Arnold Leveque's."

Another pause. "I'm afraid I don't know him."

"Another tragic affair."

"I beg your pardon?"

"He's dead."

"I'm very sorry, but I never knew the man. If you could tell me what it is you want—"

"Over the phone? Are you sure that's what you want?"

"My husband's not here at the moment," she said. "If you would leave your number perhaps he'll call you back."

"I have a tape Leveque made," I said. "Do you really want me to tell you about it over the phone?"

"No."

"I want to meet with you privately. Just you, not your husband."

"I see."

"Someplace public, but private enough that we won't be overheard."

"Give me a moment," she said. She took a full minute. Then she said, "Do you know where I live? You must, you even have the number. How did you get the number? It's supposed to be impossible to get an unlisted number."

"I guess they made a mistake."

"They wouldn't make that sort of mistake. Oh, of course, you got it from Richard. But—"

"What?"

"Nothing. You know the address. There is a cocktail lounge right here in the building, it's always quiet during the day. Meet me there in an hour."

"Fine."

"Wait a minute. How will I recognize you?"

"I'll recognize you," I said. "Just wear the mask. And leave your shirt off."

The cocktail lounge was called Hadrian's Wall. Hadrian was a Roman emperor, and the wall named for him was a fortified stone barrier built across the north of England to protect Roman settlements there from barbarous tribes. Any significance the name may have had was lost on me. The decor was expensive and understated, running to red leather banquettes and black mica tables. The lighting was subdued and indirect, the music barely audible.

I got there five minutes early, sat at a table and ordered a Perrier. She arrived ten minutes late, entering from the lobby, standing just inside the archway and trying to scan the room. I stood up to make it easier for her and she walked without hesitation to my table. "I hope you haven't been waiting long," she said. "I'm Olga Stettner."

"Matthew Scudder."

She held out her hand and I took it. Her hand was smooth and cool to the touch, her grip strong. I thought of an iron hand in a velvet glove. Her fingernails were long, and the scarlet polish matched her lipstick.

In the video she'd had the same color on the tips of her breasts.

We both sat down, and almost immediately the waiter was at our table. She called him by name and asked for a glass of white wine. I told him he could bring me another

Perrier. Neither of us said a word until he had brought the drinks and gone away again. Then she said, "I've seen you before."

"I told you we'd met."

"Where?" She frowned, then said, "Of course. At the arena. Downstairs. You were skulking around."

"I was looking for the men's room."

"So you said." She lifted her wine glass and took a small sip, really just wetting her tongue. She was wearing a dark silk blouse and a patterned silk scarf, fastened at her throat with a jeweled pin. The stone looked like lapis and her eyes looked blue, but it was hard to tell colors in the dimly lit lounge.

"Tell me what you want," she said.

"Why don't I tell you what I have first."

"All right."

I started by saying that I was an ex-cop, which didn't seem to astonish her. I guess I have the look. I had met a man named Arnold Leveque when we'd pulled him in on a sweep designed to clean up Times Square. Leveque had been a clerk in an adult bookstore, I said, and we'd arrested him for possession and sale of obscene materials.

"Later on," I said, "something came up and I had occasion to leave the NYPD. Last year I heard from Leveque, who got the word I was working private. Well, I hadn't seen Arnie in years. He was the same. Fatter, but pretty much the same."

"I never knew the man."

"Suit yourself. We got together, and he was being cagey. He told me a story about making a film in somebody's basement, a home movie with a professional touch in that they hired him to be the cameraman. Personally I don't think I could get into the mood with a creepy guy like Arnie watching, but I guess it didn't put you off stride, did it?"

"I don't know what you're talking about."

I wasn't wearing a wire, but I could have been miked like a soundstage and it wouldn't have made any difference. She wasn't giving away a thing. Her eyes made it very clear she was following everything I was saying, but she was very careful not to get caught speaking for the record.

"Like I said," I went on, "Arnie was cagey. He had a copy of the tape and he was making arrangements to sell it for a lot of money, but of course he was careful not to say how much. At the same time he was afraid the buyer might pull a fast one, and that was where I came in. I was supposed to back him up, make sure the buyer didn't take him out."

"And did you do this?"

"That's where Arnie outsmarted himself," I said. "See, he wanted a backup man but he didn't want a partner. He wanted it all for himself. Maybe he'd give me a grand for my troubles. So he kept me in the dark to protect himself from me, and in the meantime he forgot to protect himself from his buyer, because he got knifed to death in an alley in Hell's Kitchen."

"How sad for him."

"Well, these things happen. You know what they say, sometimes it's a dog-eat-dog world and the rest of the time it's the other way around. Soon as I heard what happened I went over to his apartment, flashed some tin at the super and had a look around. I didn't expect to find much because the cops had already been there, and I don't think they were the first ones in, either, because Arnie's keys were missing when they found his corpse. So I don't think I even got sloppy seconds, if you'll pardon the sexual innuendo, Mrs. Stettner."

She looked at me.

"The thing is," I said, "I knew Arnie kept a copy of the tape, because he already told me as much. So I gathered up every cassette in his place. There must have been forty of them, all these old movies that you'd turn off if they were on television. He ate that stuff up. What I did, I sat in front of my set and cranked up my VCR and went through the lot of them. And surprise, one of 'em wasn't what it was supposed to be. I was zooming through it with the Fast Forward, same as all the others, when all of a sudden the regular picture's gone and we're in a room with a teenage boy all hooked up to a metal frame like something out of the Spanish Inquisition, and there's a beautiful woman in leather pants and gloves and high heels and nothing else. I notice you're wearing leather pants again today but I don't suppose they're the same ones, because the ones on the tape were crotchless."

"Tell me about the film."

I recounted enough of it to make it clear I'd seen it. "It wasn't much on plot," I said, "but the ending was a pip, and there was this symbolic last shot of blood flowing across the floor and down the drain. That was Arnie at his most creative, you have to give him that, and the black-and-white checkerboard floor was the same as the basement of the arena in Maspeth, and isn't that a hell of a coincidence?"

She pursed her lips and blew out a stream of air in a soundless whistle. She had half a glass of wine left but she didn't touch it, reaching instead for my glass of Perrier. She took a sip and put the glass back where she'd found it. The act managed to be curiously intimate.

"You mentioned Richard Thurman," she said.

"Well, that's the thing," I said. "See, I had Arnie's tape, but what was I going to do with it? The devious bastard never got to the point of saying who the people were. Here I got a tape the principals would be happy to get back, and it would be very much worth my while to perform them the valuable service of recovering it, but how do I find them? I went around with my eyes and ears open, but short of bumping into a man walking down the street in a rubber suit with his dick hanging out, how was I going to get anywhere?"

I picked up my Perrier and turned the glass so that I was sipping from where her lips had touched the glass. A kiss by proxy, you could call it.

"Then Thurman turns up," I said. "With a dead wife, and public opinion pretty much divided as to whether or not he had anything to do with it. I run into him in a ginmill and because he's in television we get on the subject of Arnie, who worked for one of the nets before I ever knew him. And strangely enough your name came up."

"My name?"

"You and your husband. Very distinctive names, easy to remember even after a long night in a saloon. Thurman put away more booze than I did, but he got very cute, lots of hints, lots of innuendo. I figured we'd talk more, but the next thing you knew he was dead. They say he killed himself."

"It's very sad."

"And tragic, like you said over the phone. The same day he got killed I was out in Maspeth. I was going to meet him at the fights and he was going to point out your husband. Thurman didn't make it, I guess he was already dead by then, but I didn't need him to point out your husband, because I recognized the two of you. Then I went downstairs and recognized the floor. I couldn't find the room where you made the movie, but maybe it was one of the locked ones. Or maybe you redecorated since the taping session." I shrugged. "Doesn't matter. Doesn't matter what Thurman was getting at, either, and it doesn't matter what kind of help he might have had going out the window. What matters is I'm in the fortunate position of being able to do something useful for someone in a position to make it all worth my while."

"What do you want?"

"What do I want? That's easy. I want basically the same thing Arnie wanted. Isn't that pretty much what everybody wants?" Her hand was on the table, inches from mine. I extended a finger and reached to touch the back of her hand. "But I don't want to get what he got," I said. "That's all."

For a long moment she sat looking down at our hands on the tabletop. Then she covered my hand with hers and fastened her eyes on mine. I could see the blue of her eyes now, and the intensity of her gaze held me.

"Matthew," she said, testing my name on her tongue. "No, I think I will just call you Scudder."

"Whatever you like."

She stood up. I thought for a second she was going to leave, but instead she came around the table and motioned for me to inch over to my left. She sat down beside me on the banquette and again put her hand on top of mine.

"Now we're on the same side," she said.

She was wearing a lot of perfume. It was musky, which was no great surprise. I hadn't figured her to go around smelling like a pine tree.

"It was hard to talk," she said. "You know what I mean, Scudder?" I don't know that she had an accent, but there was the slightest European inflection to her speech. "How can I say anything? You could be tricking me, all wired up so that anything I say would be recorded."

"I'm not wearing a wire."

"How do I know this?" She turned toward me and put her hand on my necktie just below the knot. She ran her hand the length of my tie, slipping it inside the front of my suit jacket. She stroked my shirtfront thoroughly.

"I told you," I said.

"Yes, you told me," she murmured. Her mouth was close to my ear and her breath was warm on the side of my face. Her hand dropped to my leg and swept upward along the inside of my thigh. "Did you bring the tape?"

"It's in a bank vault."

"That's a pity. We could go upstairs and watch it. How did it make you feel when you saw it?"

"I don't know."

"You don't know? What kind of an answer is that? Of course you know. It made you hot, didn't it?"

"I suppose so."

"You suppose so. You're hot now, Scudder. You're hard. I could make you come right now, just by touching you. How would you like that?"

I didn't say anything.

"I'm all hot and wet," she said. "I have no underpants on. It's wonderful to wear tight leather pants and no underwear and get all wet inside the leather. Do you want to come upstairs with me? I could fuck you stupid. You remember what I did to that boy?"

"You killed him."

"You think he had it so bad?" She moved closer, took the lobe of my ear between her teeth. "For three days we fucked his brains out, Bergen and I. We fucked him and sucked him and let him have whatever drugs he wanted. He had a lifetime of pleasure."

"He didn't like the ending much."

"So he had pain. So what?" Her hand stroked me in rhythm with her words. "So he didn't live a hundred years, he didn't get to be an old man. Who wants to be an old man?"

"I guess he died happy."

"That was his name, Happy."

"I know."

"You knew that? You know a lot, Scudder. You think you give a shit about the boy? If you care so much about him, how come you got a hard-on?"

A good question. "I never said I cared about him."

"What do you care about?"

"Getting money for the tape. And living long enough to spend it."

"And what else?"

"That's enough for now."

"You want me, don't you?"

"People in hell want ice water."

"But they can't have it. You could have me if you wanted. We could go upstairs right now."

"I don't think so."

She sat back. "Jesus, you're tough," she said. "You're a hard case, aren't you?"

"Not particularly."

"Richard would be under the table by now. He'd be trying to eat me through the leather pants."

"Look where it got him."

"He didn't have it so bad."

"I know," I said. "Who wants to be an old man? Look, just because you can give me a hard-on doesn't mean you can lead me around by it. Of course I want you. I wanted you when I first saw the tape." I picked up her hand, put it back in her own lap. "After we've done our business," I said, "then I'll have you."

"You think so?"

"I think so."

"You know who you remind me of? Bergen."

"I don't look good in black rubber."

"Don't be so sure."

"And I'm circumcised."

"Maybe you can get a transplant. No, you're like him on the inside, you both have the same hardness. You were a cop."

"That's right."

"Did you ever kill anybody?"

"Why?"

"You did. You don't have to answer, I can feel it in you. Did you like it?"

"Not particularly."

"Are you so sure that's the truth?"

" 'What is truth?' "

"Ah, an age-old question. But I think I will sit across the table from you. If we are going to talk business it's better if we can look at each other."

I told her I wasn't greedy. I wanted a single payment of fifty thousand dollars. They had paid that much to Leveque, although they hadn't allowed him to keep it. They could pay the same to me. "You could be like him," she said. "He had a copy, even though he swore he didn't."

"He was stupid."

"To keep a copy?"

"To lie about it. Of course I've made a copy. I've made two of them. One's with a lawyer. The other's in the safe of a private detective. Just in case I get mugged in an alley, or fall out a window."

"If you have copies you could extort more money from us."

I shook my head. "The copies are my insurance. And my own intelligence is your insurance. By selling you the tape once I'm not extorting money from you. I'm doing you a favor. If I tried it a second time you'd be better off killing me, and I'm smart enough to know that."

"And if we don't pay the first time? You go to the police?"

"No."

"Why not?"

"Because the tape's not enough to put you away. No, I'd go to the press. The tabloids could run with the story. They'd know you've got too much blood on your hands to bring a libel suit. They'd make things awfully hot for you. You might never face a criminal charge, but you'd get more attention than you'd ever be comfortable with. Your husband's friends in California wouldn't be very happy to see you in the limelight that way, and your neighbors might look at you funny in the elevator. You'd pay fifty grand to avoid that kind of publicity, wouldn't you? Hell, anybody would."

"It's a lot of money."

"You really think so? I don't know if I could get that much from a tabloid, but I could get half that. If they can't sell papers with a story like that they're in the wrong business. I could walk into an office this afternoon and walk out with a check for twenty-five thousand and nobody'd say I was a blackmailer, either. They'd call me a hero investigator, and they'd probably give me an assignment to go out and dig up more dirt."

"I will have to talk to Bergen. You say it's not so much money, but it will take time to get it together."

"The hell it will," I said. "When a man runs a money laundry it's not terribly hard for him to put his hands on some cash. You probably keep five times that sitting around the apartment."

"You have some funny ideas about how business works."

"I'm sure you can have the money tomorrow night," I said. "That's when I want it."

"God," she said, "you're so much like Bergen."

"Our tastes are different."

"You think so? Don't be so sure what your tastes are until you've sampled everything on your plate. And you haven't yet, have you?"

"I haven't missed too many meals."

"Bergen will want to meet you."

"Tomorrow night, when we carry out the transaction. I'll bring the tape so you can see what you're buying. Do you have a VCR in Maspeth?"

"You want to make the exchange there? At the arena?"

"I think it's the safest spot for both sides."

"God knows it's private," she said. "Except for Thursday nights the whole area is a wasteland. And even Thursdays it's not so busy. Tomorrow is what, Wednesday? I think perhaps that's possible. Of course I'll have to talk with Bergen."

"Of course."

"What time would you prefer?"

"Late," I said. "But I can call you later on and we'll work out the details."

"Yes." She looked at her watch. "Call me around four."

"I will."

"Good." She opened her purse, put money on the table for our drinks. "I'll tell you something, Scudder. I really wanted to go upstairs with you before. I was sopping wet. I wasn't just putting on an act."

"I didn't think you were."

"And you wanted me just as much. But I'm glad we didn't do anything. You know why?"

"Tell me."

"Because this way we've still got the sexual tension going between us. Can you feel it?"

"Yes."

"It won't go away, either. It will still be there tomorrow night. Maybe I'll wear the crotchless pants to Maspeth. Would you like that?"

"Maybe."

"And long gloves, and high heels." She looked at me. "And no shirt."

"And lipstick on your nipples."

"Rouge."

"But the same shade as your lipstick and nail polish."

"Perhaps we'll play," she said. "After we've made the switch. Perhaps we'll have some fun, the three of us."

"I don't know."

"You think we'd try to take the money back? You'd still have the copies. One with the lawyer, one with the private detective."

"That's not it."

"What then?"

" 'The three of us.' I was never one for crowds."

"You won't be crowded," she said. "You'll have all the room you need."

21

I CALLED AT FOUR O'CLOCK. SHE MUST HAVE BEEN SITTING right next to the phone. She picked it up the second it rang.

"It's Scudder," I said.

"You're punctual," she said. "That's a good sign."

"Of what?"

"Of punctuality. I spoke to my husband. He's agreed to your terms. Tomorrow night is acceptable. As far as the time is concerned, he suggests midnight."

"Make it one."

"One A.M.? Just a moment."

There was a pause, and then Stettner took the phone. He said, "Scudder? Bergen Stettner. One in the morning is fine."

"Good."

"I'm eager to meet you. You made quite an impression on my wife."

"She's pretty impressive herself."

"I've always thought so. I understand we already met, in a manner of speaking. You were the boxing fan looking for the lavatory in all the wrong places. I have to admit I don't have any recollection of what you look like."

"You'll know me when you see me."

"I feel I know you already. I have one problem with our arrangement, as Olga explained the situation. You have extra copies with a lawyer and an agent, is that correct?"

"A lawyer and a private investigator."

"To be opened by them in the event of your death, and

certain specified wishes of yours to be carried out. Is that correct?"

"Right."

"An understandable precaution. I could assure you it's unnecessary, but that might not put your mind at rest."

"Not entirely, no."

" 'Trust everybody but cut the cards.' Isn't that what they say? Here's my dilemma, Scudder. Suppose we conclude our transaction to the satisfaction of all concerned and you go your way and we go ours, and five years from now you step off a curb and get run over by a bus. You see what I'm getting at?"

"Yes."

"Because if I keep faith with you—"

"I get the point," I said. "I knew someone in a similar situation once. Give me a minute, I want to see if I can remember how he handled it." I thought for a moment. "All right," I said. "See how this sounds to you. I'll instruct both parties that, if I should die a year or more after today's date, they are to destroy the material left with them unless special circumstances exist."

"What sort of special circumstances?"

"If there's a strong suspicion that I've died as a result of foul play, and if the murderer has not been either identified or apprehended. In other words, you're clear if I'm run over by a bus, or shot by a jealous lover. If I'm murdered by person or persons unknown, then you're in the soup."

"And if you die within the first year?"

"You've got a problem."

"Even if it's a bus?"

"Even if it's a heart attack."

"Jesus," he said. "I don't like that much."

"Best I can do."

"Shit. How's your health?"

"Not bad."

"I hope you don't do a lot of coke."

"I can't drink too much of it because of the bubbles."

"That's funny. You don't do skydiving or hang gliding, do you? Don't fly your own plane? God, will you listen to this? It sounds like an insurance examination. Well, you take good care of yourself, Scudder."

"I'll stay out of drafts."

"You do that," he said. "You know, I think Olga's right, I think I'm going to enjoy you. What are you doing tonight?"

"Tonight?"

"Tonight. Why don't you join us for dinner? We'll drink some champagne, have a few laughs. Tomorrow's for business but there's no reason we can't be social tonight."

"I can't."

"Why not?"

"I have plans made."

"Cancel them! What's so important you can't reschedule it, eh?"

"I have to go to an AA meeting."

He laughed long and hard. "Oh, that's marvelous," he said. "Yes, now that you mention it, we all have plans. Olga's chaperoning a CYO dance and I have to go to, uh—"

"The Boy Scout Council," I suggested.

"That's it exactly, the annual award dinner of the Boy Scout Area Council. They're going to give me a merit badge for buggery, it's one of the most sought-after awards. You're a funny man, Scudder. You're costing me a great deal of money, but at least I get a few laughs out of it."

After I got off the phone with Stettner I called a car rental agency in the neighborhood and reserved a car. I didn't pick it up right away but walked instead to Coliseum Books, where I picked up a Hagstrom map of Queens. On my way out of the bookstore I realized I was just down the street from the gallery where I'd left the original Ray Galindez sketches for framing. They had done a nice job, and as I looked at the pencil drawings behind their shield of non-glare glass I tried to see them purely as art. I wasn't entirely successful. I kept seeing two dead boys and the man who killed them.

They wrapped them for me and I paid with my credit card and carried the package back to my hotel. I stowed it in the closet and spent a few minutes studying the map of Queens. I went out for a sandwich and a cup of coffee and read a newspaper, then came back and looked at the map some more. Around seven I walked over to the car-rental place and used my credit card again, and they put me behind the wheel of a gray Toyota Corolla with sixty-two hundred miles on the clock. The gas tank was full and the ashtrays were empty, but whoever had vacuumed the interior had done a less than perfect job.

I had the map with me but I got there without referring to it, taking the Midtown Tunnel and the Long Island Expressway and exiting just after the BQE interchange. There was some traffic on the LIE but not too much of it, with most of the commuters in front of their television sets by now. I cruised around the area, and when I reached the New Maspeth Arena I circled the block slowly once and found a place to park.

I sat there for an hour or more like a lazy old cop on a stakeout. At one point I had to take a leak, and I hadn't brought along an empty quart jar, the way I'd learned to do years ago. The fact that the neighborhood was deserted and I hadn't seen a soul in the past half hour made me positively reckless, and I drove two blocks and got out of the car to pee with abandon against a brick wall. I went around the block and parked in another spot across the street from the arena. The whole street was a car owner's dream, just one empty parking space after another.

Around nine or a little past it I left the Toyota and walked over to the arena. I took my time, paying close attention, and when I got back in the car I got out my notebook and made some sketches. I had the dome light on, but not for very long.

At ten I took a different route and drove back to the city.

The kid at the garage said he had to charge me for a full day. "Might as well keep her overnight," he said. "Bring her back tomorrow afternoon, won't cost you a nickel more."

I told him I had no further use for it. The garage was on Eleventh Avenue between Fifty-seventh and Fifty-eighth. I walked a block east, then south. I checked at Armstrong's but didn't see anyone I recognized, and just for the hell of it I looked in the door of Pete's All-American to see if Durkin was there. He wasn't. I'd spoken to him a few days earlier, and he'd said he hoped he hadn't said anything out of line. I'd assured him he was a perfect gentleman.

"Then that's a first for me," he said. "I don't make a habit of it, but once in a while a man has to go and let the devil out." I told him I knew what he meant.

Mick wasn't at Grogan's. "He'll probably be in later," Burke said. "Sometime between now and closing."

I sat at the bar with a Coke, and when I'd finished it I switched to club soda. After a while Andy Buckley came in and Burke drew him a pint of the draft Guinness, and Andy took the stool next to mine and talked about basketball. I used to follow the game but I haven't paid much attention to it in the past few years. That was all right because he was prepared to carry the whole conversation himself. He had gone to the Garden the night before and the Knicks had covered the spread with a three-pointer at the buzzer, winning his bet for him in the process.

I let him talk me into a game of darts, but I wasn't fool enough to bet with him. He could have played left-handed and beat me. We played a second game, and then I went back to the bar and drank another Coke and watched television and Andy stayed at the dart board sharpening his game.

At one point I thought about going to the midnight meeting. When I first got sober there was a meeting every night at twelve at the Moravian church at Lexington and Thirtieth.

Then they lost the meeting place and the group moved to Alanon House, an AA clubhouse that has had various locations in the theater district and is currently housed in a third-floor apartment on West Forty-sixth. At one point Alanon House was between locations, and some people started a new midnight meeting downtown on Houston Street near Varick, where the Village butts up against SoHo. The downtown group has added other meetings, including an insomniac's special every morning at two.

So I had a choice of midnight meetings, and I could tell Burke to let Mick know I was looking for him, and that I'd be back by one-thirty at the latest. But something stopped me, something kept me on my stool and led me to order another Coke when my glass was empty.

I was in the john when Mick finally showed up a little before one. When I emerged he was at the bar with his bottle of JJ&S and his Waterford tumbler. "Good man," he said. "Burke told me you were here and I said he should put on a pot of coffee. I hope you're up for a long night."

"Just a short night tonight," I said.

"Ah, well," he said. "Maybe I can get you to change your mind."

We sat at our usual table and he filled his glass and held it to the light. "By God that's a good color," he said, and he took a drink.

"If you ever quit drinking," I said, "they make a cream soda that's just about the same shade."

"Is that a fact."

"Of course you'd have to let it go flat," I said, "or it'd have a head on it."

"Spoil the effect, wouldn't it?" He took a drink and sighed. "Cream soda indeed," he said.

We talked about nothing much, and then I leaned forward and said, "Do you still need money, Mick?"

"I've not got holes in my shoes," he said.

"No."

"But I always need money. I told you that the other night."

"You did."

"Why?"

"I know where you can get some," I said.

"Ah," he said. He sat in silence for a moment, and a slight smile came and went, came and went. "How much money?"

"A minimum of fifty thousand. Probably a lot more than that."

"Whose money?"

A good question. Joe Durkin had reminded me that money knows no owner. It was, he'd said, a principle of law.

"A couple named Stettner," I said.

"Drug dealers?"

"Close. He deals in currencies, launders money for a pair of Iranian brothers from Los Angeles."

"Eye-ranians," he said, with relish. "Well, now. Maybe you should tell me more."

I must have talked for twenty minutes. I took out my notebook and showed him the sketches I'd made in Maspeth. There wasn't that much to tell, but he took me back over various points, covering everything thoroughly. He didn't say anything for a minute or two, and then he filled his glass with whiskey and drank it down as if it were cool water on a hot afternoon.

"Tomorrow night," he said. "Four men, I'd say. Two men and myself, and Andy for the driving. Tom would do for one of them, and either Eddie or John. You know Tom. You don't know Eddie or John."

Tom was the day bartender, a pale tight-lipped man from Belfast. I'd always wondered what he did with his evenings.

"Maspeth," he said. "Can any good thing come out of Maspeth? By God, there we sat watching the niggers punching each other and all the time there's a money laundry beneath our feet. Is that why you went out there then? And brought me along for company?"

"No, it was work took me out there, but I was working on something else at the time."

"But you kept your eyes open."

"You could say that."

"And put two and two together," he said. "Well, it's just the kind of situation I can use. I don't mind telling you, you've surprised me."

"How?"

"By bringing this to me. It seems unlike you. It's more than a man does out of friendship."

"You pay a finder's fee," I said. "Don't you?"

"Ah," he said, and a curious light came into his eyes. "That I do," he said. "Five percent."

He excused himself to make a phone call. While he was gone I sat there and looked at the bottle and the glass. I could have had some of the coffee Burke had made but I didn't want any. I didn't want the booze either.

When he came back I said, "Five percent's not enough."

"Oh?" His face hardened. "By God, you're full of surprises tonight, aren't you? I thought I knew ye. What's the matter with five percent, and how much is it you think you ought to have?"

"There's nothing wrong with five percent," I said. "For a finder's fee. I don't want a finder's fee."

"You don't? Well, what in hell do you want?"

"A full share," I said. "I want to be a player. I want to go in."

He sat back and looked at me. He poured a drink but didn't touch it, breathed in and breathed out and looked at me some more.

"Well, I'll be damned," he said finally. "Well, I'll be fucking damned."

22

IN THE MORNING I FINALLY GOT AROUND TO STOWING *THE Dirty Dozen* in my safe-deposit box. I bought an ordinary copy to take to Maspeth, then began to imagine some of the things that might go wrong. I returned to the bank and retrieved the genuine article, and I left the replacement cassette in the box so I wouldn't mix them up later on.

If I got killed out in Maspeth, Joe Durkin could watch the cassette over and over, searching for a hidden meaning.

All day long I kept thinking that I ought to go to a meeting. I hadn't been to one since Sunday night. I thought I'd go at lunch hour but didn't, and then I thought about a Happy Hour meeting around five-thirty, and finally figured I'd catch at least the first half of my usual meeting at St. Paul's. But I kept finding other things to do.

At ten-thirty I walked over to Grogan's.

Mick was there, and we went into his office in the back. There's an old wooden desk there, and a safe, along with a pair of old-fashioned wooden office chairs and a Naugahyde recliner. There's an old green leather sofa, too, and sometimes he'll catch a few hours on it. He told me once he has three apartments around town, each of them rented in a name other than his own, and of course he has the farm upstate.

"You're the first," he said. "Tom and Andy'll be here by eleven. Matt, have you thought it over?"

"Some."

"Have you had second thoughts, man?"

"Why should I?"

"It's no harm if you do. There'll likely be bloodshed. I told you that last night."

"I remember."

"You'll have to carry a gun. And if you carry one—"

"You have to be willing to use it. I know that."

"Ah, Jesus," he said. "Are ye sure ye have the heart for it, man?"

"We'll find out, won't we?"

He opened the safe and showed me several guns. The one he recommended was a SIG Sauer 9-mm automatic. It weighed a ton and I figured you could stop a runaway train with it. I played with it, working the slide, taking the clip out and putting it back, and I liked the feel of it. It was a nice piece of machinery and it looked intimidating as all hell. But I wound up giving it back and choosing a .38 S&W short-barreled revolver instead. It lacked the SIG Sauer's menacing appearance, to say nothing of its stopping power, but it rode more comfortably tucked under my belt in the small of my back. More to the point, it was a close cousin to the piece I'd carried for years on the job.

Mick took the SIG for himself.

By eleven Tom and Andy had both arrived, and each had come into the office to select a weapon. We kept the office door closed, of course, and we were all pacing around, talking about the good weather, telling each other it would be a piece of cake. Then Andy went out and brought the car around and we filed out of Grogan's and got into it.

The car was a Ford, a big LTD Crown Victoria about five years old. It was long and roomy, with a big trunk and a powerful engine. I thought at first it had been stolen for the occasion, but it turned out to be a car Ballou had bought a while back. Andy Buckley kept it garaged up in the Bronx and drove it on occasions of this sort. The plates were legitimate but if you ran them you wouldn't get anywhere; the name and address on the registration were fictitious.

Andy drove crosstown on Fifty-seventh Street and we took the Fifty-ninth Street Bridge into Queens. I liked his route better than the one I had taken. Nobody talked much once we were in the car, and after we crossed the bridge the silence was only rarely interrupted. Maybe a locker room's like that in the minutes before a championship game. Or maybe not; in sports they don't shoot the losers.

I don't suppose the trip took us much more than half an hour door to door. There was no traffic to speak of and Andy knew the route cold. So it must have been somewhere around midnight when we reached the arena. He had not been driving fast, and he slowed down now to around twenty miles an hour and we looked at the building and scanned the surrounding area as we coasted on by.

We went up one street and down another, and from time to time we would pass the arena and take a good look at it. The streets were as empty as they'd been the night before, and the lateness of the hour made them seem even more desolate. After we'd cruised around for twenty minutes or more Mick told him to give it a rest.

"Keep driving back and forth and some fucking cop's going to pull us over and ask if we're lost."

"I haven't seen a cop since we crossed the bridge," Andy said.

Mick was up front next to Andy. I was in back with Tom, who hadn't opened his mouth since we left Mick's office.

"We're early," Andy said. "What do you want me to do?"

"Park near the place but not on top of it," Mick told him. "We'll sit and wait. If somebody rousts us we'll go home and get drunk."

We wound up parked half a block from the arena on the opposite side of the street. Andy cut the engine and shut off the lights. I sat there trying to figure out which precinct we were in so I'd know who might come along and roust us. It was either the 108 or the 104, and I couldn't remember where the boundary ran or where we were in relation to it. I don't know how long I sat there, frowning in concentration, trying to picture the map of Queens in my mind, trying to impose a map of the precincts on top of it. Nothing could have mattered less, but my mind groped with the question as if the fate of the world depended on the answer.

I still hadn't settled it when Mick turned to me and pointed at his watch. It was one o'clock. It was time to go in.

I had to walk in there alone. That figured to be the easy part, but it didn't feel so easy when it was time to do it. There was no way to know what kind of reception awaited me. If Bergen Stettner had decided reasonably enough that it was cheaper and safer to kill me than to pay me off, all he had to do was open the door a crack and gun me down before I so much as set eyes on him. You could fire a cannon and no one would hear it, or give a damn if they did.

And I didn't even know that they were there. I was right on time and they figured to have been in place hours ago. They were the hosts, and it made no sense for them to arrive late to their own party. Still, I hadn't seen a car on the street that figured to be theirs, and there'd been no signs of life in the arena visible to us out on the street.

There was probably garage space inside the building. I'd seen what looked like a garage door at the far end. If I'd been in his position, I'd want to have a parking spot indoors. I didn't know what he drove, but if it was anything like the rest of his lifestyle it wasn't something you'd want to leave out on the street.

Busywork for the mind, like trying to figure out the precinct. They were there or they weren't; they'd greet me with a handshake or a bullet. And I knew they were there, anyway, because I could feel eyes watching me as I approached the door. I had the cassette in my coat pocket, figuring they wouldn't shoot until they'd made sure I had the thing with me. And I had the .38 Smith where I'd stashed it earlier, under my coat and suit jacket and wedged beneath the waistband of my pants. It would be handier now in my coat pocket, but I'd want to have it within reach after I took the coat off, and—

They'd been watching me, all right. The door opened before I could knock on it. And there was no gun pointing at me. Just Bergen Stettner, dressed as I'd seen him Thursday night in the suede sport jacket. His pants were khaki this time, and looked like army fatigues, and he had the cuffs tucked into the tops of his boots. It was a curious outfit and the parts shouldn't have gone together, but somehow he made it work.

"Scudder," he said. "You're right on time." He thrust his hand at me and I shook it. His grip was firm, but he didn't make a contest of it, just pumped my hand briskly and let go.

"Now I recognize you," he said. "I remembered you but I had no mental picture of you. Olga says you remind her of me. Not physically, I shouldn't think. Or do we look alike, you and I?" He shrugged. "I can't see it myself. Well, shall we go downstairs? The lady awaits us."

There was something stagy about his performance, as if we were being observed by an unseen audience. Was he taping this? I couldn't imagine why.

I turned and caught hold of the door, drawing it shut. I had a wad of chewing gum in my hand and I shoved this into the door's locking mechanism, so that the spring lock would remain retracted when the door was shut. I didn't know if it would work, but then I didn't think it was necessary; Ballou could kick the door in, or shoot his way through the lock if he had to.

"Leave it," Stettner told me. "It locks automatically." I turned from the door and he was at the head of the stairs, urging me on with a bow that was at once gracious and self-mocking.

"After you," he said.

I preceded him down the stairs and he caught up with

me at the bottom. He took my arm and led me all the way down the hallway, past the rooms I'd sneaked a look at, to an open door at the very end. The room within was a sharp contrast to the rest of the building, and had certainly not served as the location for their film epic. It was an oversize chamber, perhaps thirty feet long and twenty feet wide, with a deep pile carpet of gray broadloom underfoot and an off-white fabric covering and softening the concrete block walls.

At the far end of the room I saw a king-size waterbed, with a throw covering it that looked to be zebraskin. A painting hung over the bed, a geometrical abstract, all right angles and straight lines and primary colors.

Closer to the doorway, an overstuffed couch and two matching armchairs were grouped to face a stand which held a large-screen TV and VCR. The couch and one of the chairs were a charcoal gray, several tones darker than the carpet. The other chair was white, and a maroon leather attaché case rested on top of it.

Along the wall was a modular stereo system, and just to its right was a Mosler safe. It stood six feet high and stretched almost that wide. There was another painting on the wall above the stereo, a small oil of a tree, its leaves a rich and intense green. Across the way, a pair of Early American portraits hung in matching carved and gilded frames.

There was a bar set up on a sideboard beneath the portraits, and Olga turned from it with a glass in her hand and asked what I would like to drink.

"Nothing, thanks."

"But you must have a drink," she said. "Bergen, tell Scudder he has to have a drink."

"He doesn't want one," Stettner said.

Olga pouted. She was dressed as promised in the very outfit she'd worn in the movie, long gloves and high heels, crotchless leather pants and rouged nipples. She walked over to us holding her own drink, a clear liquid over ice. Without my asking she announced that it was aquavit, and was I sure I wouldn't have some? I said I was sure.

"This is quite a room," I said.

Stettner beamed. "A surprise, eh? Here in this hideous building, in the most desolate part of a dreary borough, we have a refuge, a hidden outpost of civilization. There's only one way I'd like to improve on it."

"How's that?"

"I'd like to put it a story further down." He smiled at my puzzlement. "I would excavate," he explained. "I would have a subbasement dug, and I'd create a space running the entire length of the building. I'd dig as deep as I wanted, I'd allow for twelve-foot ceilings. Hell, fifteen-foot ceilings! And of course I'd conceal the entrance. People could search this place to their heart's content and never dream a whole luxurious world existed beneath them."

Olga rolled her eyes and he laughed. "She thinks I'm crazy," he said. "Perhaps I am. But I live the way I want, you know? I always have. I always will. Take off your coat. You must be roasting."

I took it off, got the cassette from the pocket. Stettner took my coat and draped it over the back of the couch. He did not mention the cassette, and I didn't say anything about the attaché case. We were both being as civilized as our surroundings.

"You keep looking at that painting," he said. "Do you know the artist?"

It was the little landscape, the painting of the tree. "It looks like Corot," I said.

He raised his eyebrows, impressed. "You have a good eye," he said.

"Is it genuine?"

"The museum thought so. So did the thief who relieved them of it. Given the circumstances of my own purchase of it, I could hardly bring in an expert to authenticate it." He smiled. "In the present circumstances, perhaps I ought to authenticate what I'm buying. If you don't mind?"

"Not at all," I said.

I handed him the cassette and he read the title aloud and laughed. "So Leveque was not without a sense of humor after all," he said. "He kept it well hidden during his lifetime. If you want to authenticate your end of the proceedings, just open the attaché case."

I worked the snaps and raised the lid. The case held stacks of twenty-dollar bills secured with rubber bands.

"I hope you don't mind twenties," he said. "You didn't specify denomination."

"That's fine."

"Fifty stacks, fifty bills to a stack. Why don't you count it?"

"I'll trust your count."

"I should be as gracious and trust that this is the tape Leveque made. But I think I'll play it to make sure."

"Why not? I opened the case."

"Yes, that would have been an act of faith, wouldn't it? To accept the attaché case unopened. Olga, you were right. I like this man." He clapped a hand on my shoulder. "You know something, Scudder? I think we will be friends, you and I. I think we are destined to become very close."

I remembered what he had told Richard Thurman. *"We are closer than close, you and I. We are brothers in blood and semen."*

He played the cassette and turned the sound off. He fast-forwarded through the opening in fits and starts, and there was a moment when I thought I'd got everything ass-backward at the bank and we were going to be watching the standard unimproved version of *The Dirty Dozen*. It wouldn't have mattered what was on the tape if Mick Ballou would get off his ass and hit the door, but things seemed to be dragging out.

"Ah," Stettner said.

And I relaxed, because we were watching their home movie now. Stettner stood with his hands on his hips, gazing attentively at the screen. The set was larger than Elaine's, and the image somewhat more compelling as a result. I found my own attention drawn to it in spite of myself. Olga, drawing closer to her husband's side, was staring at it as if hypnotized.

"What a beautiful woman you are," Stettner told her. To me he said, "Here she is in the flesh, but I have to see her on the screen to appreciate how beautiful she is. Curious, don't you think?"

Whatever my reply might have been, it was lost forever when gunfire rang out somewhere in the building. There were two shots close together, then a brace of answering shots. Stettner said, "Jesus Christ!" and spun around to face the door. I was moving the minute the sounds registered for what they were. I stepped backward, yanked the tail of my suit jacket aside with my left hand, went for my gun with my right. I had it in my hand and got my finger on the trigger and my thumb on the hammer. The wall was at my back, and I could cover them and see the door to the hall all at the same time.

"Freeze," I said. "Nobody move."

On the screen, Olga had mounted the boy, impaling herself upon his penis. She rode him furiously in utter silence. I could see her performance out of the corner of my eye, but Bergen and Olga were no longer watching. They stood side by side and looked at me and the gun in my hand, and all three of us were as silent as the pair on the screen.

A single gunshot broke the silence. Then it returned, and then it was broken again by footsteps on the stairs.

There were more footsteps in the hall, and the sounds of doors being opened and closed. Stettner seemed about to say something. Then I heard Ballou call my name.

"In here," I shouted back. "End of the hall."

He came flying into the room, the big automatic looking like a child's toy in his huge hand. He was wearing his father's apron. His face was twisted with rage.

"Tom's shot," he said.

"Bad?"

"Not so bad, but he's down. 'Twas a fucking trap, we came through the door and there was two of 'em in the shadows with guns in their hands. Good job they were bad shots, but Tom caught a bullet before I could take them down." He was breathing heavily, taking in great gulps of air. "I shot one dead and put the other down with two shots in his gut. Just now I stuck the pistol in his mouth and blew the back of his fucking head off. Dirty bastard, shooting a man from ambush."

That's why Stettner had seemed to be performing when he opened the door for me. He'd had an audience after all, guards hidden in the shadows.

"Where's the money, man? Let's get it and get Tom to a doctor."

"There's your money," Stettner said grimly. He pointed at the still-open attaché case. "All you had to do was take it and go. There was no need for any of this."

"You had guards posted," I said.

"Purely as a precautionary measure, and it seems I was right to be cautious. Though it didn't do much good, did it?" He shrugged. "There's your money," he said again. "Take it and get out of here."

"It's fifty thousand," I told Ballou. "But there's more in the safe."

He looked at the big Mosler, then at Stettner. "Open it," he said.

"There's nothing in it."

"Open the fucking safe!"

"Nothing but more tapes, though none as successful as the one playing now. It's interesting, don't you think?"

Ballou glanced at the television set, seeing it for the first time. He took a second or two to register the action unfolding in silence, then pointed the SIG Sauer and squeezed off a shot, his hand rock-solid against the gun's considerable recoil. The set's picture tube exploded and the noise was immense.

"Open the safe," he said.

"I don't keep money here. I keep some in safe-deposit boxes and the rest in the safe at my office."

"Open it or you're dead."

"I don't think I can," Stettner said coolly. "I can never remember the combination."

Ballou grabbed him by his shirtfront and threw him against the wall, backhanding him across the face. Stettner never lost his composure. A little blood trickled from one nostril, but if he was aware of it he gave no sign.

"This is silly," he said. "I'm not going to open the safe. If I open it we're dead."

"You're dead if you don't," Ballou said.

"Only if you're an idiot. If we're alive we can get you more money. If we're dead you'll never get into that safe."

"We're dead anyway," Olga said.

"I don't think so," Stettner told her. To Ballou he said, "You can beat us if you want. You have the gun, you're in charge. But don't you see it's pointless? And meanwhile your man Tom lies bleeding upstairs. He'll die while you waste your time trying to persuade me to open an empty safe. Why not save time and take your fifty thousand and get your man the medical attention he requires?"

Mick looked at me. He asked me what I figured was in the safe. "Something good," I said, "or he would have opened it by now."

He nodded slowly, then turned and set down the SIG Sauer next to the attaché case. I was still covering the two of them with the .38 Smith. From a pocket in the butcher's apron he produced a cleaver, its blade snug in a leather sheath. He drew it from the sheath. The blade was carbon steel, discolored through years of use. It looked intimidating enough to me, but Stettner eyed it with apparent contempt.

"Open the safe," Ballou told him.

"I don't think so."

"I'll hack her fine tits off," he said. "I'll chop her into cat meat."

"That won't put money in your pocket, will it?"

I thought of the drug dealer in Jamaica Estates, and the bluff he'd felt safe enough to call. I didn't know if Mick was bluffing and I wasn't eager to find out.

He grabbed her by the forearm, yanked her toward him.

"Wait," I said.

He looked at me, fury glinting in his eyes.

"The pictures," I said.

"What are you talking about, man?"

I pointed at the little Corot. "That's worth more than he's got in the safe," I said.

"I don't want to try to sell a fucking painting."

"Neither do I," I said, and I swung the gun around and snapped off a shot that caromed off the wall just inches to the side of the painting. It chipped the concrete, and it put a dent in Stettner's sangfroid. "I'll shoot the shit out of it," I told him. "And the others." I swung the gun toward the pair of portraits and squeezed the trigger without actually aiming. The bullet went through the portrait of the woman, making a small round hole just inches from her forehead.

"My God," Stettner said. "You are vandals."

"It's just paint and canvas," I said.

"My God. I'll open the safe."

He worked the combination swiftly and surely. The turning of the dial was the only sound you could hear. I was holding on to the Smith and breathing in the smell of cordite. The gun was heavy and my hand ached slightly from the gun's recoil. I longed to put it down. There was no reason to point it at anyone. Stettner was busy with the safe, Olga frozen with dread and incapable of movement.

Stettner hit the last number, turned the handle, drew open the twin doors. We all looked within at the stacks of bills. I was to the side, my view partly screened by the other two men. I saw Stettner's hand dart into the open safe and I cried out, "Mick, he's got a gun!"

In a film they would show the scene in slow motion, and what's curious is that's the way I remember it. Stettner's hand reaching in, fastening on a little blued-steel automatic pistol. Mick's hand, gripping the huge cleaver, poised high overhead, then flashing down in a deadly arc. The blade biting cleanly, surgically, through the wrist. The hand appearing to leap forward, away from the blade, as if liberated from its arm.

Stettner spun around, away from the open safe, facing toward us. His face was white, his mouth wide with horror. He held his arm in front of him like a shield. Arterial blood, bright as sunrise, spurted wildly from his mutilated arm. He lurched forward, his mouth working soundlessly, his arm spraying blood at us, until Ballou let out an awful sound from deep in his throat and swung the cleaver a second time, burying it in the juncture of Stettner's neck and shoulder. The blow drove the man to his knees and we stepped back out of the way. He sprawled forward and lay still, pouring out blood onto the gray broadloom.

Olga was standing still. I don't think she had moved at all. Her mouth was slack and she had her hands poised at the sides of her breasts, her nail polish a perfect match for the color on her nipples.

I looked from her to Ballou. He was turning toward her now, his apron crimson with fresh blood, his hand locked on the handle of the cleaver.

I swung the Smith around. I didn't hesitate. I squeezed the trigger, and the gun bucked in my hand.

23

THE FIRST SHOT WAS RUSHED, AND WIDE OF THE MARK. IT TOOK her in the right shoulder, I tucked my elbow in against my ribs and fired a second shot, and a third. Both entered the center of her chest, between the rouged breasts. The light was gone from her eyes before she hit the floor.

"Matt."

I was standing there, looking down at her, and Mick was saying my name. I felt his hand on my shoulder. The room reeked of death, the smells of gunfire and blood and body wastes merging to foul the air. I felt an awful weariness, and there was a dull cramp at the back of my throat, as if something was trapped there and wanted to get out.

"Come on, man. We've got to get out of here."

I moved quickly once I shook off whatever it was that had immobilized me. While he cleaned out the safe, sweeping stacks of money into a couple of canvas sacks, I wiped away any prints either of us might have left. I retrieved the cassette from the VCR, stuck it in my coat pocket, and tossed the coat over my arm. I stuck the .38 back in my belt and put Mick's SIG Sauer in my pocket. I grabbed the attaché case and followed Mick down the hall and up the stairs.

Tom was right next to the door, propped into a sitting position against the wall. His face looked bloodless, but then he was always pale. Mick set down the sacks of money, picked Tom up in his arms, and carried him out to the car.

Andy had the door open and Mick tucked him into the back seat.

Mick came back for the money while Andy opened the trunk. I tossed in everything I was carrying, and Mick returned and added the sacks of cash and slammed the trunk lid hard. I went back into the arena and checked the room where we'd done the killing. They were both dead, and I couldn't spot anything I'd overlooked. At the top of the stairs I found the two guards, and they were both dead, too. I wiped the whole area where Tom had been sitting on the chance he'd left his prints there, and I dug most of the chewing gum out of the lock so that it wouldn't be stuck open. I wiped the lock, and parts of the door we might have touched.

They were motioning to me from the car. I looked around. The neighborhood was deserted as ever. I ran across the pavement. The Ford's front door was open, the front passenger seat empty. Mick was in back with Tom, talking softly to him, pressing a wadded-up cloth against his shoulder wound. The wound seemed to have stopped bleeding, but I didn't know how much blood he'd already lost.

I got in, closed the door. The engine was already running, and Andy pulled away smoothly. Mick said, "You know where to go now, Andy."

"That I do, Mick."

"We don't want a ticket, God knows, but step as lively as you dare."

Mick has a farm in Ulster County. The closest town is Ellenville. A couple from County Westmeath, a Mr. and Mrs. O'Mara, run the place for him, and their name appears on the deed. That's where we went, arriving somewhere between three and three-thirty. Andy drove with the radar detector switched on, and even so didn't stray too far over the speed limit.

We got Tom inside and made him comfortable on a daybed in the sun parlor, and Mick went out with Andy and woke up a doctor he knew, a sour-faced little man with liver spots on the backs of his hands. He was with Tom for almost an hour, and when he came out he stood for a long time washing his hands at the kitchen sink. "He'll be all right," he announced. "Tough little bastard, isn't he? 'I been shot before, Doc,' he tells me. 'Well, my boy,' I said, 'will you never learn to duck?' I couldn't get a smile out of him, but he's got a face that doesn't look as though it's smiled much. He'll be all right, though, and live to get shot again another day. If you're on speaking terms with the Creator you might want to thank Him for penicillin. Used to be a wound like that'd turn septic on you, kill you a week or ten days down the line. Not anymore. Innit a wonder we don't all live forever?"

While the doctor worked the rest of us sat at the kitchen table. Mick cracked a pint of whiskey, and most of it was gone by the time Andy ran the doctor home. Andy made a beer last as long as he could, then had a second one. I found a bottle of ginger ale in the back of the refrigerator and drank that. We just sat there and nobody said much of anything.

After Andy dropped off the doctor he came back for us and pulled up next to the house and tapped the horn. Mick rode up front with him and I sat in the back. Tom stayed at the farm; the doctor wanted him to spend the next several days in bed, and planned to see him again over the weekend, or sooner if he got feverish. Mrs. O'Mara would nurse him. I gathered she'd performed that function before.

Andy got on the Thruway and retraced our route. We picked up the Saw Mill and the Henry Hudson and wound up in front of Grogan's. It was six-thirty in the morning and I had never been more wide awake in my life. We carried the sacks of money inside and Mick locked them in the safe. We gave Andy our guns, the ones that had been fired; he'd drop them in the river on his way home.

"I'll settle with ye in a day or so," Mick told him. "Once I count it all and figure out shares. 'Twill be a decent sum for a good night's work."

"I'm not worried," Andy said.

"Go on home now," Mick said. "My love to your mother, she's a fine woman. And you're a grand driver, Andy. You're the best."

We sat at the same table again, with the doors locked and only the light of dawn for illumination. Mick had a bottle and a glass but he wasn't hitting it hard. I had drawn a Coke for myself and found a piece of lemon to cut the sweetness some. Once I got it the way I wanted it I barely touched the damned thing.

For over an hour we spoke scarcely a word. When he got to his feet around seven-thirty I got up and went with him. I didn't have to ask where we were going, and he didn't have to go in back for his apron. He was still wearing it.

I went with him to collect the Cadillac and we rode in silence down Ninth Avenue to Fourteenth Street. We parked in front of Twomey's, mounted the steps, entered the sanctuary of St. Bernard's. We were a few minutes early as we took seats in the last row of the little room where they hold the butchers' mass.

The priest this morning was young, with a smooth pink face that looked as though it never needed a shave. He had a thick West-of-Ireland brogue and must have been a recent arrival. He seemed confident enough, though, before his tiny congregation of nuns and butchers.

I don't remember the service. I was there and I was not there. I stood when others stood, sat when they sat, knelt when they knelt. I made the indicated responses. But even as I did these things I was breathing in the mixed scent of blood and cordite, I was watching a cleaver descend in its furious arc, I was seeing blood spurt, I was feeling a gun buck in my hand.

And then something curious happened.

When the others queued up to receive Communion, Mick and I stayed where we were. But as the line moved along, as each person in turn said *Amen* and received the Host, something lifted me up onto my feet and steered me to the end of the line. I felt a light tingling in the palms of my hands, a pulse throbbing in the hollow of my throat.

The line moved. "The Body o' Christ," the priest said, over and over and over. "Amen," each person said in turn. The line moved, and now I was at the front of it, and Ballou was right behind me.

"The Body o' Christ," the priest said.

"Amen," I said. And took the wafer upon my tongue.

24

OUTSIDE THE SUN WAS BRIGHT AND THE AIR CRISP AND COLD. Halfway down the church steps Mick caught up with me and gripped my arm. His smile was fierce.

"Ah, we'll burn in hell for sure now," he said. "Taking the Lord's Communion with blood on our hands. If there's a more certain way of getting into hell I don't know what it is. My sins unconfessed for thirty years, my apron still wet with that bastard's gore, and I'm up at the altar as if I'm in a state of grace." He sighed at the wonder of it. "And you! Not a Catholic, but were you ever baptized anything at all?"

"I don't think so."

"Sweet Jesus, a fucking heathen at the altar rail, and I'm following after him like Mary's lost lamb. Whatever got into you, man?"

"I don't know."

"The other night I said you were full of surprises. By God, I didn't know the half of it. Come on."

"Where are we going?"

"I want a drink," he said. "And I want your company."

We went to a meatcutters' bar on the corner of Thirteenth and Washington. We had been there before. The floor was covered with sawdust, the air thick with smoke from the bartender's cigar. We sat at a table with whiskey for him and strong black coffee for me.

He said, "Why?"

I thought about it and shook my head. "I don't know," I

said. "I never planned it. Something picked me up off my knees and set me down in front of the altar."

"That's not what I mean."

"Oh?"

"Why were you out there tonight? What sent you to Maspeth with a gun in your hand?"

"Oh," I said.

"Well?"

I blew on my coffee to cool it. "That's a good question," I said.

"Don't tell me it was the money. You could have had fifty thousand dollars just by letting him have the tape. I don't know what the shares'll be, but they won't reach fifty thousand. Why double the risk for a smaller reward?"

"The money didn't have all that much to do with it."

"The money had nothing to do with it," he said. "When did you ever give a shit for money? You never did." He took a drink. "I'll tell you a secret. I don't give a shit about it either. I need it all the fucking time, but I don't really care about it."

"I know."

"You didn't want to sell them their tape, did you?"

"No," I said. "I wanted them dead."

He nodded. "You know who I thought of the other night. That old cop you told me about, the old Irishman you were yoked up with when you first started out."

"Mahaffey."

"That's the one. I thought of Mahaffey."

"I can see how you would."

"I thought of what he'd said to you. 'Never do something you can get somebody else to do for you.' Isn't that how it went?"

"That sounds right."

"And I said to myself that there was nothing wrong with that. Why not leave the killing to the men in the bloody aprons? But then you said you wanted more than a finder's fee, and for a moment there I thought I had you wrong."

"I know. And it bothered you."

"It did, because I couldn't see you as a man with that kind of money hunger. It meant you weren't the man I thought I knew, and that did bother me. But then in the next breath you cleared the air again. Said you wanted to earn a full share, said you wanted to go in with a gun."

"Yes."

"Why?"

"It seemed easier that way. They'd be expecting me, they'd let me in the door."

"That's not the reason."

"No, it's not. I guess I decided Mahaffey was wrong, or that his advice couldn't apply in this particular situation. It didn't feel right, leaving the dirty work to somebody else. If I could sentence them to death the least I could do was show up for the hanging."

He drank and made a face. "I'll tell you," he said, "I serve a better glass of whiskey at my own bar."

"Don't drink it if it's no good."

He tasted it again to make sure. "I couldn't call it bad," he said. "You know, I don't care much for beer or wine, but I've had my share of both, and I've had beer that's thinner than water and wine that's gone to vinegar. And I've known of meat that's turned and eggs that are off, and food poorly cooked and poorly made and spoiled. But in all my life I don't think I've ever had bad whiskey."

"No," I said. "I never had any."

"How do you feel now, Matt?"

"How do I feel? I don't know how I feel. I'm an alcoholic, I never know how I feel."

"Ah."

"I feel sober. That's how I feel."

"I bet you do." He looked at me over the top of his glass. He said, "I'd say they deserved killing."

"Do you think so?"

"If anyone ever did."

"I guess we all deserve killing," I said. "Maybe that's why nobody ever gets out of here alive. I don't know where I get off deciding who deserves killing and who doesn't. We left four people dead back there and two of them I never even met. Did they deserve killing?"

"They had guns in their hands. Nobody drafted them, not for that war."

"But did they deserve it? If we all got what we deserved—"

"Oh, Jesus forbid it," he said. "Matt, I have to ask you this. Why did you shoot the woman?"

"Somebody had to."

"It needn't have been yourself."

"No." I took a moment and thought about it. "I'm not sure," I said at last. "There's only one thing I can think of."

"Let's hear it, man."

"Well, I don't know," I said, "but I think maybe I wanted to get some blood on my apron."

Sunday I had dinner with Jim Faber. I told him the whole story all the way through, and we never did get to a meeting that night. We were still in the Chinese restaurant when they were saying the Lord's Prayer.

"Well, it's a hell of a story," he said. "And I guess you could say it has a happy ending, because you didn't drink and you aren't going to go to jail. Or are you?"

"No."

"It must be an interesting feeling, playing judge and jury, deciding who gets to live and who deserves to die. Like playing God, I guess you could say."

"You could say that."

"You think you'll make a habit of it?"

I shook my head. "I don't think I'll ever do it again. But I never thought I would do it at all. I've done unorthodox things over the years, both on and off the force. I've fabricated evidence, I've distorted situations."

"This was a little different."

"It was a lot different. See, I saw that tape during the summer and I never really did get it out of my mind. And then I ran into the son of a bitch by pure chance, recognized him from a gesture, the way he smoothed a boy's hair back on his head. Probably something his own father used to do."

"Why do you say that?"

"Because something or other turned him into a monster. Maybe his father abused him, maybe he was raped in childhood. That's one of the ways it works. It wouldn't have been all that hard to understand Stettner. To sympathize with him."

"That's something I noticed," he said. "When you were talking about him. I never got the feeling that you hated him."

"Why should I hate him? He was quite charming. His manners were good, he was witty, he had a sense of humor. If you want to divide the world into good men and bad men, he was certainly one of the bad ones. But I don't know if you can do that. I used to be able to. It's harder than it once was."

I leaned forward. "They would have kept on doing it," I said. "They were recreational killers, they did it for the sport of it. They enjoyed it. I can't understand that, but there are plenty of people who can't understand how I can enjoy watching a boxing match. Maybe what people do and don't enjoy is yet another area that's beyond judgment.

"But here's the point. They were doing this and getting away with it, and I got on their case and got lucky and figured out what they did and how they did it and who they did it to, and it didn't mean squat. No indictment, no arrest, no charges brought, not even an investigation. A pretty good cop found the whole thing so frustrating he drank himself stupid. I wasn't prepared to do that myself."

"Well, you got that part right," he said. "And then you

decided, well, letting the Universe work this out on its own is just not something I can safely do. God's in deep shit, you told yourself, unless He's got me to help Him out."

"God," I said.

"Well, whatever the hell you want to call it. Your Higher Power, the creative force of the Universe, the Great Perhaps. That's what Rabelais called it. The Great Perhaps. You didn't figure the Great Perhaps was equal to the task confronting Him, so it was up to you to take over."

"No," I said. "That's not how it was."

"Tell me."

"I thought, I can let go of this, I can turn this over, and it will all work out the way it's supposed to. Because everything always does. I know that on the days when I seem to believe in the Great Perhaps, and I still know it when my Higher Power is the Great Perhaps Not. And one thing I always know for sure—whether or not there's a God, I'm not it."

"Then why did you do what you did?"

"Because I just plain wanted them dead," I said. "And I just flat out wanted to be the sonofabitch who did it to them. And no, I'm not going to do it again."

"You took the money."

"Yes."

"Thirty-five, you said it was?"

"Thirty-five a man. Mick's end must have run to a quarter of a million. Of course there was a lot of foreign currency. I don't know how he'll make out when he unloads it."

"He gets the lion's share."

"That's right."

"And what do you do with yours?"

"I don't know. For now it's in the safe-deposit box, along with the cassette that got the whole thing started. I'll probably give a tenth of it to Testament House. That seems like a logical place to donate it."

"You could give it all to Testament House."

"I could," I agreed, "but I don't think I will. I think I'll keep the rest of it. Why the hell shouldn't I? I worked for it."

"I guess you did at that."

"And I ought to have a little money of my own if I marry Elaine."

"Are you going to marry Elaine?"

"How the hell do I know?"

"Uh-huh. Why'd you go to mass?"

"I've gone with Ballou before. I guess the current term for it is 'male bonding.' All I know is it seems to be an occasional part of our friendship."

"Why'd you take Communion?"

"I don't know."

"You must have some idea."

"No," I said, "I really don't. There are lots of things I do without knowing why the hell I do them. Half the time I don't know why I stay sober, if you want to know the truth, and back when I drank all the time I didn't know why I did that either."

"Uh-huh. What happens next?"

"Stay tuned," I said. "Don't change the channel."